Absent Friends

Duncan Swindells

Cover designed by Rob Williams at ilovemycover.com

Please follow me @dafswindells

First published: February 2020

ISBN- 9781708304027

Acknowledgments

It's nearly 12 months since I published my first novel, Birth of a Spy. I had no idea if anyone would read it or how it would be received. I've been both touched and astonished by how many of you have enjoyed the book and left generous, thoughtful reviews on Amazon and Goodreads. Many of you have asked for a sequel, so here it is and I hope you enjoy it. Of course, none of this would have been possible without the continued support of my mum, herself a great writer, who has spent hours poring over commas and apostrophes, my two boys Leo and Corin, and Georgia, my editor in chief. Thank you all.

A huge note of thanks to what became an army of proofreaders; Dan Jenkins, Holly Mathieson, Ruth Rowlands, Jenny Scott and Martin Willis. I am extremely fortunate to have had Jonathan Clarke and Adam Treverton-Jones fact check the Hong Kong sections. Craig Swindells has been my adviser on all things military and I couldn't have written the book without him. Jamie McKenzie from New Life Gym talked me through all the martial arts sequences, and was generous with his time and most crucially, gentle with me.

Danny Pollitt continued to help me with the book long after it was written, helping it be seen by the right people. I have worked with Rob at ILMC.com for several years now. I do love my cover and I hope you do too.

Writers Audrey Harrison and Martin Willis have become my mentors. To get such great advice and support from your fellow authors is a rare gift indeed.

Prologue

Fly fishing is such a rare and exacting pursuit, a mixture of patience and trickery, and the man standing in a tiny rowing boat, stripping his line into a bewitching Scottish loch knew more than he should about both. He flicked the rod back, letting the tired old cane do its work, feeling it bend and flex awkwardly under his control. The tip quivered before whipping out yards of strong, clear, floating line. As the line settled, its fine shooting tip continued to rush through the air, before coming to rest delicately on the surface. And then, finally, there is the tiny duck's feather fly, sitting up invitingly, supported by nothing more than the water itself. The man drew in a section of line, carefully repositioned his fly and, satisfied with his work, flexed his shoulders and prepared to wait. He'd had a lifetime of that, waiting. Whether on stag in a wet and windy Belfast, cooped up in a grubby hotel room in a foreign land or simply sitting in a company car outside an invitingly warm town house in the freezing cold, it seemed he was always waiting.

There were already three decent sized brownies in the

bottom of his small boat, so if this were to be the last cast of the day his trip would not have been a wasted one. Earlier in the morning he'd watched as a solitary bird of prey had dipped and swooped above him, quickly showing itself a far superior predator than he. For lunch he had toasted his aerial friend before tipping the hipflask's contents down his throat. The real reason for his visit hadn't been the fishing at all, the real reason had been to find somewhere he might clear his head and think, the fishing simply a welcome bonus.

A trout rose feet from his fly and he wondered to cover it, but judged by the swell that it was better not to. The man holding the antiquated cane boat rod and playing the floating line through his hands thought about the fly. An artificial object, created yet not real, purporting to be what it was not and always under someone else's control. Lacking in free will or its own determination and, ultimately, if successful, violently consumed again and again until eventually, worn-out and in ruins it would be discarded. But then, he thought, if the fish got wind of his little ruse, they would never rise to the fly, and instead would ignore his offerings all day long. It was about picking the right lure for the right day, if he, the fisherman, were to be believed and fill his boat with beautiful, sparkling brown trout.

He waited.

Another rise, this one moving away from the boat and his fly. It appeared to be a good fish too as its broad round back broke the surface of the water before quickly disappearing. He would try and cover that fish, try and deceive it with his gift. Quickly he stripped in the line, leaving it lying in rings on the bottom of the rowing boat. The fly was a couple of rod lengths away and so he flicked the rod back and a fresh length of line whistled past his ear as he felt the rod bend and flex. A second, well-timed flick, a subtle reposition and the line was shooting from his rod and up and off the floor of the boat. A smile spread across his face as the fly gently plopped into the water.

The man looked up at the sweeping gorse covered hillside. Under the cloud laden sky, a sudden flicker, as if someone had tilted a small mirror in his direction. There was the discreetest of cracks and the fisherman's body dropped to the floor of the boat.

1

Cambridge, Present Day

Scott Hunter woke from a dream he no longer cared to remember. He had slept a brief, alcohol fuelled sleep and dreamt bizarre and aberrant dreams of his childhood, before waking clammy and panicked. He turned onto his side and regarded the empty space next to him. He was alone. Alone with nothing more than some unpleasant memories and Amy's collection of black and white DVDs. Almost everyone had left as his world had crumbled and fallen apart. He'd watched the people most dear to him as one by one they had been inexplicably gunned down, and then, as the pieces had finally fallen into place Scott had begun to understand. He had been forced to take a life himself, to shoot a man he'd once thought a friend but who had so senselessly and selfishly betrayed him. He shifted his weight uncomfortably, the effects of the previous night's whisky beginning to wear off. He looked over the end of his bed, over the abandoned work desk and out into the world. The first soft flakes of winter were starting to fall and whiten the sky.

Whisky always left him feeling nauseous at the back of his throat. If he wasn't going to sleep, he'd contemplate lighting a cigarette. It was four in the morning. He stroked a hand over his badly shorn head. He'd taken to shaving his head whilst on the run from the police, but then continued to do so thereafter, for Hunter the daily ritual becoming an act of penance.

He reached across to his bedside table, halting as he saw the black and white photograph. It was one of a sequence. The last in that sequence. The last photograph of him with Amy, happy, smiling and together. The last photograph before the other pictures. The pictures which lay in the very bottom of his work desk. The pictures of her death, of her prone, bloodied body slumped over a bench in Hyde Park. Sometimes, when he was feeling particularly morose or drunk, or more commonly, both, he would take the photographs from their drawer and look at them, spreading them over the now pointless bed. Then he would cry. He would cry and keen so loudly.

They never did phone again, the people who'd taken this morbid collection of pictures. The man on the other end of the phone with the cultured syntax and the callously pragmatic attitude to life had called himself Lazarus. He'd offered Hunter a job, said he would be grateful to him, and then what? Hunter sat up to light a cigarette. Nothing. Nothing had happened. He'd been left alone, abandoned and forgotten, to slide who knew or cared where. There'd been a brief and, Hunter recalled thinking at the time, rather perfunctory police investigation before he'd been permitted to return to the house, not, as he had expected, to be harangued and bombarded by the media and the entreaties of the press, but, almost worse, solitude and enforced contemplation. The university had quietly disowned him. Amy, the point to his now pointless life had been violently ripped from him. His friends were dead and what little money he'd had was all but gone. Hunter was barely keeping his head above water. The snow started falling more heavily, settling in the cold night air.

Often now Hunter had taken to spending nights on the sofa, unwilling to confront the bed he'd shared with her. Bed had never been a relaxing, comforting place for him, but now less so than ever. Before there had been the ever-present hope that she would join him, but now his bed was a lonely, sterile place which he barely acknowledged and subconsciously refused to associate with sleep. More often than not he would wake on his sofa, bringing down a pillow for when the tiredness and the whisky conspired to overcome him, but Hunter never slept for long, soon waking to find the television on and the room stinking of virulent smoke and alcohol.

Eventually, as he knew he would, he stubbed out his cigarette, threw on an old dressing gown and, with the sun still hours from rising, Hunter's thoughts turned to coffee. It was just possible there was the makings of a cafetière in the kitchen, although it had been an age since he'd last visited the shops. Each time he took the stairs meant another reminder of his dead flat-mate whose body he'd discovered bent and crumpled, a small cauterized hole in his temple, the back of his head removed by the brass nine-millimetre bullet. Entering the kitchen, he found the previous day's cafetière in the sink amongst carelessly discarded cups and plates, the treacly dark coffee cracked and dry, the glass stained and brown. It would do, it would have to. He freshened it up as best he could with hot water from the kettle and left it to stew. The kitchen was in desperate need of a clean, but Hunter lacked the necessary energy or pride. When he did have money for food, he tended to waste much of it on takeaways, the remnants of which still haunted every kitchen surface. The table was a sea of chipped glasses and half-forgotten coffee mugs. He went to the fridge. A small chunk of Cheddar which was hard around the edges and starting to show tiny spots of mould, an unopened carton of milk to accompany the cereal he had neglected to buy and one apologetic carrot. The shelves in the cupboards weren't much better. In an effort to make the coffee somewhat more palatable Hunter found the end of a bag of caster sugar and tipped it into the least filthy of the mugs. The coffee was bitter and watery.

He sat at the kitchen table and took the cigarettes from his dressing gown pocket. Amy, he reflected, would have been horrified. He padded himself down, trying to find some matches, took a disagreeable slurp of the thin brown liquid and tried to remember where he'd last seen them. This was proving remarkably typical of Hunter's days. Realising that he had left the matches next to his bed, the thought of dragging himself all the way upstairs alone was exhausting and disheartening. He looked at the cooker, wondering if he could spark a ring and take a light from that? But the igniter no longer worked, so where were his bloody matches? Surely there must be a box in the kitchen somewhere for the rare occasions he actually cooked. No. He was certain now as he pulled back at the curtain of cheap whisky, there was a half-finished box in the sitting room.

He padded out from the kitchen and along the short corridor which shadowed the stairs. Hunter was about to turn right into the sitting room when something caught his eye. In amongst the flyers for kebab shops, unopened bills and all the other crap he no longer cared to be bothered with, on his doormat, where six months previously he'd discovered the envelope which had changed his life forever, there now sat another, smaller package. An A5 padded envelope, his name printed on a considered rectangle of white adhesive paper. There was no postmark and he knew better than to check if the mysterious package's deliverer was still outside. Hunter left it where it lay and instead entered the sitting room, now more determined than ever to find some matches. Then, ignoring the package a second time, he returned to the safety of the kitchen, emerging five minutes later with a fresh cup of brown water and a cigarette. He took the package into the sitting room, slumped by a tatty old sofa and ripped open one end. A set of keys fell out. A Yale door key and what appeared to be a dead bolt key, both sharing the same coloured circular ring. Inside the envelope a train ticket for later that day, a single taking him into London and then back out again to Harrow and Wealdstone in the North and a piece of paper about the same size as a business card with an address typed on it. Hunter looked at the time on the ticket and then the time on his phone. They weren't giving him long, the implication clear. Get on with it, make the decision. Now or never. He ran upstairs and threw some clothes into a rucksack, grabbed the Glock pistol he kept in a drawer in the kitchen and made for the door.

Finally, he was going to leave it all behind. The memories and the pain. Lazarus, his mysterious benefactor was presenting him with a fresh start in life, a new beginning, and Hunter was suddenly quite determined he would grasp it and never look back. His hand at the front door he stopped, threw down his rucksack and sprinted back upstairs to his bedroom. Their bedroom. Reverently he collected the photographs of Amy, disappointed with himself for having, in his haste, neglected her. Now he was ready.

***

Harrow and Wealdstone in North London is a peculiar place. A cultural hinterland, neither Harrow, with its winding lanes, artisan shops and famous school, nor Wealdstone, an anonymous stretch of North London real estate foolishly vaunting reliably high rental incomes and fought over with samurai swords and petrol bombs by a couple of aging Irish gypsy families and a steadily growing Asian community. Hunter felt it didn't know quite where it belonged or what it wanted to be. He swung the rucksack onto his back and, having consulted a map at the railway station, began to walk along a desolate stretch of dual carriageway set in half a mile of abandoned wasteland which might once have supported a petrol station. The address on the carefully printed card took him to a block of flats on the corner of a busy junction. The front doors were protected by an entry code but that small, yet crucial piece of information had been withheld from him. In any case, he didn't want to go charging in without having first observed the place. The address said 3/2, the second flat on the third floor Hunter had to presume. On the opposite side of the lights an ugly yet imposing pub which he suspected had never had a heyday but had instead started its headlong descent into obduracy mere moments after its opening. Hunter sat in the concrete front garden-cum-car park of The Falcon Pub and smoked whilst he observed the flats on the other side of the road.

His assumption appeared to have been correct. The third and

top floor was divided into four windows and two flats. Hunter could make out two distinctly different styles of décor. On the left, modern clean lines with the latest contemporary lighting units and stylish yet understated furnishings, whilst on the right the wallpaper was either stained with age or just a dirty colour from a bygone era. Unfashionable shades which could no longer be glorified with the epithet shabby chic hung from the room's two main lights. In the time that he waited Hunter smoked five cigarettes. No one came or went from the flats or the shop on the ground floor selling blinds and window sashes. The whole building seemed deserted and Hunter was about to check he was at the correct address when a girl stopped outside the shop and began rummaging through her shoulder bag. He threw down his half-finished cigarette, grabbed his rucksack and, taking full advantage of a series of red lights, sprinted across the road. The girl had found what she had been looking for and was just entering the last number into the entry keypad when Hunter joined her.

'Perfect timing,' he said breathlessly whilst dangling his keys hopefully in front of her. 'I think we're going to be neighbours. I'm moving into the top floor flat.'

She was about his height, with glasses and a short bob haircut, one lonely hairpin neatly restraining a wayward strand of blond fringe. A shirt sporting an oversized collar, crimson leather biker's jacket and a pair of shiny black boots all combining to give Hunter the impression she probably worked in the arts, perhaps as an architect or in the fashion business. Behind her designer glasses her eyes flashed blue as she inspected his keys.

'Early days I'm afraid. Haven't learnt the code yet,' he continued, hoping he was babbling just enough to appear harmless. She wasn't to understand the irony behind that statement, Hunter only needing to hear a number once to remember it immediately and start calculating its every permutation. Weighing him up the girl seemed sufficiently happy he was telling the truth and posed no threat and so showed him the 6 digit code.

'I hope I'm not going to regret this,' she said regarding him suspiciously. 'You don't have very much with you?' She left the sentence dangling, waiting for a name.

'Scott.'

'Hello Scott.'

It was obvious by her tone that his introduction was not to be reciprocated, and so he held open the door for her in silence. Inside tired stairs ascended immediately to the floors above. A pram sat spurned and dejected under the concrete edifice left by the stairs. The metal handrail's pale blue paint was cracked and peeling, and the first signs of rust were patching through. Hunter followed his nameless flatmate to the second floor. She waited for him to pass before unlocking her flat's heavy metal fire door.

'Remember, Scott, I don't want to find myself registering a complaint against you.' She laughed and disappeared inside leaving Hunter hoping his keys would fit.

On the brief landing at the top of the stairs half a bicycle chained to the railings and a sickly-looking yucca plant. After a brief waggle of the bottom security key the lock gave, then the Yale was turning and for the first time, as the door swung open, Hunter was left wondering what the hell he was doing. Quickly he undid the top of his rucksack and removed the Glock. The interior was as tired and unfashionable as he'd anticipated. A cheap, plum carpet covered the tiny entry hall and disappeared into the lounge at the front. He swung the gun up and, as he'd seen them do in the movies, bent his knees and slowly stalked into the hallway. Something had been spilt, or worse on the cut price carpet and he felt his foot squelch and slip. He followed the gun into the flat's sitting room. Empty. Hunter didn't want to hang around and it took only seconds to check the room it was so sparsely furnished, a sofa and television, nothing more. A short corridor ran from the front of the flat to the back, two doors off it plus a kitchen and bathroom.

The first room was the smallest bedroom Hunter had ever seen, opposite it another, identical in size but not in purpose. On a computer desk £5,000 worth of the latest Apple iMac Pro, sporting 32 gigabytes of RAM and a terabyte of storage. Hunter would return to examine that once he had inspected the remainder of the flat. The kitchen and bathroom were both equally spartan. He flicked open one cabinet after another and was surprised to find trays of baked beans, tinned soups and plum tomatoes, huge packs of water bottles and toilet rolls, as though whoever owned the property were preparing for the end of days, yet in the same cupboards only a single cup, plate, enough cutlery for one. Whoever was to live here, Hunter had to assume himself for the moment, would not be leaving for some time. He tried the door from the kitchen to the winding metal staircase leading to the communal car park at the flat's rear, locked and with no sign of a key. Not ideal if there were ever to be a fire. Satisfied at least for the moment that he was alone he flicked the safety on the Glock and laid it on the kitchen table eager to return to the mysterious second bedroom.

He rifled through the computer desk, empty except for some rudimentary stationary and in the bottom drawer, a mobile phone. He thought back to the other rooms in the pokey flat.

There was no landline that he could recall. He opened the phone up. It was charged and connected, and he half wondered about calling someone then decided against it. He was just returning the phone to its drawer when it rang.

'Hello, Scott, this is Lazarus. I'm extremely pleased you saw fit to accept my job offer.'

'About that...'

'You will see the flat is well stocked and you want for nothing. Am I correct?'

'Yes, that's right, but...'

'And as there is no need for anything else to be brought into the flat, I expect you to remain there until you are contacted again. Do we understand one another?'

'Don't leave the flat. Got it.'

'Someone will be in touch with you soon to talk you through the next step.'

'Which next step? I don't understand. What is the job?'

'I look forward to working with you. Goodbye, Scott.'

Hunter stared long and hard at the silent mobile phone in his hand. He half wondered foolishly and only briefly about trying to call back, but these people, whoever they were, weren't amateurs. In the end he took the mobile and its charger through to the kitchen where he was confident he could hear it from anywhere in the flat and placed it on the counter next to the toaster.

The first couple of days passed unremarkably enough. The flat certainly had been well stocked and Hunter felt no need to venture out. Instead he filled his time between cooking, watching the dilapidated old television, smoking, drinking coffee and not sleeping. He kept a constant ear open for the mobile, but after twenty-four hours he'd even stopped listening for that. The computer in his spare room interested him. It seemed to work perfectly, be connected to the internet, but there were no programs evident, no files for him to open. He toyed with the idea of going online, even checking his many email accounts, but stopped himself. There was just something about the whole enterprise which left Hunter in no doubt that whoever had appointed the flat, left the mobile phone, all of the provisions and the computer, did not intend for him to go surfing the internet and picking up old messages. He toured the nested files of the machine's hard drive for any clues, but the computer appeared never to have been used and so Hunter decided to leave it that way.

With the mobile in his kitchen still silent and untouched, day three brought with it an acute and unrelenting case of cabin fever. Hunter had always been extremely comfortable with his own company, hours of private study and coding had seen to that, but after three days of being cooped up in the tiny North London flat he needed to stretch his legs and take some air. He cooked himself some lunch and stood in the double windows at the front of the flat staring out across the busy junction of traffic lights and white vans at the pub opposite. Surely no one would mind if he were to nip across the road, buy himself a quick pint, or better still a couple of large cheap Scotches before returning to the flat for another miserable evening in front of the television wondering what the hell had become of his life. He slipped on a pair of desert boots, checked his wallet to see there was enough for a pint and grabbed his jacket from the hooks behind the door. No one would miss him. Not for an hour or so. He was just about to leave when he remembered the mobile. He scooped that up too, slipping it into a jacket pocket and trotted down the stairs past his neighbour's flat. There was no sign of her which didn't surprise him. Her flat had been unnaturally quiet for days and Hunter assumed she must have been staying elsewhere, perhaps with a boyfriend. He let the secure door click shut behind him and headed for the pub.

No one could ever have described The Falcon as a beautiful building. Even its architect Hunter mused, must have been abundantly aware of its ugliness from the moment of its inception. Sitting on the corner of a busy crossroads its main feature an unattractive triangular car park, ringed in on two sides by calf high brick walls and dilapidated low-slung chains. The third side of the triangle, the pub's front aspect, sitting diagonally to the road, facing out over unattractive North London traffic. Someone had made a passing attempt at a neo-Tudor façade, with thick black and white painted facia which wouldn't have fooled a blind man on a galloping horse. The windows were filling with old PRS stickers, dead wasps and adverts for local bands with increasingly improbable names. By the front door the now ubiquitous smouldering ash can.

If the exterior of the pub appeared unpromising, nothing could have prepared Hunter for the interior. A long, sticky and intimidating bar ran the length of the building. Dotted here and there in the main body of the room, lonely looking fruit machines blinked and beeped at no one in particular as around them deserted islands of tables and chairs sat sadly overlooked, expectantly hoping, one day, to be occupied. A huge screen silently displaying American music videos dangled from the ceiling by the toilets, whilst Don McLean sang about The Big Bopper and Buddy Holly. Hunter had a quick look about. There wasn't even anyone behind the bar, but he went and stood expectantly by it and tried not to touch anything. Finally, a disgruntled looking Irishman of indeterminate age appeared and Hunter was able to buy himself a drink. He took his pint and sat in the window seat so he might look back at the flats opposite and wonder what on earth he'd got himself involved in.

Following Amy's murder Hunter had taken two lives, neither of which had helped him come to terms with losing her. He had returned to his two-up two-down in Cambridge and sunk into a drink fuelled depression. Then there had come the perplexing offer of employment from the man calling himself Lazarus. He'd not had to consider the offer for long before accepting. After all what else was there waiting for him? He opened his wallet and wondered what he might buy for under two pounds. The bar had a deal on a dubiously dedicated whisky. Then out of money and ideas he decided to head back to the flat, but not before a quick visit to the toilets.

Hunter was washing his hands. He was aware of the door opening and closing and caught a brief glimpse of sturdy black shoes and jeans but never bothered looking up from the sink. Then he realised the other man had positioned himself quite deliberately directly behind him.

'You were told not to leave the flat. Which bit of that did you not understand?'

Hunter looked up at the mirror above the cracked and stained sink and into the heavy dead eyes of Michael Healy. The last time he'd seen him, Scott had been carrying his wounded father, desperate to get him to a hospital. Healy wore an open necked shirt beneath a black leather jacket, cruelly exposing his salt and pepper hair which Hunter noted he wore long and well kempt. In years gone by it would have been a sheer, glistening, lady-killer black, but Healy, in his early forties and probably in no small part due to the nature of his work had started to prematurely grey, his once impressive locks now shot through with fresh streaks of silver, a gunpowder stubble coating his solid jaw.

'Get back across the road before I have to tell the boss and sit by your phone. I'll be in touch soon, in the meantime do as you're fucking well told.'

Hunter spun round quickly, hoping he might take Healy by surprise, but the older man was more than ready for him and he found himself staring down the barrel of an ugly black pistol.

'Not so easy without a cricket bat in your hand, is it? Now stop fucking about and get back across the road before I lose my patience and accidentally shoot you.'

'And what if I don't?'

'You ever seen a baseball game, Scott?'

'Rounders with big gloves and silly trousers? No.'

'Three strikes is what the Yanks say, three strikes and you're out.'

'Right.'

'This,' Healy looked at the pub around them, 'is strike one. Fuck up two more times and we're done. Understood?'

'Sorry.'

'*Understood?*'

'Understood.'

'Good, and don't ever apologise to me again. Just for the record, baseball's a fine game. Next time you say something crass and ignorant like that, founded on a complete absence of information or a pathetic need to impress, that'll be strike two. Got it?'

Hunter nodded.

'*Got it?*'

'Got it.'

A tight wrinkle of a smile, but enough to let Hunter know that everything would be okay, on this occasion, probably.

'I don't understand. What *is* the job? When will it begin?'

Healy nodded, waggled the gun at Hunter to get out of the toilets and that their conversation was at an end.

'Soon,' he said to Hunter's back, 'soon.'

Then Hunter was at the double doors to the car park. He quickly looked behind him into the empty space, but Healy was gone. As he crossed the road back to the flat, slipping between the traffic, he noticed the lights were on from the flat below and caught a glimpse of movement from within, so it was no surprise when moments later and halfway up the stairs the pretty girl whom he had met on his first day, stood by her open door.

'Hi there.'

'Hello,' Hunter replied.

'I realised the other day I didn't tell you my name. It's Samantha, although I guess my friends all call me Sam, do you see?'

'What do I call you then, Sam or Samantha?'

'Why don't we go for a drink later and we could discuss it?'

Hunter drew near.

'Christ, you've been drinking already?' Sam said.

'Yeah. Sorry, maybe I'd better pass.'

'Yeah, maybe you had,' she laughed.

'Another time then,' Hunter said over his shoulder, trying to sound confident, but the door to Samantha's flat was already closing.

Istanbul, 1999

The man calling himself Mr Price strode up to the concierge desk of The Marmara Hotel.

'Good morning, I'm here to see a Mr Henderson.'

The young Turkish lad behind the counter, whose name was Yusuf, took a moment to digest this piece of information before flicking back through a black leather-bound appointments book at his elbow and announcing, with more than a hint of disdain Mr Price thought, that 'Mr Henderson is in the bar, sir.'

Yes, I bet he is.

'Thank you. Would you also mind ringing up to Miss White's room and letting her know I'm here?'

'Miss White has already left, sir,' Yusuf said, this time without consulting his thick, black book.

Mr Price, who was not easily surprised, tried to disguise it now. He tried to make it appear that that had been just one of any number of answers he'd been expecting to hear.

'I see,' he smiled agreeably. 'And when did she say she would be back?'

'She won't, sir. She's already checked out, sir.'

Yusuf consulted his leather-bound book again, found the entry he'd been searching for with his index finger, tapped at it several times as if to make sure and then looked up to address Mr Price with the direct beaming smile of one who works in the hospitality trade.

'I'm sorry you have missed her.' Worried he was not being believed he half turned the book towards Mr Price without inviting him to look. 'I remember her. She is pretty, Miss White.'

Pretty or not at that moment all Mr Price wanted to do was

reach across the counter and grab the lad by his cheap, smart jacket and tell him to stop wasting his time.

'Indeed.'

'She checked out this morning, sir.'

'You said. If you will point me towards the bar then, please?'

'Your friend left in quite a hurry. She was heading to the airport to catch a flight, I believe.'

Mr Price nodded. *Of course she was.*

'I found her a taxi,' Yusuf concluded proudly.

Terrific.

'Can you remember what time it was when she left?'

Yusuf the concierge gaped at Mr Price, who was not Mr Price.

'There's no chance I might still catch her I mean?'

'No, sir. Very early. I remember. It was easy to find her a taxi.'

I'm delighted for you.

'She seemed a little upset, if you'll forgive me for saying?'

You're forgiven, Yusuf, you're forgiven. How could you possibly know.

'Just the bar then, please.'

'Follow me, sir.'

The man Mr Price had flown nearly two thousand miles to see was slumped over a table in the darkest corner the spacious bar The Marmara Hotel had to offer.

'Mr Henderson, there is a Mr Price here to see you.'

The man calling himself Mr Henderson looked up. The events of the previous twenty-four hours had aged him considerably. That and the half empty bottle of Scotch dominating the centre of the table.

'Is there anything else I can do for you, Mr Price?' Yusuf was asking.

'Better fetch me another glass, if you wouldn't mind?'

'Of course, sir.'

Mr Henderson and Mr Price watched Yusuf the concierge disappear behind the hotel's capacious bar before either man spoke.

'What the fuck happened, Ewen?'

'That's what you're here to find out, isn't it?'

Mr Price blinked slowly and held his breath a fraction longer than was strictly necessary before exhaling.

'You slept much?'

'Not at all, actually.'

'See the lovely Miss King leave this morning?'

But before the other man could answer Yusuf returned with a sparkling tumbler which he set down next to the bottle at the centre of the table.

'Thank you, Yusuf. We'll take these up to Mr Henderson's room. Would you mind very much sending up another bottle. Mr Henderson here will pay.'

'Naturally, sir.'

Sarratt, Present Day

In the months since the shooting David Hunter had not been busy. He'd lost his spleen to a bullet and only one thing had made the subsequent lengthy recovery tolerable, he'd been reunited with his son. For a while Scott had come every day to visit him in hospital. David had told his son some, but not all, of his family's history. The boy had been inquisitive, but David had been prepared for that. He'd been preparing for such a time since the discovery of his wife's body. He'd gratefully filled in some of the blank spaces in their collective pasts, the unburdening of a life-time's secrets and lies all part of his recuperation, but when Scott had asked how it was that on the fateful night of the shooting, his eternally patient, mild mannered father, retired accounts exec and sometime gardener had so expertly stripped and reassembled a firearm David had chosen not to answer. Scott, perhaps already suspecting the truth had not pressed the point. But then, when David thought about his son and the extraordinary and tragic turns his life had already taken, he'd been forced to conclude there were as many mysteries to be unravelled there as in his own murky past. Scott had met George Wiseman and spoken with a man calling himself Lazarus, who David suspected to be the recently knighted John Alperton. He'd met and received help from two men, field agents, who David did not know, but my God he knew their type. So, whilst he was sure his son must be full of questions about his past, David was having to admit that he was equally intrigued by Scott's present. Was he about to inhabit the same shadowy, deceit filled world he had, until Land-slide? Wasn't he duty bound, based on his prior experiences, to dissuade his son from such a life? David Hunter smiled. The idea of gently coaxing his son! That stubborn streak, a mile long, had come from his mother.

After a lengthy period of recuperation, David had returned home and had almost immediately wound up back in hospital suffering with a secondary infection. The whole recovery had taken almost three months. The only thing he was grateful for, that in the Autumn his garden largely looked after itself. Now, with the first signs of Winter on its way he stood in his kitchen window and looked at the bald flowerbeds suffocating under layers of brown mulch. Soon it would be time to prepare for fresh beginnings.

David had undertaken an early spring clean of the house. He'd found a bag of old shoes, stored away for when and what purpose he knew not. None of the shoes had laces. There must have been a reason for this David supposed, but for the time being that reason eluded him. An old and decrepit pair of sandals, some worn slippers and at the bottom of the bag, his heavy black brogues. David withdrew them. They had come from one of London's finer cobblers, he could see from the stamp, the leather resole, the new heel they had put on when he'd returned them many years ago. But as he examined them now, turning them over in his hands he saw how small patches of leather had perished or been eaten away and where they hadn't been destroyed completely, they were permanently scuffed or split. These now could never be repaired. They, like him, had aged and although he struggled to admit it, withered with that age. His body was now that of a man in his sixties. As David had regularly returned to the shop in Kensington and had them lavish care and shoe polish on his brogues, now he himself was having to take regular and all too personal trips to the doctors, where he was poked and prodded by a youth little older than his son. He returned the shoes to their resting place, irrationally broken hearted at their condition, uncertain of their fate, confused by their presence, only sure that, like him, they were not what they had once been. But then that was what he did now, he kept things, old things, broken down shoes, rusty golf clubs, dusty old tax receipts and secrets, boxes and boxes of secrets. In truth David Hunter realised he had become a repository for the past.

Istanbul, 1999

Mr Henderson and Mr Price sat on the fourteenth floor of The Marmara Hotel on the edge of Mr Henderson's recently remade king sized bed and looked out over Istanbul towards the Galata Bridge, the domes and minarets of The Blue Mosque, nestling, comfortably secure of their place in the city's history. Yusuf had brought them another bottle of overpriced Scotch and the men had taken their glasses from the bar. Once Yusuf had departed, Mr Price hung up the *Do Not Disturb* sign and double bolted the door. He splashed a little tap water over his Scotch and joined his friend as they silently contemplated the view and listened to the midday call to prayer.

'Not that it isn't delightful to see you, but I was rather expecting to have the pleasure of Toby Gray's company or even Sandy?' Mr Henderson said.

'Sorry to disappoint.'

'You've come to roll up the op?'

'Seems like you've made a pretty good job of that yourself,' Price replies taking a sip from his glass. 'What went wrong?'

'Might be easier to tell you what went right.'

'When did you start drinking?'

'I don't remember.'

'From the moment I heard you were coming out here with Pat I knew it was a mistake. Why was she sent anyway? Did you have something to do with that? Long weekend in Istanbul, did you fancy that?'

'I was told to blood the new recruit,' Mr Henderson replied tiredly.

'A safe pair of hands?'

'Your words not mine. Sandy gave me all that crap about novice hurdlers and first time over the sticks, old son.'

'I don't buy it.'

'Believe it or not, neither did I.'

'So, what the hell happened?'

'The chap we were supposed to meet was a no show.'

'It can't be as simple as that. Just because an asset doesn't turn up is no reason to fly me out here to conduct the grand inquisition. What was the reason for him not coming do you suppose?'

'I suppose because at about midnight, four hours after we should have been meeting him, the Turkish Police were fishing his headless corpse out of the Bosphorus. I suppose that *might* have something to do with it?'

'Fuck.' Mr Price went immediately to the bathroom and returned with a glass of water for their Scotch. 'Fuck.'

'They turned up here not an hour later like a herd of bloody elephants and all the subtlety and stealth of a Russian tank parking up at the end of your street, lights flashing, sirens on, the whole bit.'

'What about King? How did she walk away from all this?'

'A perk of being the new girl, I suppose? No one knows or cares who you are, so you quietly slip away into the night. I, on the other hand, was probably flagged the moment they saw my ugly mug at the airport.'

'Nice of her to stick around though, lend a bit of moral support.'

In a defiant act of concentration Mr Henderson carefully places his glass on the table which sits in the window. 'I sent her home.'

'You did what?'

'I sent her. No point in the pair of us getting screwed over.'

'And why are you not entertaining the Turkish Police with this crock of crap?'

Mr Henderson loosened the new bottle's cork and poured them both a healthy measure holding up his glass and waiting for the other man to return his stare. Mr Price, already knowing what to expect on the opening of a new bottle, looks away and then, reluctantly, back.

'I take this glass into my hand,' Henderson begins. 'Come on,' he insists, 'you never know, this could be the last chance we get.'

'But it's different every time. Must we?'

'Yes, we must. And you're missing the point, as usual. I take this glass into my hand,'

Albeit unwillingly Price joins in, 'And drink to all that's here.' Now both men finding their rhythm, 'For we don't know where we shall be this time another year.'

Henderson, encouraging his friend; 'We might be dead,'

And Price indulging *his*; 'We might be slain,'

Henderson again now and with renewed purpose and real feeling; 'We might be laying low,'

And finally together once more as they look out over the roof tops of ancient Istanbul, 'We might be in a foreign land and not know where to go,' followed by howls of drunken laughter at the relief of it all. The anthem of their disparate little brotherhood.

'Slange var,' Henderson the Scot.

'Absent friends,' Price the Sassenach, 'fuck 'em!'

Followed by a clink of glasses.

'I'm really worried. There's a whole side of this you're not seeing and I can't show you,' says Henderson.

'Anything I can do to help?'

'I don't think so. Just promise me you'll be there when it all comes out?'

'We'll see.'

'Thanks. Listen, let's get out of here, at least for the evening. There's a great little restaurant I've found. It's just around the corner.'

Mr Price thinks about the offer. 'I'm sorry, I'm going to have to pass. I'd advise you make that your last though,' he holds up his empty glass in a silent and reductive toast, 'you know what has to happen tomorrow?'

'Back to London?'

'I'm afraid so, and it isn't going to be pretty.'

'I know.'

Mr Price stands and moves to the door.

'Get some rest, lay off that stuff for a while and I'll see you in the morning.'

2

Harrow, Present Day

Hunter spent the next six days obediently camped out in the claustrophobic little flat waiting for the phone to ring. He had lost count of the number of times he'd washed the few clothes he owned or tidied the minimally appointed space. He rearranged the stores, first alphabetically and then in order of priority. He started to exercise, primarily to ease the monotony and then gradually to improve himself, but – after over a week of tedious incarceration Hunter was just about ready to walk away from the smothering North London apartment and the job he'd been offered. The nonspecific, no fee, no paperwork to sign, no work involved job he had been offered and which seemed likely never to transpire. As he contemplated his future, and with the uncertainty of each passing day he was drawing closer and closer to one inevitable and disturbing conclusion. There never had been a job. He'd had a friend at university, a good friend, who'd enjoyed a practical joke and the more elaborate the better. If Alec hadn't been shot to death this could easily have been his doing. Hunter should pack up the few possessions he had and leave rather than wait another day.

His insomnia, which had only worsened on his arrival in Harrow, was allowing him to brood over the problem of his future nearly twenty-four hours a day. But, having suffered with the condition for much of his adult life, Hunter and insomnia, like Frank and Alice, had become devoted if dysfunctional lovers. When he did sleep, he dreamt predominantly of his childhood but also intermittently of dead people, long forgotten faces and broken promises. When awake he became strangely obsessed with the mobile phone he'd discovered in the computer desk, sometimes carrying it with him everywhere, even through the night, whilst at other times, concerned that by his very presence he was in some way preventing it from ringing, he would leave it on the kitchen table, only then to feel utterly beholden to it, unable to venture too far away should it ring. And so, eventually, after ten days of enforced contemplation and borderline incarceration, Hunter finally gave up. He packed away his possessions and was working out his next move, when the doorbell rang. Hunter opened the door to the same sunken eyes he'd seen in the pub.

'My name is Michael Healy. You may call me Michael, or Mr Healy, although that does make me sound like a geography teacher, so let's stick with Michael. You may not call me Mike, Mickey or any other derivative of the word Michael. Got it?'

'Got it.'

'Good. We're going for a drive.'

A blacked-out Audi A4 was parked in the bus lane outside the flat. The same blacked out Audi Hunter had seen outside his house in Cambridge and the same Audi they had observed

George Wiseman's South Kensington apartment from, but this time Hunter was getting in the front.

'Where's...?'

'Bob? Retired, after your last little stunt.'

'I'm sorry.'

'Don't be, least of all for him. He's not, miserable old bastard. Only too glad to be away from this lunacy.'

Hunter decided it might be preferable to just look out of the window rather than try and engage Michael in any further conversation.

They drove west across North London, through Sudbury and Wembley and then down past Ealing into South Acton or Chiswick, depending on what you would have your taxi driver believe and whether you were buying or selling. Healy slowed before turning into Radnor Road, an avenue lined with naked silver birch. Commuter belt, for people with well paid jobs, but either not enough money to move out to the sticks and suffer the commute, or not enough courage. The road was fully parked, cars only needed for the weekend when the kids were back from school. An unremarkable collection of Georgian two-up two-downs populated by mid-level lawyers and solicitors, journalists and media types. The pub presiding over one end of the road, a melting pot of greed and racism and all washed down with sub-standard beer and the background promise of violence. Every other house had a motorbike or scooter hidden beneath waterproof covers and ready for the morning's bustling commute. Healy parked up at a corner looking back along the row.

'Now what?' Hunter asked.

'If you take a walk down that street, past the pub, you'll find a parade of shops. I'll have a cappuccino and a croissant.' Michael Healy had been waiting for years to say those insignificant words.

Hunter stepped out of the car and thrust an open fist at Healy, who looked back and through him. Hunter's hand remained there and so, reluctantly Healy scrabbled for his wallet and found a tenner. 'And don't bother coming back without either,' he concluded, settling in his seat.

So, this was it, Hunter thought as he negotiated his way into Chiswick, this was the long-anticipated job he was secretly being groomed for. He was getting pastry. And then, as if from nowhere he saw Amy standing by the café in Kensington, W8, a coffee in one hand, a paper in the other, waving to him. That had been the last time he'd seen her, or at least the last time he cared to recall. She'd been his world and now, because of him and his actions, she was dead. On the opposite side of the road a shamelessly corporate American coffee chain. Not for the first time it occurred to Hunter to walk straight out into the busy London traffic. But then Mike Healy wouldn't get his fucking croissant, would he?

They sat in complete silence for nearly an hour, then Hunter could bear it no longer.

'Exactly what are we doing here?'

'Watching.'

'What?'

'Not what. Who.'

'Who then?'

Healy looked at the clock on the Audi's dash.

'Just another few minutes.'

Hunter struggled to see which of the many houses Healy might be observing. He caught a quick glance at the clock. Two minutes to eight. Whoever it was would be leaving their house on the hour, presumably to catch a train into London and a well-paid job. At a minute to eight, front doors began opening and then a steady trickle of disgruntled looking office workers emerged for the day. Not one of them Hunter noticed, provoking the slightest reaction from Michael Healy.

They continued to wait until, at thirteen minutes past the hour a front door halfway down on the opposite side of the road flew open and a middle-aged woman burst onto Radnor Road. She appeared to be about to slam the door behind her, but then, remembering, disappeared back inside only to return moments later clutching a well-travelled leather doctor's bag which she threw over her shoulder before marching off towards the nearest railway station.

Michael Healy glanced at the clock, removed a small and rather crumpled jotter from his jacket pocket and scribbled something down.

'Was that our "who"?

'Well done,' Healy replied with more than a trace of sarcasm.

'Who is she?'

'Miss White.'

'Real name?'

'Try not to be a complete arse Hunter.'

'Sorry.'

'And stop apologising.'

Hunter was struggling. No small talk. No stating the blindingly obvious. Intelligent questions only, please.

'Why are we watching her?'

'Because it is what we have been instructed to do,' Healy continued curtly.

'By who, Lazarus?'

Healy ignored the question and sipped at the dregs of his coffee. 'Tell me about Miss White.'

'I'm guessing she's sixtyish?'

'Not bad. Fifty-seven actually. Physical description.'

'Five-eight? Shoulder length, no longer white-grey hair. A little overweight. Is that fair?'

'Fairness has nothing to do with it.'

'Okay. Overweight then.'

'How many pounds?'

'I don't know.'

'200, 220?'

'Okay.'

'Clothes?'

'God, I don't know. She looks like she got dressed in the dark. Some sort of knitted thing. Is it a kaftan?'

That at least deserved the briefest of reactions from Healy, and Hunter was pleased to see him hide a smile.

'Go away and find out.'

'What?'

'This is what we do, for today at least. You can't give a detailed description of our Miss White there if you don't know what she's wearing, so go away and find out. Start with her footwear?'

'Boots?'

'What sort of boots?'

'Brown boots?'

'Those, Mrs Healy informs me are called knee high boots.'

'As distinct from?'

'You need to know this shit,' Healy continued ignoring Hunter, 'it matters. Now, demeanour?'

'She was a bit frantic.'

'Good. What type of frantic? Upset, husbands run off with his secretary frantic? Just had an unpleasant letter from the Inland Revenue frantic or just every day, running late frantic?'

'Yeah, sure, probably going to miss her train.'

'Or shit scared she's going to miss an assignation with a Russian operative called Vlad who could have her killed, frantic?'

'Oh, I see.'

'I doubt it. Trust me she's like that every morning.'

Hunter thought the idea that he would ever trust Mike Healy was an amusing one but chose not to share it.

'Where was she going?'

'To get a train into town.'

'Possibly, but we shouldn't presume. Which train?'

'How the hell should I know?'

'Find out.'

Hunter was beginning to get more than a little frustrated with his new teacher's unreasonable approach.

'Who are you working for Michael, John Alperton?'

It was a stab in the dark, a name Hunter had heard Wiseman use and the mention of it now did seem to ruffle Healy's feathers.

'In time you'll come to understand that we have any number of masters. This,' Healy said hiding a smile at the irony of his comment, 'is our morning's exercise.' He reached across and popped open the car's glove compartment. 'There's a phone for you. Don't get too excited, it's nothing fancy, simply for us to keep in touch.'

Hunter turned the phone on and opened up its menu screen. Healy hadn't been kidding. It was about as basic as they came.

'You'll see there are a bunch of messages already on there to make the thing look a bit more used. Scroll through the contacts. *M Gym*, that's me. If I want you here, I'll send you a text, *See you at the gym* that sort of thing, and a time. You're to get yourself over here ASAP. Understand?'

Hunter understood, and so Michael Healy fired up the Audi and headed back to North London, their first lesson at an end.

'Day one. Don't get any funny ideas about sloping off across the road,' Healy said outside the flat on Wealdstone Drive. 'Keep your eye on that phone and I'll see you soon.'

Hunter slammed the Audi's door shut and prepared himself for another miserable evening in front of the television. No sound came from Samantha's flat as he passed and then he was searching for his keys. Hunter took off his jacket and began pacing up and down the thin corridor which connected the front and back of the flat. He was trying to process the events of the day, trying to remember everything Healy had taught him or tried to teach him. Everything about the strange woman they had observed on and off throughout the day and Healy's many instructions and requests. Hunter walked past the second bedroom for the umpteenth time. Healy seemed to have given him the green light to use the computer, so he fired up the iMac and went on-line. He found a pad and pen in one of the table's drawers, tracked down the website he'd been looking for and began taking notes. In a separate window he brought up two maps of London and in a third a series of tables and graphs. Scott Hunter licked his finger and turned a fresh page. He spent several hours glued to the computer's monitor. Then at ten o'clock his new mobile phone buzzed with a message from his mentor. He would try and get some sleep so as to be able to meet Healy in Chiswick at eight o'clock the following morning.

***

At eight-thirteen they watched Miss White walk to the end of the road where she turned by the pub and disappeared towards Chiswick.

'Where's she going?'

'Chiswick Park Tube.'

'You're quite sure about that? What about South Acton?'

'South Acton's on the North London Line and goes, well nowhere really.'

Healy stared at Hunter, a long and, for Hunter, uncomfortable stare.

'Okay, nowhere interesting.'

The stare again.

'She's not going to South Acton, okay? First off she's walking in completely the wrong direction and secondly, even if she walks all the way around the block and doubles back, there won't be another train from South Acton in either direction,' Hunter consulted the Audi's dash, 'for at least another eighteen minutes, so why's she rushing? Doesn't make sense. She's going to Chiswick Park Tube.'

'Why there and not Turnham Green?'

'You said yourself. She's carrying a few extra pounds. She's a fifty-seven-year-old woman. Chiswick Park is a third of a mile away. The average walking speed for a woman in better shape than her is under three miles an hour. She's giving herself an extra couple of minutes, and anyway, Turnham Green on foot's another seven or eight minutes away. Why would she bother?'

'Okay,' Healy conceded reluctantly, 'then where?'

'My guess...' Hunter began before seeing Healy's expression and realising that guessing was clearly off his menu. 'She's going into town. Westminster,' Hunter said with renewed confidence.

'She could be going to...'

'Richmond or Ealing Broadway?' Hunter interrupted. 'I know. But she isn't.'

'How can you be so sure?'

'Because the next train west isn't until eight-thirty and even at her pace she'd be ridiculously early for that. So, like I said, why would she be rushing? She's going to catch the eight-twenty-three into town from Chiswick Park. Platform 2. She'll arrive at Westminster with enough time to get a coffee and a bagel before her nine o'clock meeting.'

Healy smiled. 'Not bad, Scott. Not bad at all. Have you had breakfast?'

'No.' Here it comes Hunter thought and after all that, the morning coffee run.

'Got any money?'

'Barely enough to get here.'

Healy presented him with a crisp new twenty-pound note.

'Go and get something to eat. There'll be nothing to do here until about four. Miss White may like to run late, but she is nothing if not consistent. If there is, I'll text you, otherwise, be back here for three-thirty.'

Hunter looked at the note in his hand. Aside from the immense sense of gratitude at having some cold hard cash in his pocket, this was validation. He was doing something right. He wasn't sure what that was yet, but something.

'Thanks, Michael.'

'Don't.'

And the Audi's door was slamming and Hunter relaxed. There had been a brief, unsettling moment verging on friendliness, but now everything was back to normal. He left Healy and walked into Chiswick.

When he returned at exactly half past three having bought a paper and some cigarettes and relaxed for the first time in weeks, he couldn't be certain, but the machine that was Michael Healy appeared to have been asleep. They sat in silence for almost half-an-hour, any sense of familiarity or closeness a distant memory, and then they were watching Miss White approach from around the corner by the pub. So, this was her routine. She walked along Radnor Road, staying on the opposite side of the street. Then she walked right past her house, hardly giving it a second glance. To Hunter's horror she continued walking towards them. As she came closer and closer to the car, Michael Healy suddenly turned on Hunter and started an animated conversation about the previous evening's Champions League result. Hunter found himself responding, even though he had no idea what Healy was talking about, and then Miss White was gone, and Healy stopped just as suddenly as he had started.

'Notice anything odd about our Miss White, this afternoon?'

'Why didn't she go straight home?'

'She's walking anti-surveillance. And your next question should be, why is a mid-level civil servant with less than five years on her mortgage walking anti-surveillance?'

'Because she's not a civil servant?'

'You wanted to know why we're here, and that I suspect, Mr Hunter, is very much why we are here.'

That night, after he'd been dropped back at the flat in Harrow and exhausted and hungry from hours of sitting listening to Healy and waiting for Miss White to return, Hunter went to the kitchen to fix himself something to eat. Stocks were beginning to run low and he was examining the contents of his fridge to see if there were the makings of a basic pasta when he felt the phone in his pocket vibrate.

Good work today. Check your post.

Hunter had only just returned to the flat. He'd walked in through the front door and there had been no post, not even a flyer from the fast food joints nearer town. Time was getting late and the postal service had surely long since packed up for the day. Perhaps Healy meant for him to check his email, but that seemed unlikely too. He padded out of the kitchen, up the short corridor to the flat's front door. Outside, on the mat, a large cardboard box full of provisions; eggs, rice, cereal, fresh milk, cheese, chocolate biscuits, coffee, fresh butter and even, Hunter noted with a smile, a small bottle of Bells Whisky and a carton of the cigarettes he smoked. He carried the box through to the kitchen and decanted his reward.

He was just about to light himself a celebratory cigarette and crack open the whisky when the doorbell rang. Immediately terrified it must be the police or worse, Michael Healy, he pressed his eye cautiously to the peep hole. Samantha, the attractive girl from down the stairs.

'Hi. I was wondering if you'd like to buy me a drink?'

Hunter was in the mood to celebrate and even if they just

went to the grotty pub across the road, the idea of spending an evening with Samantha was extremely attractive.

'I can't. I'm sorry.'

'Oh, I see.' She didn't just look disappointed, she looked offended too.

'I want to,' Hunter stammered, 'it's just, I'm not supposed...'

I'm not *supposed* to what? Leave the flat? She'd think he was a lunatic or a mummy's boy or on remand or all three.

'I just fancy staying in. Do you mind?'

Samantha was smiling again.

'I see you've been to The Falcon then. Sure, why not. Do you want to come to mine? I've got wine, there might even be a beer somewhere at the back of the fridge?'

He wouldn't be leaving the flats, not technically, and he could take his mobile phone with him. It was the perfect solution. Michael had said he'd done good work and he was in the mood to celebrate, but he didn't want to celebrate alone.

'Sounds great.'

Samantha's flat was exactly how Hunter had imagined it. She stopped in the tiny hallway to remove her shoes and so Hunter followed suit.

'Come through,' she said cheerily, disappearing into the sitting room.

With the exception of a print depicting a vivid blue swimming pool there were tasteful yet, to Hunter's eye, largely incomprehensible contemporary reproductions hanging from the walls. A television set not dissimilar to the one in his flat had acquired the feminine touch, covered in a colourful Indonesian batik. Dried flowers rested on bookcases packed with Kandinsky and Rothko, Ravilious and Hepworth. Next to the ornamental mantelpiece a thinly distended brass of a woman with huge feet and carrying a child.

Hunter had been right, and for the second time in twenty-four hours was feeling pleased with himself.

'Nice flat,' he said relieved that she had not wanted to see his.

'Wine or beer?'

'Either,' he shrugged, 'I don't mind.'

He followed her along a corridor, past two closed doors to bedrooms as small as his he had to assume and through to the kitchen which lay immediately below his own, although that was where any similarity ended. Samantha's kitchen was altogether cleaner, sparkling pots and pans hanging from stainless steel racks and everywhere modern fixtures and fittings. She went to the fridge and reached out a bottle of wine. A pair of glasses already waiting on the kitchen counter. She made a joke of presenting him the bottle.

'Will this be to sir's liking?' she said, laughing nervously.

'Perfect.'

She splashed some wine into the glasses and handed him one. Hunter watched a delicate hand artistically tuck a wayward wisp of blonde fringe behind her ear.

'Where are you studying?'

'Middlesex Uni. I'm in my last year. History of Art. You?'

Hunter was so pleased with himself he nearly blurted out his entire life story.

'I'm just looking for a job. It's my first time in London and I could really do with making a fresh start.'

Samantha moved closer to him and Hunter realised he was enjoying the closeness. She raised her glass. 'Well, here's to fresh beginnings.'

'Fresh beginnings,' he smiled.

East London, 1999

And so Mr Price had been sent home in disgrace, his tail firmly between his legs, unhappy expressions painted on all who knew him. Mr Price, or at least the man calling himself Mr Price was the only one who seemed not in the slightest bit concerned. There were rumours, Christ when were there not rumours, there had even been stories about King and Gray. There had been rumours of unhappiness at home, of fights and arguments. His co-workers speculated that it was these unwanted intrusions into his work life which ultimately had resulted in the loss of one Ewen Connolly and as a consequence, Landslide. Everyone agreed it was such a terrible shame, what with Mr Price having a young family and all. The service for its part and following a period of masochistic self-recrimination, quietly turned in on itself. First there had been Moscow, which had been bad, then there was Landslide, which had been worse, and finally the perceived defection of Ewen Connolly, a trusted and well liked, if junior agent, which had been the disaster to end all disasters and all under the nose of one of their own. And as if to add insult to injury, not just anyone but one of their finest. One almighty fuck up after another, was what people were whispering. Heads, as Sandy Harper was so fond of saying, would surely roll.

The man they were calling Price wasn't surprised when, after a dignified pause, the telephone in his room at The

Marmara rang. The only surprise had been how long it had taken. Quietly he was pleased. At least they thought something of him, were trying to spare him what remained of his dignity. It also meant he was going home, away from the scene of the accident. Accident because no crime, that he was aware of, had been committed. The voice on the other end of the line advised him not to screw around anymore but to get his arse back to London. The plane would be leaving in less than three hours. Oh, and a word to the wise, best you don't drink too much at the airport old son, people will want to speak with you when you get back, old son. He packed his meagre possessions into his small suitcase. It didn't take long. He'd not bothered to unpack the few clothes he'd brought with him. A last check through the bathroom. His toothbrush and paste. Then downstairs to reception. The bill on his room had already been settled and so he asked the friendly concierge to flag him down a taxi and he would be on his way. A plane ticket was waiting for him at the British Airways desk. Mr Price found a bar and ordered a large Scotch, and then another.

He wasn't surprised, this middle-aged man masquerading as Mr Price, to find himself met at Heathrow by a nondescript individual in an altogether forgettable grey suit and black tie holding a board with his name on. Mr Price it said in thick, boorish writing. He almost laughed.

'15c?' he asked perhaps more cheerily than the circumstances allowed.

He was not surprised when he received no response. Nor was he surprised when the man refused to speak to him all the way from Heathrow to Aldgate in London's East End. He would probably have done the same under the circumstances. Pleasingly the route the man took was the route he would have taken. At least he would have got that right.

The flat the man drove Mr Price to had once belonged to the German Lutheran Church. What, to a casual passer-by, might have appeared to be a cobblestone courtyard was in fact a two hundred and fifty-year-old graveyard which, if there were heavy rain, came alive in a morbid dance of phalanges and phalanxes as centuries of fragmented bones fought their way to the surface.

The church let out a couple of rooms to students for a nominal fee and on the top floor and out of anyone's way was 15c. Subsequently, in the noughties when property prices had risen faster than Christ himself, and with the church finding itself on hard times and surrounded by the world's banks and vacant flats owned by foreign oligarchs, the clergy had seen the light and converted the bulk of the space into financially more lucrative town houses and the service had moved on. But in 1999 it remained, the quiet neighbour who was seldom if ever in, always paid its bills on time and never so much as squeaked a word of complaint. The service bought in cheap functional furniture which was quickly bolted to the oak floorboards. A corner of one room was treated for damp, but otherwise the wallpaper had remained – sagging sorrily and torn in places. An internal wall was replaced with a gigantic one way mirror and the door to the bathroom removed, along with most of the other internal doors, the general consensus being escape from a third floor window covered in bars, even had it been possible, would only have ever resulted in one outcome.

15c was stark, unwelcoming and loved by all who worked it. The tube station was two minutes around the corner, a greasy spoon next to that and an old fashioned East End pub across the street run by a modestly threatening individual called Dave who regularly baptised his beer with a bucket of water and always poured the drip trays back into the barrel. Local villains of no consequence who boasted loudly that nothing had ever been quite the same since Ronnie and Reggie went away easily rubbed shoulders with CID detectives who were quietly inclined to agree. And then there was Brick Lane. A stone's throw on the other side of the Whitechapel Road, the world-famous row of all-night curry houses.

Mr Price's avuncular chauffeur showed him up three flights of stairs and into a room Mr Price had frequented many times before, except he was usually on the other side of the glass or at the very least the metal table screwed securely into the floor.

The styrofoam cup of lukewarm coffee from the café around the corner, the ancient and battered Pernod ashtray, no doubt liberated from its café in Paris, the cigarettes given gratis, none of this shocked or surprised Mr Price. Even when the irascible Sandy Harper entered wearing an egg and bacon tie but devoid of its provenance and an ivory linen jacket which looked like he'd slept in it, Mr Price barely registered his arrival. Even when Sandy threw down his lighter and a thin manila envelope which slid across the formica threatening to spill its contents onto the floor, Mr Price remained implacable. Sandy scraped a chair across the floor and sat down noisily. Mr Price had a feeling he already knew the ultimate destination of their meeting. He'd been on Sandy's side of the table often enough. There would be platitudes and lies but not necessarily in that order and then Mr Price would be asked one question too many. A question he hadn't an answer for, or not a plausible or perhaps most importantly, a palatable answer for. Then he would, metaphorically speaking of course, be required to clear out his desk, take the envelope, such as it was, and without a bad word, a backwards glance or a fare thee well, fuck off, sunset or no, never to come back. These people, and he was quick to acknowledge the irony, these people did not believe in the proverbial returning bad penny. Once you were out of the door, you were out. Colleagues you had once eaten with, travelled with, perhaps even slept with, would no longer cross the road to wish you well or enquire after your health. Once you left, you were dead to them. Sometimes literally.

Mr Price withdrew a Marlboro from its battered soft packet.

'Been to The States I see.'

'The duty-free's the only thing that keeps me going back.' Obligingly Sandy Harper pushes his lighter across the table. 'But what am I saying. You're quite the traveller yourself these days,' he continues, taking a cigarette for himself. 'Sticky spot we find ourselves in.'

'Agreed. Although by we I take it you mean me?'

'Quite. How's your boy doing by the way?'

Mr Price flicked open the zippo and drew long and hard on the Marlboro.

'Fuck off Sandy. Don't try and climb inside my head, you wouldn't like it there. Let's just get on with it shall we.'

Sandy Harper took back his lighter a degree more forcibly than he'd intended and returned it to the table.

'Absolutely. Tell me about Ewen Connolly then. Which legend was he using?'

'Henderson.'

'And you?'

'Robert Price.'

'And what about Landslide. What do you know?'

'Nothing. Landslide wasn't my op remember? I was just dragged in to make everything right. All yesterday's news by the time I got there. Just the de-brief to take care of.'

'Connolly?'

'Exactly.'

'What did he tell you?'

'Said he went but that Landslide was a no show.'

'That it? *He* went, not the girl?'

'That's what he said.'

'You're sure?'

'Quite sure, yes.'

'I smell horseshit. Where was the meet?'

'Quaint little apothecary in The Grand Bazaar. The tourists get picked up as they leave their hotels and shown the sights before ending up in Uncle Hakan's shop. Cosy little room round the back just perfect for picking their pockets, metaphorically speaking naturally.'

'Naturally,' Sandy drawled. 'You been?'

'First thing I did when I got off the plane.' Not strictly true, but Sandy wasn't to know. 'Fits the bill rather nicely. Slightly off the beaten track. Sort of place you'd have to know about. Pretty sure that if you wanted some privacy for a while the owner would turn a blind eye, for the right price.'

'And when Landslide was a no show how long did Connolly wait?'

'Told me thirty minutes, which I'd have said was about twenty too long.'

'Me too, unless he was trying to impress?'

'Seems unlikely, under the circumstances. He said he'd

checked out the place well enough. Round the block half a dozen times. More than necessary wouldn't you say, particularly if you thought the guy you were there to meet was never coming anyway?'

Sandy choose to ignore that observation.

'Was it empty? I mean, *did* he pay the chap off?'

'He said there'd been no need.'

'No need, why would there be no need? There's that smell again, fresh from the stables. What did Connolly do next? Straight back to the apartment? Kiss and a cuddle with Miss King?'

'He said not. Took a walk down to the Bosphorus for an hour of quiet reflection and navel gazing.'

'Did he now?'

'Wanted to collect his thoughts before calling it in I suppose.'

'You suppose? Jesus. And he said he'd gone down to the river? He actually said that?'

'I can check my notes if you'd like?'

'Don't play the fool, it doesn't suit you.'

'Down to the river, contemplate the Almighty for a while then back into town and send the flash to London.'

'Why not straight away? Why did he spend so long at The Bazaar first and then the river?'

'You'd have to ask him, Sandy.'

'No can do, old son. That was your job, wasn't it? To make some sense of the five-star cock-up that was Landslide. And what the hell was King doing all this while?'

'Ewen said she was to wait for him at the hotel, but it seems there may have been a young man.'

'Young man?' A slice of prurience in Sandy's tone.

'Young Turkish lad.'

'Oh, this just gets better.'

'Only what I'm told. All third hand, but she was seen by someone at the hotel with a man who was most definitely not Connolly.'

'This is un-bloody-believable.'

'Plus, I got the feeling that Ewen was covering for her.'

'Sunday afternoon shag?'

'She wouldn't be the first, Sandy.'

'You're supposing rather a hell of a lot, if you don't mind me saying, old son? For one, you're supposing that this Turkish Don Juan was just that and not one of Connolly's Russian friends.'

'Sandy,' Mr Price admonishes.

'Well, did you press him on it?'

'Played his cards extremely close did Ewen. Why don't you speak to Pat King? She's in a much better position to tell you who she was sleeping with than I am.'

'No can do, old son. She's vanished off the face of the earth.'

'By which you mean?'

'She's in a safe house in Belsize Park and not talking to anyone.'

'Not talking to you?'

'That's what I said.'

'On whose orders? George? Toby? That son-of-a-bitch Alperton?'

'Your guess, as they say, is as good as mine.'

'Bullshit.'

'Now, now, let's not forget ourselves. Although it does appear our first port of call is to find young Abdul and drag his sorry arse in here,' Sandy says very much to himself. 'This is horrible, just horrible. All we know about him is he was young and Turkish. Christ, he could have been anyone. Kemal bloody Ataturk for all we know.'

Sandy Harper took a moment to steady himself. There was no way on earth he was going to carry the can for this, no way on earth.

'Alright, let's address the more vexing issue of Landslide. Where the hell is our man out of Moscow?'

'If I knew that, I'm not sure there would be quite such a need for this conversation.'

Sandy reaches into the file sat precariously at the table's corner and withdraws a photograph.

'Our man?' Mr Price asks.

'Hard to say, isn't it? Fish have had quite a good go at him.' Sandy pauses, trying to gauge the other man's reaction. 'Plus, his hands and feet have been hacked off and he's been decapitated.'

'Russians?'

'My guess. If this is Landslide, is there any reason for me not to believe your pal Ewen Connolly wasn't responsible for his rather ignominious demise?'

'The Turkish Police certainly didn't think so.'

The man they were agreeing to call Mr Price reached for another cigarette. Had this always been their intention, after Viktorija's death? Give him a job they suspected would go wrong, let him fuck it up, no thanks to Messrs King and Connolly and then, after the compulsory roasting, put him out to pasture like one of Sandy's old nags? Had he become, after her death and now the consummate balls up that had been Istanbul and Landslide, tainted in some way, despite neither ever having been directly attributed to him and never mind what Sandy Harper might have to say to the contrary? Suddenly he was the operative for whom things went wrong. People were injured, or worse, targets went missing or damn well disappeared altogether. Body parts were found washed up on foreign shores. He wasn't certain that he wouldn't have done exactly what Sandy Harper, the educated idiot was doing. He could imagine the naysayers, the prophets of doom. For God's sake make sure to steer well clear of him, the man's a menace.

'Alright then,' Sandy was continuing, 'tell me about Connolly. Could they have made him when he entered the country?'

That had certainly been Ewen Connolly's theory recalls Mr Price.

'Wouldn't imagine so, unless they'd been tipped off.'

That should get him fired up.

'Tipped off? Tipped off by whom?' Sandy enquires querulously. 'What are you implying?'

'I'm not implying anything.' Except that he was of course. 'I'm just exploring all the avenues, Sandy.'

'Well explore another avenue. Tipped off indeed.' Sandy Harper exhaled a long, thin plume of smoke. 'Tell me about your relationship with the Scotsman.'

'Are you asking if I knew him?'

'If I were?'

'Then you'd be playing particularly dumb and I can't imagine why.'

'Do you know him?'

'Come on Sandy you know damn well I know him.'

'Just playing the game, old son.'

'Well play a different game?'

'What about her?'

'King?'

'Yes. Friend?'

'Of whose?'

'Of yours, old son.'

'I wouldn't say so, no.'

'More than that then? Special friend? Lover? Talk about Landslide across the pillow?'

'You tell me. What is it you think you know, Sandy?'

Sandy pushes the packet of cigarettes across the table.

'I think you helped Connolly fly the coup. I think we made a grave misjudgement letting you bring him in, or try to, and I think the pair of you are up to your pretty little necks in it. That's what I think. Now, are you going to tell me where he is?'

'Have you checked his apartment?'

'Very fucking funny. You finished interviewing him at The Marmara on Monday evening at six o'clock?'

'Half past.'

'I do beg your pardon. Half past six. Then what?'

'He asked if I'd like to get something to eat...'

'Very pally.'

'I'm trying to tell you. We'd been drinking all day, he said there was a place he knew, in town, near The Blue Mosque, said the food was good.'

'And you said?

'No thanks. Not a nice position to be in with anyone least of all...'

'A close personal friend?'

'Exactly.'

'Godfather to your kith and kin, wasn't he?'

'Still is, as far as I'm aware.'

'Touché. So, you turned down dinner with your old pal, godparent, confidant. Then what?'

'I walked into town. Needed a change of scene and a sober up. Fresh air.'

'In Istanbul?'

'Touché.'

'You're walking the sweet-smelling streets of Istanbul, taking the night air. Meet anyone you know?'

'No.'

'Sure?'

'Quite sure.'

'Nice quiet stroll then, cup of sweet apple tea and straight to bed?'

'That's more or less it.'

'More or less?'

'Yes.'

'Sleep well?'

'Extremely.'

'Alone? No sweaty little shepherd boy to keep you warm?'

'Fuck off, Sandy.'

'Simple enough question.'

'*Yes*, I was alone.'

'Thank you. And Mr Connolly, what do you suppose he was up to?'

'How the hell should I know? Maybe he went to the restaurant?'

'Ah yes, the fabulous little romantic bistro by the Bosphorus.'

'I never said that.'

'Just testing.'

'Well don't.'

'If not the restaurant, where did he go?'

'I really have no idea. I'd imagine he'd have waited until I left and then begun preparing his exit.'

'No touching farewell speeches? No arrangements to meet in Paris? Secret assignation. Split the loot?'

'Sandy, what are you talking about?'

'You expect me to believe he just left Istanbul completely unaided? No help from King? You? A cold third party?'

'I don't know.'

'Our Russian friends, you suppose?'

'If you say so.'

'Picking up their man. Spiriting him back to Moscow. Ticker-tape parade or whatever the Commie equivalent is. Slap up lunch at the Metropol, handshakes all round at the Kremlin, dancing girls and vodka, then vanish forever?'

'Have you gone quite mad? This is Ewen Connolly we're talking about.'

'Why did you let him go so easily?'

'I didn't let anyone go at all. But let me tell you this,' Mr Price continues, on the verge of digging a hole for himself, 'yes, maybe, I would have tried to help him.'

'Thank you.'

'For what? Oh, do grow up Sandy. I'm not admitting to anything, I'm simply saying that perhaps it would have been the right thing to do.'

'The what?'

'The right thing to do. Jesus, Sandy, what would you have done in my shoes? He was, *is*, my friend and he was terrified Sandy. You know Ewen as well as anyone. You know the sort of man he is, and he was scared, Sandy, very scared. So, you tell me, what would you have done in my shoes?'

'This isn't about me, and the problem is,' Sandy said slamming his fist down hard on the table, 'that I can't ask Connolly myself, because, after spending all day with you getting pissed and accounting for his part in the unconscionable fuck up that was Landslide, he buggered off in the middle of the night to God only knows where. *My* guess is you put him on a train. Quick kiss and a cuddle at Halkali Station, pat on the bum and pack him off to Sofia? Bucharest? Vienna? With a promise he'll write and another, firmer promise, that he'll never come back?'

'No.'

'Come on. No one's believing this straight to bed nonsense.'

'I'm telling you. That's the way it went.'

'Russians then?'

'Your guess is as good as mine.'

'That's very funny. You potter off on your own sweet lonesome and he what? Waits in the foyer for a man called Vlad in a bear skin hat and a copy of *Crime and Punishment* under one arm who'll carry his luggage for him?'

'How many times?'

'Or perhaps *you* carried his bags for him?'

'We've been round this.'

'Trouble is, old son, people are wanting answers, and you don't seem to want to give me any.'

'Can't give what I don't have, *old son*.'

'You do see my predicament though?'

'I do. London got your balls in a vice?'

'Something like that. Afraid to say it, but like it or not, heads will roll.'

'Not yours though?'

'Certainly not.'

'Mine?'

'Possibly. Perhaps we'll be seeing a little more of you at the golf club, you know, once this blows over?' Sandy is standing now, pacing the small room, clicking and clicking the lid of his zippo, in a world of his own. 'He's always done such good work until recently. So I say, like the fool that I am, do this for me, you know, after Moscow, get your arse back in the saddle, if you follow me? Go out to Istanbul, I say, nice cosy little trip, I say. Take the girl with you. Fresh faced little thing I'm told. So, take the girl for a bit of company, the food will be great, well good at least, the weather, if you like that sort of thing, seasonally clement. Make the most of it. I mean I was quite candid with him, you know, don't play with the scenery and all that, window shopping only, you understand?'

The man calling himself Price nodded slowly. How typical, how absolutely bloody typical of Sandy Harper to somehow find a way to make this about him.

'Bags packed, I said? Good. Have a nice holiday, try not to spend too much time on your back, oh and don't forget about Landslide. Get the girl to do some of the work, if she can drag herself out of bed. You put your feet up, let someone else take the strain. But then what is it the Scots are always telling us? The best laid plans of mice and men?'

'Don't be bloody funny, Sandy.'

'Oh, I'm sorry. Touched a nerve have I? Well boo hoo, David. Boo fucking hoo.'

3

Sam's flat, Harrow, Present Day

When Hunter finally awoke he felt as though his head might explode. Recently he'd had more than his fair share of hangovers, but nothing approaching this, added to which there was something cold and metallic jammed up hard against the bridge of his nose. Slowly he peeled his eyes open. Michael Healy stood over him, the titanium endcap of a suppressed Walther PPK resting just above Hunter's nasal bone.

'Who's been a stupid boy?'

Nothing except a fierce blinding pain at the back of Hunter's skull and the overpowering urge to vomit. But the expression on Healy's face told him, in no uncertain terms that that was not an option.

'Know much about pentothal? Flunitrazepam?'

'The date rape drug?' Hunter managed.

'Well done. First they give you that, then the pentothal. It's a tongue loosener. Naughty little cocktail. You see once you start to talk, you just can't stop. You gas away, blabber blabber blabber, all sorts of interesting crap, just pouring out of your mouth, and there you are, powerless to stop it. But then that's what I love about you Scott, how little you know. There isn't anything of any real interest in there anyway, is there?' Healy said, tapping Hunter's delicate skull with the pistol.

Hunter thought his head, full of information or not, was about to fall clean off his shoulders, and that that might have been a blessed relief. Healy obligingly removed the gun and Hunter was able to sit up and look around Samantha's flat. The little furniture there had been, all gone. The paintings he thought he could have done himself, gone, the table, the chairs, everything down to the rug by the electric fire, all gone, leaving just the sofa bed he had collapsed on. He stared at where the dining table had been. The legs hadn't even left a dent in the carpet.

'Pretty was she?'

'Very.'

'Plenty of them.' Healy took a seat next to him on the edge of the sofa. 'You ever do anything as stupid as that again and I'll take you out back and shoot you in the head myself. Now get up.'

'I can't.'

'*Get up*. Now.'

'Does she work for you?'

'I said get up.'

'Does she?'

'What's the matter? Ego dented, is it? Really thought you could pull a bird like that? Get up, we've got work to do. Oh, and for your information, that's strike two. One more and then we're done. Got it?'

'Got it.'

***

Hunter took in the makes and models of the cars parked bumper to bumper along Radnor Road. He'd had to ask Healy to pull over so that he could buy a bottle of water and a packet of paracetamol, which he had, reluctantly, agreed to do. He still felt sick from the after-effects of the drugs he'd been given, but his eyes were hurting a little less.

The cars showed a great deal about the people who owned them and inhabited the semi-detached houses. Clean and all wearing their residents' permits like upper-middle class badges of honour. 4x4s and estates sparkled in the early morning light. Family cars with trite messages in their rear windows inviting other drivers to take care, back seats groaning with boosters for little princesses.

Hunter was rapidly recognising their registration plates. Some might have said learning, but Hunter didn't need to apply himself in any way to the task, he simply looked at the combination of numbers and letters and they stuck. There was a red Vauxhall Astra parked outside Miss White's house. The car looked filthy, unappreciated and out of place amongst its neighbours, as unremarkable as it was possible to be. Drab functionality, superseded by the kind of cars which raced for attention through the glossy pages of the weekend's colour supplements, advertising a better life, with improved fertility and career prospects.

'You might want to cut back a little on the booze,' Healy said unnecessarily, 'otherwise that glittering career of yours will end up being nothing more than a rumour round the water cooler.'

They spent the day in relative peace and quiet with Hunter

struggling to stay awake under Healy's watchful eye. Then, at a little after four, as the street started to crowd with returning office workers, Hunter caught sight of the object of their attentions. Miss White, in a burnt ochre poncho, voluminous emerald trousers and a pair of white cowboy boots was walking purposefully back towards the house.

'Holy cow,' Hunter spluttered 'what has she come as today?'

'That's nothing,' the other man said with a sigh, 'you should have seen what she was wearing last week.'

Hunter decided to make the most of Healy's improved mood. 'Michael, what am I being trained for?'

'Why would you imagine I have the slightest idea?'

Hunter was prepared to concede that point. If information was being withheld from him, it was only fair to assume it was being withheld from Michael Healy too. Both men watched in silence as Miss White walked past their car and disappeared in the direction of the pub. Time to try a different tack then.

'Who are you?'

'You know who I am.'

Not particularly helpful and Hunter was sensing Healy's benevolent demeanour ebbing away.

'When will I be told what's going on?'

'When I am. You're wasting time.'

'Whose time?'

'Yours and mine. Listen, I don't want to be here anymore than you do.'

'Why are you here then?'

'Because I was told to be and because I've a wife and daughters back home and because you'd be surprised to what lengths people will go to for the ones they love.'

Michael Healy caught himself, uncomfortable at having said too much. Hadn't this been part of the trouble with Bennet his old partner? They had crossed that line into each other's personal lives and then everything had changed and not for the better.

Hunter, sensing his mentor's awkwardness, decided against spouting a reassuring platitude, and instead looked away and up Radnor Road.

How far, he wondered was *he* prepared to go for the people he truly cared about? Who were the people he cared about? He had not done enough for poor Amy and for that he suspected he would never forgive himself. His father had gone to extraordinary lengths to protect him from the barefaced truth of his mother's suicide, to such an extent in fact that for years they had hardly spoken. Hunter realised, as he silently observed the recalcitrant Healy out of the corner of his eye, just how few people there were in the world he truly cared enough about to go that extra mile. Perhaps it was that selfish narcissism which fuelled him and the man to his right, although he sincerely hoped not. He hoped he was not turning into his grandfather and he prayed he would never be as broken as Professor Frederick Sinclair.

'Listen, once they think you're ready...'

'I am ready.'

'Once I think you're ready,' Healy continued correcting himself, 'you'll be given your instructions.'

'I think I'd like to know who I'm working for first.'

'Not a chance.'

'Why? Look at it from where I'm standing, you could be anyone.'

'The door's right there,' Healy said, flicking off the Audi's locks. Hunter reached for the handle. 'A word of caution though. Remember what you know so far and think what may happen to you if you decide to walk. As it stands, if everything goes belly up, we can wash our hands of you.' Hunter knew just what that might mean. 'The flat in Harrow? Burned, no trace left. You? You never existed. I'm sorry Scott, but it's that simple.'

'Total deniability.'

'Total.'

'So you do know what I'm to be used for? *If everything goes belly up*, you said.'

'A figure of speech nothing more.'

'Bollocks.' *One last try.* 'Who's Lazarus?'

'Not a chance.'

Hunter watched as Miss White returned on the opposite side of the road, checked her coat pockets for keys and unlocked the front door to her house.

'This is nothing to do with deniability, is it?' Hunter said. 'You need a fresh face, someone no one knows, not so you can deny any knowledge of them, but because you don't trust your own. I'm right, aren't I? Jesus, do *you* even know who you're working for?'

'What is it you think we do here, Scott, what do you think this is all about?'

'Catch the bad guys? Protect the public?'

'It's about even numbers.'

'I don't follow you.'

'As opposed to odd, Scott.' Healy said cutting in. 'Black and white but never grey. We're here to stop the whole world from simply sliding into the abyss. We don't deal in rights and wrongs, trust me we're in no position to. Our job is to just keep this sorry exercise on the tracks and make sure the whole damn show goes on. Got it?'

'Got it,' Hunter said without being completely convinced he had.

'We're done for the day,' Healy was saying. 'I'm sure you can find your own way home. Oh, and I'll see if they can't help a little with tomorrow's breakfast, put a little money in your pocket. Sit by your phone.'

At the flat Hunter opened up a fresh window on the iMac and went straight to his on-line bank account. In his current account and to his extreme delight more money than he had ever owned.

The following morning and Hunter was fixing himself some breakfast when he heard the text come through.

Sorry, I can't give you a lift today. See you at the gym. Hope you can make the usual time?

He glanced at his phone. That meant he had exactly one hour to get from the flat in Harrow to West London and all under his own steam. If he took the bus and caught a train to Baker Street, changed to the Circle Line and then to the District Line and if each of his connecting trains happened to link up Hunter thought it was just possible. He threw back his coffee, grabbed a clean hoodie from his bedroom and headed out.

At the junction outside the flat he caught an H14 into Harrow. Hunter was taking his seat, pleased he had stepped straight onto a bus and about to flick through an abandoned copy of The Metro when, seconds before the doors closed and with the bus ready to depart, a man leapt on. Slightly older than himself, early thirties Hunter speculated, a wiry little guy with an athletic physique wearing sweatpants, dayglow trainers and a hoodie not dissimilar to his own. He had a short-cropped beard and bald head and was panting from his run. Hunter watched him pay for his ticket and returned to his paper.

At the station the bus terminated. Hunter climbed the steps to Harrow and Wealdstone tube and joined a shortish queue. With his ticket bought he walked down to the platform and stood patiently waiting for the train into town. The man in the gym gear did the same. Hunter went to examine the tube map and looked back up the platform at him. He was starting to identify a type and there was something about this man which he'd seen before. Outwardly the practised lack of concern, the learned disinterest in the world around him, but underpinning all that a twitchy reluctance for eye contact and a masked state of high alert. Was he being followed? He'd not come far from the flat and he was taking the same route as many hundreds, thousands of Londoners did each day. But there was something about this man which was making Hunter uneasy. A train was approaching the platform. If he caught it and providing the rest of the transport system cooperated he would make his meeting with Healy with a few minutes to spare. The train screeched to a halt and Hunter stood obediently allowing passengers to get off. He shot a look up the platform. The guy in the sweats was doing the same. Anyone who was getting off had done so and people were already barging on and searching for seats. Hunter held back. So did the guy in the sweats with the bald head. The doors started to close. Hunter reached into his pocket and withdrew his mobile phone, pressed it to his ear and embarked on a singularly one-sided conversation as the train slid out of the platform. A quick look up and to his right was all that was needed. He saw the back of the man as he walked off and up the platform. Hunter found a train timetable to busy himself with and continued his imaginary conversation. He would now probably be late for his meeting with Michael Healy, but he needed to find out who this was at the other end of the platform and whether they meant him any harm? Was he in some way related to his pernicious neighbour? Hunter looked up at the array of security cameras guarding over the station. Another tube train was due to arrive in a couple of minutes. The journey into London would buy him some valuable thinking time.

Hunter was headed for Baker Street. It had been several months since he'd last been there but he still had a clear mental picture of the various waiting areas and the levels they were on. As the train drew in, with the man in gym gear at the far end of his carriage, Hunter slipped his hoodie up and over his head.

Baker Street was crowded and chaotic with tourists, commuters and students. Hunter took the stairs to one of the busier concourses brimming with screens displaying platform information and train times. He stood in a shop front next to the public toilets and pretended to study the information boards. The man in the sweats took up his position to Hunter's left looking through a rack of magazines. The station was so hectic it crossed Hunter's mind that, when the next busy train arrived and disgorged its consignment of passengers he could seize the opportunity, blend in with the crowd and lose his man. But what if he wasn't just being observed, what if he was the target of an attack. What if, after his conversation the previous day, Healy or more powerful men than Healy, had decided they had no further use for him, no use for someone who drank to excess and fell prey to the first pretty smile which came along. Hunter wasn't prepared to take that risk. The journey had bought him some time and so he held back patiently. A number of trains later he spotted the person he'd been waiting for. A young man, perhaps a year or two younger than himself, probably a student, in jeans and a T-shirt and looking somewhat the worse for wear. He was heading for the gents toilets. Hunter took his wallet, found the change for the barrier and a twenty-pound note.

***

Scott Hunter sat on the Hammersmith and City train. He would be over an hour late for his meeting and wasn't even sure that Michael Healy would still be there. He'd watched the student leave the toilets, a fresh twenty-pound note in his pocket and Hunter's hoodie pulled tight over his head. He'd watched the man in the sweats fall in step behind him and then Hunter had jumped on the first available train. It had taken him east and away from where he'd needed to be, but once he'd satisfied himself he was no longer being followed he'd retraced his steps. A forty-five-minute walk down the Goldhawk Road and across Chiswick Common and there was Healy's car. He tapped on the window, the lock sprang up and he climbed in, for once relieved to see his mentor.

'You're late.'

'I know. I think I was followed.'

'Okay,' Healy nodded, 'let's start with a description.'

'Thirty-year old male Caucasian. A bit shorter than me, maybe five-ten? Bald with a short cropped dark beard. Oh, and he looked like he worked out. Not muscle bound, you know, but fit, really fit. And he was wearing all the gear too.'

Healy raised an eyebrow, encouraging Hunter to continue.

'Gym gear. Latest trainers, sweats and a hoodie,' Hunter concluded proudly. 'Shook him off at Baker Street Station.'

'That true?' Healy asked looking in the rear-view mirror.

'Yeah. Slippery little bastard this one.'

Hunter spun round. The man with the bald head, dark beard and gym sweats half smiled back.

'This is Gary Williams. Don't be fooled. He' looks like a scrawny little shit, but he's a complete hard arse. He'll be your combat and weapons instructor.' Hunter stuck out a hand, and Williams looked at it. 'Gary, this is your new intake, Scott Hunter.'

'Great,' Williams said, raising an eyebrow in Hunter's direction. 'Come on then, I'm over there.'

He hopped out of the back of Healy's car and made towards a yellow Fiesta parked two lengths back. Hunter looked to Healy who nodded.

'Remember Scott, three strikes. Do as you're told and don't fuck up.'

Hunter let himself out of the car and followed the pigeon-toed Gary Williams.

They set off on the A4 towards Hammersmith and Earls Court.

'Mikey tells me you're the next big thing. Bright as a button he says.'

Hunter didn't know how to respond so decided to say nothing.

'I'm going to enjoy beating the shit out of you.' Williams continued all smiles, behind the facial hair a pair of black twinkling eyes and a mischievous grin. 'No one makes me look stupid and gets away with it. Mike says you come from quite an interesting family?'

Again Hunter chose to say nothing and so they continued along The Thames in silence. Williams turned over the Chelsea Bridge and wound his way down past the Battersea Dogs Home to Clapham, South London and an ugly series of businesses housed under a Victorian railway viaduct.

Hunter followed him to the last of the arches. The front had been entirely boarded over and a rudimentary door cut out. Williams produced a key and undid the padlock before stepping inside. An electric light automatically flickered on and Hunter was surprised to see in the wall opposite an altogether more modern steel door and a numeric keypad. Williams stepped up and input the code. The door beeped twice and swung open as more lights flickered on. Disappearing before them from a metal gantry, hundreds of steps descending deep underground. Hunter followed Williams down into the bowels of South London.

'In the September of 1940,' Williams said over his shoulder, 'at the height of The Blitz, they built eight of these subterranean air raid shelters to house members of the public during the bombing. Abandoned after the war we requisitioned one in 1989 and converted it to our needs. Hear that?' A low grumble from overhead. 'That's the Northern Line. We're actually lower than the underground here. Sorry, there's no lift.'

After what seemed like an eternity they reached the bottom of the steps and another steel door and another keypad. Williams input the code and held the door open for Hunter.

'Welcome to the service. This is where we store pretty much everything. There's a live fire range at the far end and my gym's just there on the right.'

Hunter stared down the long straight corridor with its arching roof. It wasn't a huge leap to imagine the place full of terrified Londoners cowering from Hitler's bombs. At regular intervals along the corridor fresh shafts branched off. These seemed much more modern than the space they were standing in but every time Hunter tried to pause long enough to see what they contained, Williams grabbed his elbow and hurried him along. In the distance the distinctive dull thud of a firearm being discharged.

Finally at their destination Williams led Hunter into a room which had been padded from floor to ceiling in crash matts. Punch bags hung from the roof every ten feet or so and in one corner a soft drinks dispenser hummed quietly. 'This is going to be your classroom for a while. There's a changing room at the back there with showers and a bog. You'll find everything you need.'

In the room a bench with a choice of sweatpants and tops. Hunter found something he hoped would fit and got changed.

'Over the next three months I am going to teach you the absolute basics of self-defence. This will not turn you into a one-man killing machine, this will not turn you into Bruce Lee or Jackie bloody Chan. You'll be able to look after yourself and that's about all. Mikey gave me your number. When I want to see you, you'll get a text. We'll work five days out of every week.'

'What about Healy?'

'Not my problem. You sort it out with Mikey. Do you understand?'

'Understood.'

'When we're done here you'll spend some time on the range

learning how to use a variety of firearms. You ever fired a gun before?'

'I've fired a gun a total of three times into the body of Frederick Sinclair, killing him. So, yes, I've fired a gun before.' One mighty beat. 'I've also bludgeoned a man to death with a wooden rowing paddle, but I'm sure you know that. You ever killed anyone?'

Hunter took Williams' silence as a yes. Stupid question really from the look of him.

'So, you know what you're doing with a weapon. This should be quick and simple.'

'That's not what I said. I've shot a gun precisely three times. That's all and I can't say I remember much about the experience as I was a little pre-occupied trying to prevent my father from bleeding to death.'

'Oh yeah? I don't really care. Get over there and warm up.' Williams flicked a finger towards the other side of the gym. Hunter nodded, turned and began moving across the room towards a wall of focus pads and body shields.

There was the soft patter of Williams's feet and then silence as the wiry little man launched himself at Hunter. His bony shoulder blade thundered into the middle of Hunter's scapula sending him sprawling to the floor.

'*Never* turn your back on an opponent, even for a second,' Williams bawled at him.

'I didn't know we'd started.'

'Especially if that opponent is me,' Williams finished, bouncing on the balls of his feet. 'Come on, get up.'

Hunter hauled himself up and off the mats and stared at Williams. Hunter was not a big man, not a powerful man, but surely to God he could knock over Williams. Hoping he might surprise his new instructor he ran headlong straight at him.

A hop and a jink and he flew past Williams and collided painfully with one of the many punchbags dangling from the ceiling, but not before Williams had landed a fierce blow to his chin. Hunter fell to the floor and sat rubbing his aching jaw.

'This is good,' Williams said with a grin. 'I thought Mikey said you were bright, but this is fun. If you carry on like this, you'll be so knackered I won't have to work so hard taking you apart. Now, do you want to learn something or shall I just watch you crashing into things all day? Either's good with me.'

'Teach me,' Hunter said.

'Okay,' Williams nodded taking something from his hoodie pocket. He bent down and with a piece of chalk drew a long white line between them. 'Let's start with some basic holds and controls. The object of the exercise is to get your opponent across the line.' Now it was Hunter's turn to nod. William's stood to one side and gestured to the spot where he'd been standing. 'If you'll just go over there?'

Hunter walked over the line and took up his position where Williams had asked him to.

'Nice work genius. See how easy that was?'

'You tricked me.'

'No. I asked you nicely and you cooperated and so we both got what we thought we wanted and no one got hurt. It doesn't always have to be the other way, is all I'm saying.'

Perhaps, Hunter thought, there might be a little more to Gary Williams than first met the eye?

'Let's try it again, but this time I promise not to be so nice. Give me five.'

Hunter stared at his instructor, bewildered.

'Come on Einstein, it's how we start. Gimme five!'

Hunter put out his hand and Williams slapped it.

'Now, fist bump.'

Williams held out his fist and so Hunter did the same. But then suddenly the wiry little man had hold of his outstretched arm, hyperextending Hunter's elbow. Before he knew what was happening Williams was behind him, Hunter's arm painfully pushed up his back, the smaller man's other arm around his throat grabbing at his shirt. Hunter couldn't move. He could barely speak, but his feet had never left the mat. Never crossed the line. 'I thought... you were supposed to get me... over the line,' he continued struggling to maintain his balance.

'I changed my mind. Anyway, what you going to do about it?' Williams pushed his mouth close to Hunter's ear. 'I'm going to break you down, Einstein. Then, once I'm done doing that, I'll build you back up again, if you're lucky. Now all you have to do when you've had enough is tap out. Had enough?'

'No,' Hunter said, determined not to give Williams the satisfaction.

Williams drew Hunter's arm a fraction higher up his back until he thought his elbow might explode. 'Had enough?' he repeated. With his free hand Hunter tapped out and fell to the floor.

'Like I said, break you down, build you up.'

Hunter spent the remainder of the day being drilled relentlessly by Williams and then, when he was exhausted and thought he couldn't possibly take any more, Williams led him down an endless corridor, away from the entrance and towards the sound of gunfire. A long, narrow vaulted space served as the service's shooting-gallery. A counter extended at right angles to the range, brimming with firearms of every size and description. Hunter thought he recognised a couple of the guns. There was a Glock like the one he kept in his kitchen in Harrow. At the far end of the range the silhouette of a rifleman brandishing a weapon across his chest.

Williams followed him into the cramped space.

'You'll need these,' he said holding up a pair of yellow ear mufflers, 'and these of course.' He placed a heavy carrying case at one end of the counter. Inside, boxes and boxes of differently sized ammunition.

Despite what Williams may have been thinking to the contrary, Hunter wasn't simply apprehensive about being this close to so many firearms, he was horrified.

'I expect you fancy a pop on this?' his instructor said picking up a huge shining revolver and spinning its chambers, 'or maybe you're more of a SIG man?'

Hunter didn't have the heart to tell him.

'Well, I think we'll start you on this. It may not look like much and you almost certainly haven't seen it in the films, but it's been good enough for the British Army for the last I don't know how long, so it's good enough for you.'

Williams picked up a utilitarian looking weapon and handed it to Hunter.

'This is the SA80 assault rifle,' Williams continued, ramming in a magazine. 'It's a good bit of kit, whatever anybody says, close quarters or up to 500 metres. You'll want to zero it in first, so put some rounds down on the target.'

Hunter looked at the gun. A harsh mixture of black and dark earth metals, unforgiving bold functionality without any other consideration. He turned it over, reluctantly making the unfamiliar familiar and powerfully conscious that in his hands he held a deadly instrument. He traced a finger down the practicable hand guard following a deep scratch which cut through the paintwork revealing naked metal beneath.

'When you're done playing, I'll show you how to clean it. You can leave it on the counter for the time being, but remember, the armourer will give it a once over tonight and if it's in any way dirty,' Williams paused, finding the tiniest spot of grease to emphasise his point, 'today's session in the gym will seem like a bloody picnic. Got it?'

He opened a fresh box of brass and thumped it down next to Hunter. Williams showed him how to click the rounds into the magazine, where the safety was and how to align the sights.

'Let's see what you got, Einstein.'

Hunter pressed the butt of the rifle into his shoulder, squinted down the range and tried to steady himself. Williams kicked at his feet, repositioning them, then, content he was ready, Hunter snatched at the trigger. An abhorrent crack, the thumping bolt of the recoil, a cheery tinkle as the redundant casing landed on the concrete floor and then the most incredibly emotive smell, like the weapon itself, unyielding and harsh.

The round flashed past the silhouetted soldier leaving no impression and then the dull thud as it hit the wall of sandbags at the far end of the range and a puff of recriminatory dust.

'I thought you said you'd done this before?'

Hunter thought about setting Williams straight but instead shuffled closer to the sights and prepared to fire again.

'Bit of work needed there, genius,' Williams added unhelpfully as another round missed its target. 'Finish that box and I'll go get us some more ammunition.'

***

Central London, Present day

For a man of his rank and position, Sir John Alperton had proved remarkably easy for Sandy Harper to track down. His secretary had made half a dozen well-judged phone calls to a selection of august shirt shops and tailors across town. Whilst none were keen to discuss their clientele, especially customers as respected and revered as Sir John, they were delighted for the opportunity to badmouth the competition. Each shop understood the Knight's standing in the security world, but whilst he might have dealt with matters of national and international influence and consistently dined at the top table, some things in life, a £15,000 suit made from pashmina wool imported especially from Nepal for instance, were simply more important.

One particularly indiscreet purveyor of fine Egyptian cotton had caught wind from a man who knew a man that a neighbouring tailors had recently taken delivery of a bolt of Merino grey wide chalk-stripe, and with the talk on Jermyn Street that Sir John was in the market for a new suit, it wasn't a huge stretch to track him down. When Sandy's secretary had placed a speculative phone call the tailors had been so cagey as to instantly incriminate themselves giving Sandy plenty of time to straighten his tie, throw on an old Herringbone and catch a cab across the river. Ten minutes later he was standing at the door of Pettigrews of London,

Gentlemans' Outfitters since 1752. There followed a short yet animated conversation with the shop's owner and then he was addressing a beleaguered John Alperton as a crouching Wilfred Pettigrew fussed and agonized over an unusually contrary inseam.

'Jesus, Sandy this better be good. Isn't there a horse race somewhere you should be at? What about Bridget, can't she deal with whatever it is?'

'Not this, no.'

'Well spit it out then.'

Harper looked down at the man at Sir John's feet who was devotedly pinning a capricious hem.

'Wilfred should probably have a higher security clearance than you, Sandy so come on, what is it?'

'I bumped into an old friend of mine from Five yesterday. Name of Frank Cassatto mean anything to you?'

'No. Should it?'

'He's an American. Hack working in Hong Kong. Friend of mine ran into him over here. Drunk as a lord and terribly talkative.'

'I'm sorry Sandy, what has any of this to do with me? If you're going to come and harangue me every time a friend of yours meets a drunk journalist, well, I don't know, I shall have to find a new tailors.'

A pained Mr Pettigrew looked up from pinning a wayward trouser leg.

'Of course I would never do that, there's a good chap. Look Sandy, you've upset Wilfred. Go on, what did your drunk American have to say?'

'He was asking a lot of questions.'

'I thought you said he was a journalist? That's what the blighters do isn't it?'

'About Landslide.'

Sir John stiffened and looked long and hard at himself in the shop's mirrors. 'Pettigrew, give us a moment would you, there's a good chap?'

'Is everything alright, Sir John?'

'Quite alright thank you. Sandy here is just bleating on about a long dead friend, nothing to concern you. I just need a quiet moment that's all. If you wouldn't mind?'

'Naturally, Sir John,' Mr Pettigrew smiled obsequiously then made for the door, pausing as he passed Sandy Harper. 'I could probably measure you up for something a little smarter, sir, once I've finished with Sir John of course?'

But before Sandy could answer, Pettigrew had turned and vanished leaving the two men to talk in private.

'What does he know, your Yank?'

'Not as much as he thinks he does. Just doing a spot of fishing. Nothing concrete.'

'But he's been talking to someone?'

'Ewen Connolly.'

John Alperton would tell Mr Pettigrew he didn't want the suit now. He'd pay for the man's time, that would be expensive enough, but quite suddenly Sir John Alperton never wanted to see that suit ever again.

'You're quite sure?'

'No, but it makes a lot of sense you'd have to agree?'

Alperton had never put much stock in agreeing with Sandy Harper, but he was forced to concede there was a certain logic to what he was suggesting, and he reluctantly supposed, there had to be a first time for everything.

'Who else have you told?'

'Just you and Toby Gray. He doesn't know I'm here, for the record, but I thought you should know.'

How uncharacteristically gallant of you. What's the real purpose of your visit? Alperton wonders. Sandy Harper wasn't in the business of doing favours for anyone, least of all him, so why are you here, really? Sandy was standing in front of the shop's triple dressing mirrors tugging peevishly at his Herringbone simultaneously in three directions.

'Rumour has it you've a new jockey in the stables?' he says over a shoulder, as casually as the situation will allow.

Ah, now we're getting to it. Come on then Sandy, let's take a little dance shall we? I'll lead.

'News to me.'

'I was told he's quite the chip off the old block,' Sandy continues, petulantly turning his back on the mirrors.

You sly old bastard. A duck and a spin. Drop in Landslide to stir the waters, but now we're getting to the real grist of it, aren't we Sandy? This is the real substance you slippery bastard, the real heart of the matter.

'Genuine thoroughbred. Plenty by the way of pedigree, if you follow me?'

It would be pretty damn difficult not to. Someone was going to pay for this. Hard to imagine who Sandy could have been talking to though. Bridget was the height of discretion. Healy then? Again he was pretty discreet too. Bob Bennett, his old partner had not long retired so it shouldn't have been him.

'Sounds fascinating Sandy, a real find. I am pleased for you.'

'I've heard he's already seen the jumps and taken to them like a hunter.'

Oh, this was just excruciating.

'Really?' Raised eyebrows and a look of consternation mixed with a shrug of incomprehension. The dance they'd taken together fast approaching its coda. 'Where exactly are we going with this Sandy?' Alperton speeding things along now, happy to have had his card marked, but suddenly eager to find a new partner.

'Was half hoping I might take him off your hands for a little while, give him a trot out along a nice deserted beach somewhere. Somewhere quiet. I hear China's very nice this time of year. The food's fucking awful of course, the weather's pretty terrible too come to think of it, but the suits are cheap and the people are charming. What do you say? Give the lad a run out, stretch his legs? Might do him some good? Never know, could be beneficial to the both of us?'

'It really has been lovely seeing you, Sandy. Don't hesitate to keep in touch. Oh, and I'll be sure to let you know if I hear anything of your mysterious stallion.'

'Very well then.'

'Wilfred, I think Sandy here has said all he's come to say. If you wouldn't mind seeing him out?'

'It would be my pleasure, sir.'

***

After a long day sat with Michael Healy observing an empty house in W4 Hunter was about ready to go home. Healy was sending him on his way and making arrangements for the following day when there was a tap at the window.

'Thought I might find you two love birds here. Come along Einstein, work to be done,' Gary Williams said, leaning into the car.

Hunter looked at Healy who smiled and shrugged.

'No rest for the wicked it seems.'

Hunter dragged himself from Healy's car and followed Williams to his, already dreading what was to come. They set off towards South London, Williams clearly in high spirits.

'How was your day then, with Mikey? I couldn't stick it, just sitting there all that time doing nothing,' Williams said answering his own question. Hunter grunted a reply.

'So, what's the deal Scott? You got any brothers, sisters?'

Hunter wondered if this was some fresh test, dreamt up by Healy and executed by Williams and so elected to say nothing.

'Don't want to talk, huh? I understand, after all, we're not here to discuss your family are we? You'll have to forgive me though, I'm kinda interested in you, Scott Hunter. Mikey's let one or two fascinating little things slip the other day.'

Now Hunter was feeling less communicative than ever.

'He dropped some light reading material off at my place yesterday. Your entire nasty little life story in fact, all neatly bound and wrapped in a shiny new folder, courtesy of John Alperton, I'd imagine.'

Hunter continued to stare out of the passenger window as South London went by and wondered whether an hour with an SA80 assault rifle might not be preferable to listening to Gary Williams.

'You know what, Harpo Marx, I think I'll just swing by mine and pick it up.'

Williams turned off their usual route and then they were threading their way through the backstreets of West Norwood. He turned into Boden Road and parked up outside an anonymous Victorian mid-terrace.

'Wait there, Einstein.'

When Williams reappeared he was clutching a manila folder which he threw onto Hunter's lap.

'Help yourself,' he said.

'I'd rather not, if you don't mind.'

Williams pulled back out into traffic.

'I think we'll start with some target work today,' he said enjoying himself.

That came as some relief to Hunter. Days of practice and he was now able to hit the target, but rarely the figure at its heart. Williams often left him to struggle with the onerous rifle alone and today Hunter was looking forward to the solitude.

Once at the range he pulled on his ear defenders and safety glasses and was trying to recall all he'd learnt from his previous visits when Williams joined him.

'Seems as though Mike was right,' he said resting Hunter's file on the counter next to the boxes of ammunition and shouting. 'You're quite an interesting guy, Scott Hunter.'

A round tore down the range missing its target. Williams flicked open the folder.

'Cambridge educated, eh. Posh then?'

Another bullet spat from the assault rifle missing its mark.

'Make sure you're relaxed, but still holding the weapon firmly. I guess you're smart because that's what Mike keeps telling me. Good at codes it says here although I'll be honest with you, I didn't understand this bit much.'

Hunter's next shot caused the target to flutter, but nothing more.

'Make sure your sights are correctly aligned,' Williams said before returning to the file. 'Now we're getting to the good stuff. Your family. Jesus Christ. Your grandad was a Nazi.'

Hunter gripped the trigger more firmly and a round tore through the centre of the target.

'That's bad man. Remember, *squeeze* the trigger, don't snatch at it. And your dad was one of us but then had to leave in disgrace.'

Two more rounds join the first.

'Steady your breathing and apply the pressure more slowly and evenly. Your girlfriend was murdered right in front of you and your old lady topped herself.'

Hunter filled the body of the target and tried to keep firing long after the hollow click of an empty magazine.

'And I thought my family was messed up,' Williams added shaking his head.

Hunter unclipped the magazine, slammed it down on the counter next to the box of brass, took off his safety goggles and walked out.

'Nice shooting,' Williams shouted after him. 'Don't forget to clean your weapon, Scott and close the door on your way out.'

The banks of the Thames, Oxfordshire, Present Day

Sandy Harper and John Alperton's meeting in Pettigrew's off Jermyn Street hadn't gone unnoticed, John Alperton not being the only one to buy his suits there. Toby Gray sat in splendid isolation overlooking the Thames beneath a bank of singularly British clouds. He drew a hand across his face, tired and concerned.

Rose Tree Cottage in Oxfordshire had been in the Gray family for generations and had witnessed the rise and some might have argued, fall of the family seat. Like the fields opposite, which in the Second World War had played host to the RAF, but were now being put to more peaceful pursuits, covered as they were with black plastic pillows of silage, Rose Tree Cottage and its inhabitants had had a turbulent history. His brother, Lucian, whom he rarely if ever saw now sat in a form of quarantine in the House of Lords, a casualty to their lineage, a handmaid to their class.

He didn't know a lot, this man of few words, just that Sandy and Sir John had been spotted consorting off Jermyn Street. That snivelling little sycophant Harper had been only too eager to tell him of Frank Cassatto's indiscreet conversations. The American had been shooting his mouth off about Landslide to anyone who'd buy him a drink, which in itself shouldn't have been a problem, but Harper and Alperton, now that was a very different concern. Harper was spiteful and cheap, but Sir John could be vindictive and merciless and so the less they had to do with Landslide the better.

Gray waved at a pleasure boat as it spluttered past, no doubt on its way to the pub around the next bend. There had been a time when he wouldn't have been far behind it. There had been a time when he would have struggled home from the South Bank, already having thrown down a few along the way, slewing his car across the driveway, clumsily thrown on something a little more relaxed, gone to the boathouse at the end of the garden which ran straight into the Thames and drunkenly rowed himself the couple or three miles through meandering loops and bends to The Three Locks Pub. But then everything had changed. The pub had changed hands at roughly the same time he had stopped drinking. He'd been back once or twice since, but it was full of new money in knee length shorts and trainers wearing yachting tops a hundred miles from the nearest beach and out to impress peroxide dyed princesses in leopard skin print, redolent tattoos and 6 inch stilettos and so Gray had retreated to the sobriety of Rose Tree Cottage. Money, he reflected sadly, had spoiled almost everything. But then there was much to be proud of too. His work, he hardly liked to refer to it as work when it felt more like a vocation, his work had been a success. He had, quietly and efficiently played his part, done what he had set out to do all those years ago when he'd first been approached by a cigar smoking George Wiseman. He had changed the world, and of that if nothing else, he should feel justifiably proud. A wry smile spread across Gray's face as he thought of his achievements and another gin palace swept past on its way up The Thames.

This situation with John Alperton though. This would have to be nipped in the bud, and quickly otherwise there were others who might wish to become involved; Hedley-King for one. There was another too, who had been implicated all those years ago and might choose to involve himself once more. A canal barge of champagne swilling bourgeoisie chugged noisily past and Tobias Gray smiled a biddable smile and raised his glass of orange juice.

Yes, better to head Alperton *et al* off at the pass and to that end a visit to The Traitors Gate in Bermondsey was probably in order. He withdrew two mobile phones from his jacket pocket, selected the appropriate one, found the number he had been searching for and pressed the phone to his ear.

***

As he'd promised, Gary Williams set about systematically breaking Hunter down. Day after day of gruelling exercise. Warm-ups, warm-downs and circuit training, followed by hours of wrist locks and breaks, goosenecks and cavaliers, soft defences and hard takedowns and all ending in much the same way, with Hunter's face being ground painfully into the crash mats and Williams encouraging him to tap out.

Eventually Hunter had had enough. Every inch of his body ached from the relentless training and with no end in sight, his spirit broken and Williams still enthusiastically bouncing on the balls of his feet like an overexcited pit bull, he decided it was time for a fresh course of action. It would be madness he reasoned to continue to do the same thing again and again and ever expect a different outcome.

'That's it. I quit. You can keep your stupid job and your crazy training routines and your hours of sitting in cars waiting for nothing to happen, I quit.'

Gary Williams looked down at Hunter and smiled.

'I told Mikey I'd break you,' he said shaking his head, 'There's no shame in it. Not everyone's cut out for this type of work.'

Hunter exhaled slowly and Williams couldn't be certain that he wasn't on the verge of tears.

'I tried my hardest,' he said, 'I mean, I did as much as I could, you know?'

'I know. You did pretty good, Einstein. Sometimes all the brains in the world can't make up for good old-fashioned brawn.'

Hunter seemed about to speak again but instead said nothing, staring at the gym mat between his feet and that utterly intractable white chalk line. He wiped at his nose with the sleeve of his shirt.

'Don't feel bad. Hey, can I get you something, a glass of water?' The kind-hearted Williams now that he'd proven his point.

'I'll be fine,' Hunter muttered.

'You sure? Come on, up you get.' An outstretched peace offering. Hunter took Williams's forearm in his hand and Williams did the same. Then Hunter swept his leg around violently as he'd been instructed and made contact squarely behind Williams's knee. In the same instant he yanked down hard on the casually extended arm and Williams was tumbling forward and over the white chalk line. Hunter was up and on him before his instructor had the faintest idea what was happening. With one hand he forced his bearded face hard into the crash mat, the other took control of his wrist, twisting his thumb away from his fingers until his instructor cried out in pain.

'Tap out!' Hunter yelled in his ear.

Williams grunted and kicked beneath him with all the desperation of a wounded animal, so Hunter raised his arm backwards until he was sure it would dislocate at the shoulder.

'Tap out, for Christ's sake.'

Another grunt and Hunter grabbed the fingers of Williams's right hand. 'Tap out now or I break them,' he shouted, pulling two fingers one way and two the other. Gary Williams reached back and with his free hand tapped Hunter's thigh.

***

Bermondsey, London, Present Day

The Traitors Gate Pub in Bermondsey, South London, sits at the corner of a busy junction, its curved double doors opening out onto the street. It's presided over by "Shoeshine" Ian, a short stocky man in his early fifties whom the service trust implicitly. At the age of twenty-five Shoeshine had inherited the Traitors Gate when his father had died prematurely from a heart attack. The pub, like Shoeshine, is Millwall through and through. The Traitors had become a shrine not just to his dead father but to the highs and lows of his football team. No one in the service could quite remember when they'd started frequenting the pub, or who had discovered it. Like many aspects of the service's long history it had become the stuff of tall stories and half-truths. Behind its bar, behind the footballing memorabilia and scarves, postcards and currencies from around the world, behind the foxed glass and *Free beer tomorrow* stickers, behind all of that, one nondescript door. But it was this singularly uninteresting portal which guaranteed Shoeshine Ian need never pour another mediocre pint or dispense a disappointing glass of lukewarm white wine ever again, if he so chose.

They'd arrived at fifteen-minute intervals, three men and a woman. Each, after placing a perfunctory drinks order and having handed over their mobile phones to be stored carefully in a shoebox kept beneath the bar, head for the toilets at the rear of the pub. To the left of the two public toilets a third door marked *Private Staff Only*. One by one they open the door and disappear down a long flight of steep stairs. First to arrive is Sandy Harper, the most junior of the quartet. He hands in his phone and takes a gin and tonic, lemon would be lovely thank you and could he have a little more ice. Fifteen minutes later, Sir John Alperton. The barman, already knowing Sir John is coming, has an excellent bottle of claret decanted and waiting. Patricia Hedley-King is next to arrive. She will have a G&T please, and don't even think about stinting on the G. Last to arrive to his own party, Tobias Gray, big white chief and master of all he surveys. A glass of fruit juice and a slice of orange with ice for the teetotaller.

At the bottom of the stairs a small square room with a round table and just enough chairs. Each knows their place. Gray sits as far from the door as is possible, the position of power from where everyone can be observed. His three reluctant disciples wait patiently for him to speak. Hedley-King smokes nervously.

'Ewen Connolly, once of this parish, ex-army, ex-service, defector and traitor,' Gray begins like Pilate preparing to wash his hands.

'Strong words,' Hedley-King offers up meekly, knowing her place.

'We know where he is,' Gray announces triumphantly.

'You're quite sure,' Sandy says, playing the game for everyone else's benefit.

'Noisy Yank,' Gray continues, suddenly subdued and cross with himself for using such a lazy epithet.

'Is there any other type?' Sandy again, playing the stooge this time.

'We should bring him in,' Hedley-King, stabbing angrily at a cigarette butt before expressing herself more confidently.

'For once I am inclined to agree,' Sir John finally speaks up. 'Tobias, where do you stand on this?' But Gray seems distracted as he gently cradles one hand in another and does not answer. 'Sandy then, what are your feelings?'

'No secret. I never trusted him. If we're sure where he is, I suggest we snatch him and find out what he's been telling our Russian friends all these years.' An unnecessary touch of chicanery on Sandy's part but he is quietly proud of himself. After all, he should not know what he knows.

'Chinese, actually. I think you'll find Connolly has been hiding out in China,' Alperton puts in helpfully. 'Oh, don't look so surprised, Sandy. I hear things too.' Oh good, we're all playing the same game, they think.

'And you're quite sure he defected?' Hedley-King again. A genuine question though.

Gray, who has been unusually quiet lets one knee gently settle over another, his long elegant leg tilting towards the only woman in the room. 'Quite sure, yes.'

'How else would you explain his behaviour?' Sandy chips in a shade too sanctimoniously. 'Although, what am I saying? You were the last to see him.'

'I don't like your tone, Sandy,' Hedley-King counters, 'and just for the record,' she pauses to light another cigarette, 'I never thought he was a traitor and I was *not* the last to see him, as you damn well know.'

'He is being dealt with too.' Tobias takes control. 'So, it seems we're in agreement. Connolly has some explaining to do.' Gray looks from one to the next, gauging their opinion, egging them on.

'Agreed!' they cry like some second-rate chorus. And as easily as that Ewen Connolly's fate is sealed.

***

Healy watches them depart. First to leave, that fraud Sandy Harper. Then one of the big hitters, Sir John Alperton. Whatever has gone on down there must have been serious. But Sir John is not alone. There, next to him, at his arm and talking earnestly, Miss White. What the hell is she doing here? Once they're gone, at ten o'clock, Healy locks the Audi and enters the pub. Toby Gray is standing awkwardly at the bar waiting for him.

'I'm worried Michael. They think they've found Ewen Connolly.'

Ewen Connolly. A name Healy has heard, but only whispered. A blot on the service's copy book from way back when and thought by many to be no longer. Difficult for Healy to imagine what interest there could possibly be in him now.

'Where?'

Gray holds up an envelope. 'It's all in here, Michael. I'd prefer it if he came back under his own steam you understand, answered a few questions, that sort of thing, but you should have heard them in there, baying for blood. Added to which, I have a notion that when he defected,' Gray pauses to adjust a sleeve and stare meaningly at the floor, 'he may have had help.'

'From inside?'

'Exactly. It was almost certainly one of them I'm afraid; Alperton, Sandy, Miss White,' Tobias Gray sips down the last of his orange juice, 'or David Hunter. That would certainly account for how fired up they all are. In truth if Connolly had just vanished off the face of the earth never to return, I would have been quite happy. Grown old and died out in Beijing or wherever he is. But if one of them was his handler, helped him disappear, then potentially things are about to get pretty sticky. How's your young gun getting on?'

'Good. He's smart, resourceful. Williams tells me he's mastering the basics. He'll do fine.'

'Glad to hear it. He'll need to be if he's to track down Connolly.'

'I didn't say he's ready, he's got at least another couple of months training to complete.'

But Gray appears not to have heard Michael Healy.

'His orders.'

Gray looks grimly at the long thin envelope and slides it across the bar where it is pocketed by Healy.

'Does he know?' Gray looks up from his drink, bothered by the questioning of his authority. 'That you think his father's involved I mean?'

'No,' Gray continues impatiently, 'And best to keep it that way until we're absolutely certain, if you wouldn't mind?'

'And Miss White?'

'I know you'll have questions, Michael.' Healy has heard this speech before and he knows the way it's destined to turn out. 'I'm sorry. You'll have to take this under advice. Continue with the surveillance. Only once I'm certain of her involvement, or lack thereof, will you be briefed.'

4

Clapham, South London

At the end of yet another session with Williams, Hunter was surprised to find Michael Healy waiting for him in the gym's subterranean changing rooms.

'Things are moving along a little quicker than we might have anticipated. Gary tells me your training's going well.'

'Really?'

'Well, what he actually said was you'd almost mastered some of the more rudimentary techniques, but coming from Gary, that's high praise indeed. He's a tough little bastard, Scott, but I think he's been genuinely impressed with your dedication.'

Hunter had stripped off and was heading for the showers, a towel wrapped around his waist.

'Before you go, I've something for you,' Healy continued holding up a thick grey envelope. 'Your legend.'

'My what?'

'You've got until tomorrow morning to learn everything there is to know about Simon Frost.'

Hunter was confused. Up until then they'd been observing a woman. Healy had called her Miss White whilst tacitly admitting that that was not her real name. There had been weapons training, not to mention hours of arse kickings from Gary Williams. Now he was crapping on about a legend, whatever that was, and asking him to bone up on someone called Simon Frost.

'Who the hell is he, Frost?'

Healy smiled and threw down the envelope on the bench. 'He,' Healy said somewhat theatrically, 'is you, Scott. He is you. I'll see you both bright and early tomorrow morning and Scott...'

'Yes.'

'There absolutely *will* be a quiz.'

Later, back at the flat, Hunter spread out the contents of the envelope Healy had left him on the sitting room floor. Next to him a pad and pen he'd found in the computer desk, by his side a freshly opened packet of cigarettes and a smallish Scotch over ice.

There was everything, from school reports - Simon Frost had attended a Grammar in Hertfordshire, which was just close enough to the truth to make it easy for Hunter to remember - to reports on the course he'd supposedly taken in journalism at university. Utility bills, a scratched and snapped National Insurance Card, and even a tax return in his new name. A driver's licence with a photograph he didn't remember posing for, supermarket loyalty cards and a reward card for a coffee chain he had never frequented but where he was pleased to see he only needed two more stamps for a free cappuccino. A new mobile phone with a fresh set of presumably fictitious friends. But this was all the window dressing, all the flotsam, the real substance was in a thirty page spiralbound dossier which outlined every aspect of Simon Frost's life, from his blood type, O Neg., and naturally the same as Hunter's, to allergies, sexual preferences, which football team he supported and which satellite television company he'd subscribed to in order to support them.

Hunter took a healthy swig from the tumbler, found a cigarette and settled in for the long haul. All the numbers; car registrations, insurance policies, bank details, home, work and friends' telephone numbers came easily to him, but he found he was struggling to recall some of the more emotive aspects of Frost's life; favourite foods, pubs he frequented, his family background. After a little thought Hunter began assigning each of the different elements of his alias's life a different number. Once there was a numerical value attached to a thing Hunter found he could play with that figure in his head, finding a home and a meaning for it and, most crucially, remembering it. But even with this new technique there was a hell of a lot of information in the file in front of him to plough through before his next meeting with Healy. He went to the kitchen, rinsed out his whisky glass and put the kettle on.

Then there was his assumed profession. Journalist for the London Evening Standard. Hunter hadn't the faintest notion about journalism. He could see why it had been chosen. It could open otherwise firmly locked doors and might ease his passage in certain conversations, but he was going to have to be exceptionally careful how much he revealed about himself. According to his legend he was very much the office junior on the staff. That suited him rather well. He could play the teaboy all day long. He set to work memorising the company's address in Kensington and their telephone numbers. Then there were all his fictitious workmates. More names, numbers and hobbies. And as Hunter took it all in, this man's life, his life and yet not his life, and he tried to absorb the collection of photographs scattered around his feet, not of him but of Simon Frost, this recently introduced stranger he was rapidly having to acquaint himself with, he couldn't help but be reminded of a very different sequence of pictures, the photographs of Amy he'd scooped up in his hurry to leave his old life and Cambridge behind. Photographs he would have to relinquish if he were successfully to begin his new life as Simon Frost.

***

A cloud of faces swam in Hunter's mind, all his own, yet not. Strings of figures, all known to him, yet not, accompanied the faces encircling him like amiable snakes. A passport photograph here, a driver's licence picture there, patrolling chaotically through his mind. He tried, from his position twice removed, to do what he did and establish some connection with the swirling digits, to bring a degree of order to them, to connect them to the faces, but off in the distance there was something or someone preventing him, a third element entered his dreams, rhythmic and relentless, like the pattern of a drum beating through his thoughts. As the drum grew ever louder Hunter understood that he must leave this place, and then there was Gary Williams, morphing from his own.

I'm going to enjoy beating the shit out of you.

Williams is beating on an old and cracked punch bag which, as it spins and rotates under his fists, becomes Hunter, who slowly begins to rise and rise until he is conscious and painfully aware of the crick in his neck. He has fallen asleep surrounded by paperwork, empty coffee cups and a half full ashtray. He's half sitting half lying on the living room floor, his head propped awkwardly on the sofa behind him, the rest of his body bruised and aching from days at the gym.

And someone is beating out a tattoo on the flat's front door and even before he can drag himself from the floor, Hunter knows with a horrifying certainty who that person is.

'Strike three?'

'No, not today, Scott. Let's call it a foul ball,' Healy says elbowing past him and making for the kitchen. 'Get yourself dressed, I'll make us a coffee, we're going for a drive.'

***

Healy parked up near Notting Hill Gate.

'This is us.'

Hunter wondered what they were doing there. Another person to trail, a house to be observed, surely not more firearms training?

'Come with me.'

He followed Healy from the car, down a small side street, past an open-air picnic area and into a park. Hunter was not a Londoner and so one piece of highly manicured parkland looked much the same as any other, but his knowledge of the capital over the past few months had improved sufficiently that as they walked in silence through tree lined avenues, his heart began to sink. To his right he recognised Kensington Palace, in the distance The Italian Gardens and past them The Serpentine, curving south and east towards Knightsbridge. Then, as he knew they would, they arrived at Frampton's monument to Peter Pan. Hunter's mind was suddenly swimming with images he had struggled to repress. George Wiseman, the irascible old boy who somewhat reluctantly had helped him realise just who his family had been. A chase from this place, pursued by a nameless man whose grandfather, Otto Kästner, had been, like Hunter's, a Nazi war criminal. But above all, Amy Proctor. His Amy, lying on the very bench Healy had brought him to, blood stained and dying.

'What's going on? What are we doing here?'

'You're done.'

'What do you mean "you're done"? You told me you weren't kicking me out,' Hunter said, realising just what the whole process had come to mean to him.

'I'm not. This is where it begins, Scott. Williams tells me you're ready, says you can throw an okay punch, although he wasn't as happy with your work on the range. He thinks that without the required emotional connection you aren't just a poor shot, you're bloody awful. Is that true?'

Hunter gave a noncommittal shrug.

'Well either way, now you need to decide. Are you going to leave your mark or carry on as you have been and let life just happen to you? But first you have to deal with this.' Healy spread out his arms. 'You have to face and come to terms with this. It's not going anywhere. You lost someone special to you, I get it. We've all been there. And now you're alone. No friends. No one. Get over it and get on with it, because this is never going away. It will always be with you,' Healy tapped the side of his head, 'up here. So, find a way. Don't let it define you, because it will. Use it to make you stronger, not weaker, faster not slower. This is it, Scott. You're on your own from now on. Got it?'

Hunter was beginning to understand. To understand what his father must have gone through when his mother had died.

'Got it.'

'Look, you can screw around feeling sorry for yourself for the rest of your life or you can stand up and be counted, do something important, something which might actually matter. Personally, I couldn't give a shit either way, but you're young and from what I've seen you're smart, so stop wasting time and get on with being in control of the here and now. Take it from me, I spent far too many years in someone else's shadow trying to do the right thing. Today's Monday. Deal with Monday, however you do that, that's up to you. Sod Saturday and Sunday, sort Monday. When Tuesday comes along, get stuck into Tuesday.'

'Thanks, Michael.'

'Don't Hunter. You're ready.'

Healy found a black and white photograph and a plump white envelope in the inside pocket of his leather jacket and handed them to Hunter.

'You're to fly out to Hong Kong, first thing. There's a passport in Frost's name with all the relevant visas. You're working as a journo for The London Evening Standard. The rest's up to you. They want you to find someone. Ewen Connolly, possibly going as Ewen Henderson or Elias Hoffstetter.'

'German?'

'Swiss. It's possible he's fled to mainland China by now so first you'll need to track down this man,' Healy continued, pointing at the photograph. 'Frank Cassatto, foreign correspondent to one of our broadsheets, low life drunk and recreational drugs user fighting out of Brooklyn, New York. My advice, start at the Admiral Nelson in Tsim Sha Tsui district of Kowloon. Chances are he'll be there. Otherwise you might try The Shamrock or the Prince Regent, all drinking holes for expats and septics. If you don't get any joy there, just flip over a few decent sized boulders in Wan Chai, he's bound to come scuttling out eventually, especially if he thinks there's a drink or a line of coke in it for him. When he's not writing a column, he's been known to do the odd bit of freelance intelligence gathering for our American cousins. Don't get any funny ideas though, he's only in it for the money, so don't bother trying to appeal to his sense of decency, because he clearly doesn't have one. Sell to the highest bidder, that's Cassatto's motto.'

'Is there a photograph of Connolly?'

'No. Nothing current.'

'How am I supposed to know when I've got the right man then?'

'24172738'

'What the hell does that mean?'

'Don't shoot the messenger, Scott. Just what I've been told. Listen this guy disappeared twenty years ago. We're dealing with scraps I'm afraid. Once you've found him let me know. Use the email address on your phone. You'll need a...'

'VPN in China, I know,' Hunter said. 'I'll bounce my location over a secure network back to a server in the UK or basically anywhere that isn't China. That way it looks like I'm on a local network and not one in Beijing.'

'Good boy. Don't send the message, just save it in your drafts. We'll monitor your email and communicate with you in the same way.'

'What makes you think this guy, Connolly, is going to want to talk to me?'

'Landslide.'

'What?'

'Landslide. If you can find Connolly, I'm told that should be enough to focus his attention. I believe it was an op which went bad years ago. No one's ever been desperate to talk about it and so I didn't. In fact, I got the distinct impression that certain people wanted as little to do with Landslide or anything connected with it as possible.'

'Why? What happened?'

'Like I said, at the time it was better not to ask, so I didn't, but I do remember a lot of worried looking faces. A lot of powerful people in anxious little huddles whenever the subject came up. And then, for whatever reason, it all blew over. No doubt some other new horror came to overtake it.'

'Why the interest in it now? If Landslide was such an embarrassment then, why not leave it dead and buried, why bring it up again?'

'Who knows? All I've been told is that this guy, Cassatto, on a layover from the US of A back to Hong Kong was heard shouting his mouth off about Landslide to anyone who'd listen. Truth is he'd probably run out of money and didn't have anything at all other than perhaps the name. Whistling in the wind if you ask me. Probably heard it in a bar on the Lockhart Road, thought it might buy him a night in a fancy hotel or a bag of Columbian marching powder, and decided to chance his arm. Anyway, he's where I'm told you should start. Got you a little something, call it a going away present.' Healy reached in a jacket pocket and produced a phial of pills. 'You don't sleep much, do you? Slip a couple of those under your tongue.'

Hunter shook the tiny canister Healy had given him and tried to digest this new information. When he looked up Healy had turned and walked back the way he had come, leaving him alone as George Wiseman had done many months before. He watched his mentor retreat into the park and then he did the only thing he could, the only thing he thought Healy would want him to. He sat on the bench where Amy had died and tried to let her go. She was not coming back. Hunter looked across the Serpentine with its crazy collection of ducks, at the tree he and George had hidden behind on that day and tried to accept. Slowly, as he sat and smoked and Hyde Park and London continued around him, Hunter began to embrace his solitude and to understand it a little. He was starting to feel stronger as an individual, bolder and less reliant on others. He was a very different person now. He had done things, terrible things, which had changed him forever and he'd been forced to acknowledge, perhaps there would never be another Amy, he did not know, but for now at least, he felt strangely determined. Today was Monday and so he would get on with Monday.

He stubbed out his cigarette and turned over the envelope in his hand. A single white adhesive sticker with his name printed on. He opened the envelope. A plane ticket, a passport in the name of Frost with his photograph, a healthy bundle of dollars, US and Hong Kong and a banker's card in the name of Simon Frost held together with a rubber band and a sheet of paper carefully folded in three. Typed on the paper a formulaic and utterly anonymous email address.

Hunter opened the airline ticket. He'd always fancied going

to Hong Kong, although he had a feeling this was not going to be a relaxing fun filled vacation with time for sight-seeing and shopping. He looked at the time and date on the ticket.

Back at his cramped North London flat Hunter quickly threw some clothes into his rucksack and went online. He opened a search engine and typed in Ewen Connolly. There were several Ewen Connolly's spread across the globe, of all ages and professions, some alive, many not. Hunter was thinking what an exhaustive task it would be to trawl through them all when it occurred to him, these were all easily identifiable, with a web presence and therefore, almost by definition, none of them would be the man he was looking for. His employers could easily have undertaken the same search he had performed in seconds. The Connolly he was looking for had in some way slipped off the grid, otherwise anyone could have found him. Hunter turned his attentions to the 8 digit number. On the bus back to the flat he'd considered the many possibilities and permutations, and the more he thought about it, the more there had been. An account number for a British bank, but then without the name of that bank the account could be anywhere. Passport numbers were 9 digits in length, an ISP address 10. If it were a telephone number then it was lacking an area code and so Hunter discounted that too. He started to look further afield. Swiss bank accounts comprised of 16 numbers, so perhaps this was just one half of an account shared by Connolly and someone else? Then the idea of foreign countries led him to look at the number in a completely different way. What if it wasn't an account or reference number at all, but a location. Degrees of longitude and latitude were often given to 8 places. Admittedly he only seemed to have one set of coordinates but he was growing desperate. Hunter looked at the

24th Meridian east of Greenwich. It certainly dissected some interesting places, descending across the Arctic and Atlantic oceans before hitting Europe and Belarus, the Ukraine and Estonia, all countries that until 1991 had been behind Churchill's Iron Curtain. And then there was Libya.

The 24th Parallel by contrast ran through Saudi Arabia, China and again, Libya. Now Hunter used the 8 digits as both longitude and latitude. A small village on the border of Libya and Egypt. Hunter couldn't imagine how it might tie in with Ewen Connolly, but it was something.

***

He settled back in his seat on the British Airways flight from London Heathrow to Dubai. Next to him an appalling woman from the home counties with a large nose and a face like a vulture who had started complaining the moment she'd sat down and appeared set to continue berating the cabin crew for the next eight hours. Hunter wondered whether the severity of the plait in which she wore her hair was in some way constricting the flow of blood to her brain. His only comfort, that he could kill her with his bare hands simply by jamming his thumb into her eye socket. Instead he slipped on the complimentary headphones and chose to ignore her. All he had with him, the few clothes he'd packed, a laptop and an overwhelming sense of not knowing what he was doing. The name of the man he'd been sent to find meant nothing to him. Ewen Connolly could have been anyone. He might be dangerous or he might need help, he could be anywhere and perhaps most troublingly, he might not even be alive. The same could be said of Frank Cassatto he thought as he looked at the

American's black and white photograph. A thin youthful face, dark slick back hair, black intelligent eyes and a strong dimpled chin. Hunter slipped a couple of Healy's pink dramamine tablets under his tongue and washed them down with two whisky miniatures sweet talked from the stewardess. He was no stranger to sleeping tablets. After his mother had hanged herself he had experienced a slow yet terrifying breakdown, which had been as painful as it had been inexorable. A succession of doctors and psychiatric nurses had prescribed endless combinations of uppers, downers, anti-depressants and sleeping tablets which had only exacerbated his condition. At university a well-meaning student had offered him herbal pills the size of jacket buttons and these had proven to be the last straw. Hunter had felt as if he were drowning and had sworn off medically assisted sleep for good. Then Amy had died and suddenly all bets were off. Now he'd pop any tablet available if it promised respite from the waking world. Thirty minutes later, as the stewards buzzed around his neighbour and with the plane's engines droning monotonously in the background Hunter slipped into an uneasy slumber and dreamt of a time long past.

A warm smiling face, a caring hand on a young boy's shoulder, kind words delivered in a soft lilting accent. The boy's face creased in a gigantic smile as their guest talks quietly and passionately with his father. The boy does not know this man, although he has met him before, but he cannot remember his name. He is not a name, he is his father's friend who brings chocolate and once, when he was very young, a small red teddy bear covered in pretty white spots from somewhere called Germany. They decide they will call the bear Aloysius, which makes the man laugh. The boy is pleased to make his father's friend laugh and wonders where

Germany is. The boy's mother is happy and smiling too, when often she is sad. She laughs and jokes with their guest and then, as if following a silent command, retreats to the kitchen to prepare special food; the man's favourite, an apple dessert covered with pastry, sweet with raisins and served with ice cream. Sometimes, when the man visits, he stays, and he and the boy's father sit up long into the night drinking drinks he is not allowed and talking in hushed tones. The boy wonders what they can possibly be saying that is so important and makes his father, who is usually so jolly, look so serious. On one occasion he sneaks downstairs and tries to listen to their hushed conversations. It is the only time he ever remembers his father become angry. He's sent back to bed and does not spy on his father and his friend ever again. Sometimes, when the man stays he is still there for breakfast. The boy loves breakfast with his father's friend. He looks pale and sweaty and his eyes are a strange colour, but he tells jokes and funny stories and uses words his father would rather he did not. The boy loves that. Other times, when the boy wakes up early – full of excitement – their guest has already left. Perhaps he is a postman the boy thinks. But always when he stays he tells the boy a bedtime story. These are the boy's favourite things. He could listen to the man's stories forever, in his soft thick accent. They're full of action, danger and excitement and make his father sigh and roll his eyes. The boy wonders if he could make up such fantastic stories and where they come from. Perhaps the man is a writer. At bedtime there is always a fight, with his father saying he should get some sleep and the man saying "Let him have one more, David. Let him have one more and then we'll talk." His father always lets him tell one more story and then he tries to sleep, his head full of armies, explosions and a place called Ireland. The boy wonders if Ireland is near

Germany. And then, something has happened, and quite suddenly the visits stop. The boy never sees the man again and quickly the memory of him fades and the boy forgets him altogether except in his dreams. There are other visitors, but none bring him gifts and none bring him chocolates and soon all that is left of his father's friend is a small red bear with delicate white spots called Aloysius which has come from somewhere far away.

5

Somewhere in London's East End, 1999

Jesus, Gray and his trained monkey Sandy Harper are here.

Someone had gone out of their way to find the sparsest, ugliest room. The only view through the bars of its one mucky window; drainpipes and chimney stacks and precious little by way of natural sunlight. The walls stark and naked except for the green and white Exit sign which hangs uselessly above the only door. In the centre of the room a bare formica table with dull metal legs unceremoniously bolted to the floor; square and functional and wearing a discoloured and chipped teapot under a tatty chequered cover. Four cups and saucers had been found but only three spoons. Some of the cups match, others do not. A small handled silver quaich full of sugar cubes, a pair of tarnished silver tongs and a jug of semi-skimmed make up the wretched ensemble. If the service had been a show on Broadway, it would have folded quickly, quietly and without ceremony.

Ewen Connolly had heard about this place but had never thought it would be quite such a dump. He took in the two empty chairs around the table at 15c. Who, he wondered, could they possibly be for? He had no idea of the nature of their meeting. He'd been summoned and had obediently done as his masters had bidden. Now he pulled himself up to his full height, stuck out his chest towards Sandy Harper and did what he did best. Waited. There had been a huge amount he had resented about the British Army; the shit pay, the long hours on stag when his mates had been heading into the local town with girls on their arms and of course that prick of a drill Sergeant. But none of that pissed him off more than the look on Sandy Harper's face, like something had crawled under his nose and died. The Rupert's Rupert, with his half an inch of ivory cuff, his pushed back blonde hair which he couldn't leave alone and his bloody tie pin. Sandy Harper was just the sort of Englishman Connolly hated; loud, arrogant but above all else pleased with himself and for no discernible reason. Harper had his head so far up Toby Gray's arse he must have been able to see his tonsils. Connolly tried not to smile at that. Why give the prick the satisfaction?

He looked out of the corner of his eye at Gray. Now he was a different kettle of fish all together. Probably hadn't come from quite the same money as Sandy. He'd used his brains to get to the top. There were stories. Of course, there were always stories. Stories of the part he'd played in Berlin in '89. Of his meteoric rise through the ranks of the service. Stories of the coups he'd led, the people he'd brought down, the horses he'd traded, the men he'd dispatched, the backhanders he'd taken and handed out, the malfeasance and the villainy, but by contrast with his underling, Gray was a self-effacing, self-contained, objective man of few words and long hours at the bar. So, who would be joining this awkward little gathering, and to what end, Connolly wonders?

Gray coughs, shifts in his seat and resettles himself. He appears about to light a cigarette, then, thinking better of it, pushes his lighter around the table distractedly.

'Shall we make a start?' Sandy's voice; impatient and impertinent.

'Why not?' Gray replies in cheerily censorious tones. 'Well then, Ewen, why don't we take this opportunity to listen to your side of the story re Moscow before John shows up. Shall we start with the girl? Attractive I'm supposing?'

So that was why he'd been summoned, to dish the dirt on John Alperton. Jesus. And that prat Sandy was staring at him and grinning like a bloody hyena about to bring down an antelope.

Don't you say a god damn word about that man, do you understand? Alperton's words ringing in his ears. *You stick to what we discussed, do you understand?*

What was that saying about rocks and hard places?

'Aye. She was pretty enough.'

'Who made the first move?' Now it was Sandy's turn to gently turn the screw. Connolly tried to think what Alperton would have done. He would have played it for laughs and seen if they went for it.

'Love at first sight, Sandy.' *Like you and one of your bloody horses.*

'Who made the first move?' but now without even a hint of a smile.

'I think he did. I don't know, I wasn't exactly sat on the end of the bed.'

'Alright. How often did they meet and where?'

'Every couple of days. His hotel mostly. Sometimes they went out for dinner.'

'Where?'

'Georgian place. Chikovani's.'

'Any good?' Sandy's smile has returned, regrettably.

'Couldn't say.'

'And this lover's tryst was going on for how long, would you say?'

'Couple of weeks.'

'Then what?' Still Sandy asking all the questions and getting most of the answers.

'Then one day John shows up at the allotted time and place and there's no Viktorija, just a big brute of a Russian.'

'The brute have a name?' Gray is still with them it appears.

Ewen shakes his head. 'Sorry. Just the dead drop, then the walk off. No idea.'

'Unlike Aleksei to change his MO.' Connolly tries not to flinch at the mention of the name, unsure whether he is supposed to know or not. 'Don't suppose he contacted John,' then the most almighty beat whilst Gray lights up, 'to tell him of the change of routine I mean?'

'Not to my knowledge, no.'

They move on, as if the name has never been spoken.

'Your knowledge is looking a little sketchy,' Sandy says, being a prick as usual and for no good reason.

'And then what?' Toby Gray again, gently getting them back on track.

How much to tell? How much of this did they already know or at least suspect? Alperton had said not to mention the man at the restaurant. They seemed happy enough with what he'd told them thus far. He would stick to their plan.

'He went looking for her.'

'You're going to make me cry, Connolly. Romeo goes off in search of his Juliet, how touching. Then what?'

'I trailed him for a few days.' Then immediately realising the error of his ways and before that idiot Sandy can jump on it. 'Four days.'

'Thank you.'

'For four days, cafés, bars mostly. The park a couple of times. Restaurants obviously.'

'Well obviously.'

'Alperton still made all his drops though. Then he found her, in a bar by the river.'

'And?'

'There was a hell of a stooshie.'

'Argument?'

'My guess, yes.'

'Then?'

'Then Alperton took a taxi back to his hotel on the other side of town. She followed him about ten minutes later.'

'She wasn't the only one to follow him though, was she? How many men?'

Sandy was moving quickly now, showing a few of his cards along the way.

'Two.'

He hadn't seen them until it had been too late. Would it be necessary to tell them that?

'And where were you whilst all this was going on, Connolly?'

No, clearly it would not.

'Following the girl back to the hotel.'

'Don't get smart. Did you make them?'

Here we go, Drill Sergeant Sandy bloody Harper.

'No I did not,' *you bastard.*

'Perhaps we'll come back to that later, Connolly?'

Gray looks to his left, checking his subaltern. Thank you, thinks Connolly, for the reprieve, however brief it may prove to be.

'What happened next?'

'I thought I'd go up and have a nosey. Took the stairs. Got to the end of the corridor. You could tell something was up. Halfway down Alperton's door was wide open. Hell of a racket coming from inside if you know what I mean? Raised voices, but not Russian I don't think.'

'What then?'

'Chechen.'

'Bloody Chechens.' A rare slip of Gray's mask.

'What did you do?' Sandy again.

'The only thing I could, I turned around and walked. Didn't need to see what was going on to know.'

'Nice of you. Thought you'd leave him to it?'

'My brief, remember?' The brief he had so flagrantly ignored. 'Observe, but don't get involved.'

'Quite. What exactly did you do then?'

'Waited. I sat it out until they'd left and went to find John.'

'John?' Sandy is incredulous at the perceived over-familiarity.

'Alperton.'

'Yes. Just before we cut ahead to the scene of the accident,' Sandy smiles at that, 'these two men?'

'Hired hands. Professional killers. FSB, I don't know.' *Except that of course I do, or at least I have my suspicions. Strong and deeply worrying suspicions.* 'Muscle, nothing subtle you understand?'

'Clearly. So, once you could be of no further use, you decide to show your face.'

'That's not how it was.'

'No? Do tell.'

'If I'd followed *your* brief I'd have walked straight to the embassy, first plane home, don't look back.'

'But you didn't, did you?'

'No.'

'Why not? Conscience get the better of you?'

Ewen Connolly could have reached over, grabbed the back of that smug bastard Sandy Harper's head and bounced it off the table, hopefully breaking his nose.

'Something like that, yes. I checked the corridor out first to make sure the heavies had gone, then back to the room. John was on the floor trying to revive the girl, but I could tell from the moment I saw her...'

'Go on.'

'Huge gash on her forehead,' Connolly says running a finger over his own head in an effort to convince himself.

'How?'

'Pushing and shoving, so I'm told. She fell. There was a marble table. My guess, she cracked her head on the edge as she fell and that was that.'

Gray moves in his seat for the umpteenth time. 'How was John?'

'How would you expect? Distraught. Angry. Surprised to see me of course and confused as fuck, I expect. I made him clean up, we locked the room, checked out of the hotel and found somewhere to lay low for a few days.' *Not entirely true but true enough.*

'Safe house?'

'All arranged before I left London for just such an eventuality.'

'Address, of this safe house please?'

'16 Grimau Street. Squalid block of Khrushchevka flats in the Akademichesky district.'

Sandy looks to his master. Gray nods his approval.

'They should be bloody torn down.' This at least is true he thinks.

'Thank you, Ewen.' Soothing Gray again. 'And then what?'

'Once things had settled down we went straight to the embassy and you know the rest.'

'Your days holed up in Moscow, you and Alperton stay put?' Sandy probing again, like an animal trying to extract the last juicy grub from a rotten tree trunk.

'Yes.'

'Just you, John Alperton, a steady flow of Moscow's finest vodka and your thoughts to keep you company?'

'That's right.'

'Not tempted out for an evening of dancing girls and strip joints?'

'No.'

'Didn't try and track down our friend, see what he might have had to say about the whole sorry affair?'

'And how would we have done that? Listen Mr Harper, I know the drill better than most in these situations. We sat tight and only made the move to the embassy after forty-eight hours, per your orders.' He turns to include Toby Gray in the conversation, eager to get away from Sandy's analytical stare.

'Well, that was very well done of you.' Sandy is being supercilious again and Connolly has to fight every instinct not to grab his tie pin and jab it in his eye.

'I'm sure you did all you could, under the circumstances. And thank you for being so candid,' says Gray being disarmingly reasonable.

Not as candid as I might have been, thinks Connolly.

'Sandy, would you mind?' Gray once more, this time gesturing towards the door.

Sandy Harper stands, straightens his tie, adjusts his trousers and reluctantly attends to the door, leaving Connolly, Gray and an awkward silence.

'Jesus, this place is a dump,' Connolly says hoping to ease the tension, 'is there really nowhere else we could meet?'

'I'm sorry you feel like that, Ewen,' Toby Gray replies calmly, 'and no, there is not. Added to which, I happen to rather like it.'

Connolly apologises quickly and both men listen in silence to Sandy Harper.

'If you would like to come in now, please,' he says without an ounce of warmth.

Connolly sits to attention again as John Alperton enters the room.

'Ah, John, you know everyone,' Gray says, stamping his authority on the proceedings.

'How are you, Toby?'

'Fine, fine, thank you.'

Which of course they all understand to mean he is anything but.

'Sorry I'm late. Mind if I smoke?' Alperton putting himself at ease.

'Traffic on Carnaby Street must be worse than usual,' Sandy says in a stage whisper but to no one in particular.

'Fuck off, Sandy. For your information I was with our friends from across the pond, but I wouldn't expect *you* to understand, bit above your pay scale.' Alperton is finding his cigarettes and adjusting his jacket, whilst never bothering to look up. What the hell was that bedwetting sycophant Sandy Harper doing here, he thinks? Best to put the little toad right in his place and quick about it. 'Do be sure and send your wife my regards.'

'Gentlemen,' Gray urges, sensing there is a danger of tempers boiling over and determined to play the peacemaker at any cost, 'If you wouldn't mind?'

Connolly is still staring at that fifth empty seat whilst Toby Gray fiddles with his cigarettes again. *Who could it possibly be meant for? George Wiseman, the only man Tobias Gray's in awe of and whom Connolly has only met on one other occasion? Surely not George. Things are bad clearly, but that bad? What about that unconscionable little shit Frederick Sinclair? No, he'd be too tied up with his new job at the university, and in any case, no one could bear to have him around. They'd all agreed there was just something about the man. It was only George's good word that ever brought him to the table and even then he suspected a reluctance on the old boy's part.* Gray is fiddling with his cigarettes again causing Connolly to want to grab them, scrunch them up and hurl them across the room.

If you want to listen to what we have to say, sit still and listen.

Instead he's relieved when Gray picks up the packet, extracts a cigarette and lights it.

'And I believe you know Ewen Connolly?'

'Connolly.' A matter of fact nod, one chap to another.

'John,' Connolly mumbles awkwardly before returning to drill holes in the vacant seat with nothing more than his empty stare, as he listens horrified to John Alperton relate his side of their sorry tale. Every now and then Sandy pulling him up on one point or another.

'But Connolly here said you never left Grimau Street until it was time to go to the embassy, that the truth, John?'

'That's not quite how I remember it.'

'You *did* leave the house then?' An incredulous Sandy Harper, directed at John Alperton.

'No. But I remember Connolly leaving briefly, on one occasion.'

Fantastic. After all he'd done for him, they were going to paste him into a corner – make him look like the traitor and hang him out to dry.

'Really? Are you quite sure? Connolly here assures us he knows the ropes, better than most I believe you said? Perhaps you're mistaken John?'

'It was only briefly. I expect we needed something to eat?'

This was just like being back in the bloody army, being stitched up for something he hadn't done, well not really.

'Yes, I expect so. Popped out for some blinis and caviar, eh Connolly?'

Gray is looking distractedly at his watch. 'I think I've heard enough, Sandy. Why don't we skip ahead, perhaps return to this later? I think we should move on to the next item on the agenda, Miss King will be joining us shortly.'

King? Pat King? What the hell was she doing here? She hadn't been in Moscow, thank God.

'I've invited Connolly here to run our next operation on the ground.'

Naturally this is the first Ewen Connolly has heard of such a thing, but he says nothing and faces the front whilst John Alperton sits patiently and examines his fingernails, his continued presence at this meeting unnecessary. There had clearly been some discrepancies with Connolly's account, he mused. That had been a shame but understandable surely considering the circumstances. Why the Scot had felt the need to lie about the safe house in Moscow he couldn't imagine. Certainly Connolly had broken from procedure by leaving but no one around this table was going to call into question his dedication. None of them may have liked him very much, he was a rough diamond that was for sure, but he'd saved Alperton's neck hadn't he? So what if he'd had to get out of the safe house for an hour or two? They'd have probably killed each other if he hadn't. Mind you, better they concentrate on the Scot than on what *he'd* been up to.

Alperton tried to remember, filtering out some of the events of his last few days in Russia's capital. Hadn't the Scot returned with fresh supplies, bread, some cheese and of course something unspeakable to drink? Finding bread could have taken him an hour alone. The door opened and John Alperton put it from his mind.

Patricia King enters, still in her thirties and terrified. She smiles meekly at the assembled group, whispers a general hello and, with nobody making the slightest effort to find her a seat or introduce themselves, draws up a chair.

So, they'd drafted in a new recruit. Connolly had mentioned her during their enforced incarceration in Moscow. Now that

Alperton thought back to their time in the unspeakable flat on Grimau Street, the Scot had mentioned her a number of times. In fact, now that John Alperton cared to give it his full attention, Connolly had spent a great deal of time talking up the service's latest recruit. He looked at her now. She was not unattractive he supposed, handsome in a rather pleasing way. Her hair was a little in need of attention and her clothes were, well, frankly horrendous, but John Alperton was forced to concede there was something about her.

'Who could do with a cup of tea?' Sandy simpers, appearing intent on playing mother, like the child who rushes for the keeper's gloves and pads enjoying the sensation of singling themselves out as in some way different. He looks around at the select group. The recently arrived and clearly chippy John Alperton in a natty herringbone and today sporting, and pulling off, a paisley neckerchief. Toby Gray, the grey man in every respect, impassive and imperious, the epitome of clinical impartiality. His clothes were just as Sandy found him, boring and accountable. Ewen Connolly, the Scot, and therefore not to be trusted. Sandy hadn't wanted him present at this meeting at all. He was a squaddie, a grunt, discharged from the army for some drunken brawl, a whole rung or more beneath him on the ladder. Connolly would do as he was damn well told and need not be consulted. He sat there in his jeans and a T-shirt, pawing at a packet of cigarettes in the manner of a man trying and failing to quit. His lighter, or Sandy speculated, his matches nowhere to be seen, slowly folding and unfolding the packet which was surely about to break under his ministrations. If Connolly were indeed trying to quit, Sandy would enjoy his first puff of the day and make sure the Scotsman got a good lungful too. He slid a cup and saucer across the formica at him. Connolly observed the tea suspiciously before drenching it in milk and noisily drowning a couple of sugar cubes.

'Looks a bit pissy to me,' he mutters.

'No doubt you were expecting something stronger?'

'What do you mean by that?'

Alperton smiles to himself, having seen this display before. Toby Gray does not. Pat King shuffles in her seat and hopes that no one will notice her.

'Don't pay any attention to him,' Gray chimes in, 'he's trying to make you feel uncomfortable. It's what he does,' as though he collects moths or speaks in sterile puns. It's just what he does.

Sandy chooses, on this occasion, to ignore his superior and present John Alperton his tea. *Sandy*, the only word of thanks before a splash of milk joins the pale brown liquid. Lastly their lord and master, Tobias Gray, his lips chapped, eyes puffy from a lifetime of long nights at the bar. He spins his cup through half a turn, hoping perhaps it will aid in any taste, but declines to add either milk or sugar. No words of thanks are proffered, well-made tea the least of his entitlements. There not being enough cups to go around, Pat King is conveniently forgotten. It crosses her mind to speak up but then she returns to her unanswerable prayer that a wide and bottomless pit will fantastically appear and swallow up the whole bloody lot of them.

'Gentlemen, Lady,' Sandy begins turning to address Connolly, 'We want you to pop over to Istanbul, scoop up a new pal of ours and bring him back here.' He glances at Toby Gray for his approval. So, not entirely your call then, John Alperton thinks. 'Take Pat King here with you. I believe you know one another?' Connolly nods and King returns the gesture. Then

Sandy continues as if she weren't there. 'She's pretty green, but it's all remarkably straight forward stuff, it'll give you a chance to show her the ropes.'

'Make sure that's all you show her, please Ewen,' Gray chimes in, to her obvious embarrassment and ribald chortles all round. Connolly feels himself colour. 'We want you to make contact with an asset coming out of Romania.' Gray pushes an envelope across the table. 'You'll refer to him as Landslide.'

There are stolen glances and someone stifles a barely concealed gasp as Connolly nods professionally and takes the envelope. Landslide is the asset they have all heard of, right down to the lowly Patricia King, but know nothing about. He or she is the super-source, the fount of all the intel Gray has ever produced over the years, a veritable oracle. A quick peek inside is all Connolly needs to confirm his worst suspicions, a black and white photograph of a man stepping from a car. Nicely taken, good angle on the face, not too much shadow. He lets the photograph slide back inside its envelope and remembers the last time he's seen that face.

'Where and when?'

Tobias Gray takes charge now that there are serious matters to discuss. 'The Grand Bazaar, quiet little apothecary, King here's already got the address.' She nods, and no one questions how it has come into her possession. 'Sunday, eight o'clock in the evening. That gives you two a couple of days to do a spot of sightseeing, get properly acquainted. Why not make a long weekend of it? You might even like to take the charming Ms King here for a spot of Baklava, Connolly.' More obsequious chortling. 'We've taken the liberty of putting you up in The Marmara, it's new, on the other side of the river, a fifteen-minute cab ride into town. Don't forget to keep the receipt.'

'He won't.' Sandy again.

'Then what?'

'Rumour has it that Landslide is looking for a change of scene. Pissed off with his current surroundings. You're to make contact, see how the land lies and if there's any way we can aid our new chum.'

'Report back and await further instructions?'

'Very good,' Sandy purrs, enjoying the idea of handing out instructions to the Scot. 'Once we're certain he's the genuine article we'll look at extracting him. You're just to keep him under observation until then, make sure he's as happy as a sandman and that no one nobbles him in the meantime.'

'Will he be alone?'

'To the best of our knowledge,' Gray continues catching his stride now. 'He's currently holed up just outside Bucharest. His masters believe he's taken a girlfriend up to the log cabin he owns near Barvikha.' Alperton looks up from his tea. *So, he's a Russian. Now this is interesting.* 'We're banking on him not being missed until Monday morning, by which time, providing you don't balls it up of course, he should be well on his way to a nice cosy little mid-terrace two-up two-down in North London.'

Ewen Connolly knew the man they were calling Landslide. Perhaps that was why he'd been chosen? He knew he wasn't Romanian. He could easily identify him with or without their photograph. He glanced around the table and wondered if Sandy Harper or John Alperton realised who it was they were dealing with. He suspects, from their calm demeanour, they do not. He's certain in fact that John Alperton does not. Another good reason for sending him and not someone a little higher up the food chain. He would have to be careful. The man he was going to meet in a quiet little apothecary in Istanbul could be extremely dangerous. Connolly had witnessed it with his own two eyes.

'A weapon?'

Sandy looks to his master. Gray shakes his head. 'I'm afraid not, Ewen. Too risky by far. If you get turned over by the Turkish Police they'll have a field day and we can't afford any awkward questions. In any case, we want Landslide alive and well please, and with the minimum amount of fuss. You'll find a one-way ticket back here,' Gray continues, gesturing towards the envelope, 'and a Finnish passport under the name Lucas Petterson.'

Definitely Russian then, Alperton thinks. Only the Russians can pull off Finnish with any degree of conviction.

'Understood. What if there's trouble?'

'Make certain there isn't. Use King here if needs be.'

'Understood.'

'In fact,' Sandy chimes in, 'we were wondering if she shouldn't be the one to make contact?'

John Alperton who has been holding his council up to this point coughs twice and leans into the conversation, 'Is that wise? She's very young and, unless I've missed something, completely lacking in the necessary experience.'

'I can vouch for her,' Gray replies curtly, thereby drawing a line under any further discussion. 'She'll be ready, won't you?' he continues as if finally remembering King is in the room. 'Ewen can oversee, but it should all be straight forward enough, so please don't balls it up.' This last remark aimed squarely at the Scot. 'It's all been agreed.' Gray pushes his saucer of tea around listlessly for a moment, suddenly in a private meeting of his own.

'It's all been agreed,' he mutters to himself again. Then he reaches into the cavernous pockets of his overcoat and produces a hipflask. Alperton catches Sandy Harper's eye across the table but nothing is said.

'Anyone mind If I...?' Gray askes as much to himself. And in that second the other three men know they have lost him. Gray, for whatever reason, is a spent force, a hunted animal, weak before the chasing pack.

'I'll take a shot of that,' Ewen Connolly, the man with the least to lose replies, forgetting himself. He's long since tired of his tea and isn't enjoying the direction of their conversation. 'What are you having?'

'Brandy. Nothing special I'm afraid,' Gray says holding out the flask.

'Second thoughts, I'll pass,' Connolly says, perhaps remembering himself.

Gray makes a feeble show of offering Sandy, Alperton and even Patricia King the flask before screwing its cap back on and replacing it in his overcoat. So, that's it, Alperton thinks, it's barely eleven o'clock and you're reaching for the bottle already. Perhaps Toby Gray is finally feeling the strain, perhaps he is about to relinquish his crown. But to whom, surely not that toad Sandy Harper?

Having listened to his seniors have their say, the temptation for Ewen Connolly to re-open the envelope which lies on the table in front of him is almost overwhelming. What, he wonders, would they think if he were to tell them just who this man, the man they have all agreed to refer to as Landslide, really is? And what were they playing at sending in the young girl opposite him when he was far better placed to positively identify him? He liked Pat King, perhaps a little too much. They'd worked together before and he had bought her a couple of drinks following one particularly successful op. She had shown all the signs of becoming an excellent agent.

'Is this a honey trap?' he hears himself ask.

'Couldn't hurt,' Sandy coos.

And for that reason alone Connolly isn't comfortable with the idea of putting her in the same room as Landslide.

'Are we sure he wants to come over? There's no danger we're being set up?' he asks out of a sense of obligation and a desire to steer the subject away from Pat King. All eyes turn on Toby Gray. Landslide has always been his super-source, the asset so hot, so invaluable to the cause that, up until now, only Gray himself has been allowed to deal with him.

'I am quietly confident that he wants to come over. If I am correct, Gentlemen, Miss King, this could be quite a feather in our cap.'

'No sense in asking for a name?' Alperton asks.

'None at all, John, sorry.'

Absolutely none at all, Ewen Connolly silently concurs. He watches as a pair of flies chase each other up and down the mirrored wall which dominates one whole side of 15c and wonders what disgusting paths their lives have taken, and then he regards the men sat around their rudimentary table, sipping badly made tea together. He's about to damn them all to hell when he catches himself in the mirror as the flies continue their fetid tango. Seeing himself he's suddenly forced to contemplate who might be on the other side. It was inconceivable the Americans could be involved, this had a very homegrown, inhouse feel to it. The Russians then? Less likely still. Wiseman, the bluff old boy with his cigar and fair play sensibility? Or, Wiseman's superior? Surely there was no one above old George, except, he thinks with a smile, God himself. Yes, he might have been George's boss, at a push. Connolly steadies himself. In all likelihood there would be no one more than a nameless worker bee and a 4-track reel to reel. He goes back to staring at his own reflection and puts recent events, both past and present, from his mind. Just the Lord God all bloody mighty then.

'Once he's on home turf I'll make sure you're properly introduced,' Gray continues, addressing John Alperton. 'Until then, I'm afraid it will have to be left in the capable hands of Connolly here and Miss King. I'm sure you'll have no end of questions for him, once he's here.'

I'm bloody positive you will, thinks Connolly.

John Alperton grunts. Why the hell has he been dragged into this meeting then, to oversee Sandy's nauseating little power game, or worse still to witness his anointment as poor old Toby Gray's successor? Talk about having your nose rubbed in it. One thing to be passed over for the top job, quite another to have it happen right in front of you. There was nothing for him to contribute until Landslide, whoever he proved to be, was back in Britain, so why waste his time listening to Sandy stating the bleeding obvious? 'Consider my interest officially piqued,' he says as much to himself as to the assembled company.

6

Hong Kong International Airport

Having travelled for over twenty-four hours Hunter was almost relieved to escape from the airconditioned surroundings of a succession of enormous airports and step into the oppressive humidity of Chek Lap Kok island. A young Hong Konger wearing the latest sports clothes and a pair of fluorescent white trainers welcomed him with a confident grin and a hastily conceived cardboard sign.

'Mr Frost?' he asks rhetorically.

Hunter nodded.

'Follow me please, Mr Frost.'

Thanks to Michael Healy's little pink dramamine tablets Hunter had slept more than expected. Despite which he knew the moment he slumped in the red and white taxi and it rolled out of the airport and into the sticky midnight air that he would soon fall asleep.

'Where to, Mr Frost?'

'Do you know the Admiral Nelson Pub?' Hunter yawned, too tired to cover his mouth.

'Tsim Sha Tsui, I know it.'

The lad checked his watch. Hunter had lost all track of time. All he knew now was that it was dark and he was exhausted.

'But it closes in fifty minutes. I will try, Mr Frost.'

Hunter looked at the clock on his phone which had helpfully reset itself. It was ten-past one in the morning. He watched distractedly from the back of the cab in a haze of jet lag and sleeping tablets as they left the airport and crossed the never-ending Tsing Ma bridge. He remembered his final briefing in Hyde Park. It had been short and not particularly sweet. Go to Hong Kong and find a man calling himself Ewen Connolly or Henderson, or Hoffstetter or, more likely, none of the above. Yes, it will be like looking for the proverbial in a haystack. Go and find him anyway, and when you've found him contact us. No, we don't have a photograph for you. The only photograph we have was taken a thousand years ago. First you must find an American called Cassatto. He's been seen by a none too reliable source of ours propping up the bar in the Admiral Nelson Pub in Kowloon. That is where we recommend you start. Good luck and if you don't find Connolly, don't bother coming back.

When Hunter had asked how he could be sure he had found Connolly or Henderson or whatever the hell he was calling himself now, Healy had repeated an 8 digit number. It wasn't much to go on but he'd accepted the envelope which Healy had thrust into his hand and thanked him, which he was now regretting.

They'd sent him out there to chase ghosts, fairy tales and phantoms. The man could as well be dead as alive, but they'd never mentioned that possibility had they? And what the hell was Landslide? A codename for what? A twenty-year-old operation gone bad. It must have been of quite some importance for all this fuss. And who the hell was Ewen Connolly anyway? An operative, but no one had wanted to say whose. It was all probably irrelevant. Even if he were still alive the chances of tracking down one man in a country boasting a population of over a billion was next to impossible. It would end up being the longest wild goose chase and the shortest service career in history. They hadn't even booked him a return flight. He clutched the bag next to him and fell back to sleep.

'Mr Frost, Mr Frost, we are here.'

Hunter looked out of the cab window. Although he was six thousand miles from home, the sight which greeted him could hardly have been more British. The pub was decked out in red, white and blue bunting, gasping baskets of flowers hanging from every available support and on the pavement a wooden chalkboard light-heartedly advertising a forthcoming rugby tournament. Were it not for the fact that the whole front side of the pub was absent and spilled out directly onto the pavement, Hunter could have been in Trafalgar Square. He paid the cab and made for the entrance just as a phalanx of well medicated tourists was leaving. Hunter elbowed past them and into the pub's interior, where portraits of its titular maritime hero, old advertisements for Ireland's most famous black and white export and neatly embroidered polo shirts adorned every square inch of the walls. A smartly dressed young Australian bartender who looked as exhausted as Hunter felt welcomed him.

'I'm sorry, mate. We're closing up for the evening,' he said expertly flipping another chair over and sitting it on a table.

Yeah, I can see that, Hunter thought, even though it feels strangely like the middle of the afternoon.

'I've just got off a flight from London and I was supposed to meet someone here, I know it's late.'

The Aussie pulled at his waistcoat and repositioned a bar stool. Sensing the man was desperate to leave for the evening Hunter produced the photograph Healy had given him.

'I was supposed to meet him here,' he said, holding up the picture for the barman to inspect.

On the flight he had imagined this moment. He'd imagined all the possible reactions, all the possible outcomes, from confusion to violence. Hunter readied himself. But the man opposite him burst out laughing.

'Bugger me, that looks like Frank.'

'You know him then, Frank Cassatto?'

'Know him? We all know Frank, I mean he doesn't look much like that these days but... what's he done now?'

'I just need to talk to him, ask him a few questions, that's all.'

'Yeah, well you better join the bloody queue mate. We've got one or two burning questions of our own, like when's he going to clear his bloody bar tab?'

Hunter wondered what he'd stumbled into. Who was this man, Cassatto?

'I'll be sure and let him know,' Hunter replied. 'He's not here then?' The barman just laughed. 'Any ideas where I could find him?'

'There can't be too many places around here that'll still serve him. You might want to head over to Hong Kong. Then again I guess you could always try the Jockey Club out at Sha Tin.'

'Thanks. I don't suppose there's a hotel round here is there?'

'I'd try up by the harbour front, although,' he continued looking at his watch, 'might be a bit late for that. Otherwise there's a few up near the park.'

Hunter thanked him again and turned to see if he could find another cab. The months of training left unhelpfully behind, now he was confused and desperate to crawl into bed, but Scott Hunter was not too tired to understand that, in a foreign land, far from the protective ministering of Michael Healy and his superiors, he was now extremely vulnerable.

***

The next day Hunter slept in, waking just before midday in a hotel and not for the first time since arriving in Hong Kong not entirely certain exactly where he was. He showered and threw on some fresh clothes. In the hotel's reception he picked up a map and a helpful concierge pointed out where they were. The hotel was situated at the north end of Kowloon Park, just off the Austin Road. Where, Hunter asked somewhat sheepishly, should he go if he wanted something to drink. The receptionist checked his watch, smiled knowingly and pointed to an area on the other side of the park.

Hunter grabbed something to keep him going from the 7-eleven across the street and began walking south along Nathan Road and towards the Star Ferry terminal on what, under different circumstances, would have been nothing more than a glorified pub crawl. Nathan Road was long and busy and lined with the aerial pillars of smothering banyan trees, the pavement crammed with traders and tourists. In a bid for some pavement of his own Hunter cut in and onto Haiphong Road and past the shirt and suit shops and the grubby store fronts with their lurid pictures of scantily clad young Asian girls. He walked past the shops where for forty-five dollars US, fish ate the dead skin from your feet. The shops dripping in flashing neon that looked like strip clubs but weren't and the dark doorways leading to stairs and the strip clubs that were. Passed shop after shop selling each and every mobile phone imaginable where twice a day giggling schoolgirls checked their social media status before heading home to unwitting parents. And along the way he stopped in at every watering hole, every French café, Australian sports bar and faux London pub to show Frank Cassatto's photograph until he'd reached the harbour with its vibrant collection of stalls and kiosks selling guided tours and boat trips to the surrounding islands.

Know him. Of course I know him, he owes me money. So, if you find him, you can tell him I'm looking for him too.

Hunter had the same conversation over and over, in bar after bar, pub after pub. For every owner Cassatto owed money to there was another who had barred him.

Caught him dealing coke out of the gents. I don't know why you're after him, but I'd suggest you find him before I do. You're wasting your time, by the way, he's completely broke. No one here'll touch him. My bet is he's over on the island. Why don't you start around Central and work your way along Lockhart Road. That's where the bars are.

At the pier Hunter considered getting on the ferry which would take him across the harbour and to Hong Kong itself, but, not having quite finished with Ashley Road he turned on his heel and began north and back up towards the park, stopping in at an Australian themed bar with its own Chinese rock band and a clientele of drunken Brits fuelling up before the flight home. He showed the owner his black and white photograph of the American, but he shrugged his shoulders and refused to comment so Hunter moved on to the next place, a London Pub where the migrant landlord recognised the photograph immediately but hadn't seen him in weeks. And then, finally in an Irish bar hidden away on a side street off the Ashley Road and boasting all day breakfasts, chilled Guinness and attractive Malaysian waitresses he had some luck. Hunter navigated the steep flight of steps off the street and into a dark sea of bar stools and high tables patrolled by smartly dressed girls in emerald green skirts and matching waistcoats taking orders and making small talk with lonely businessmen, homesick expats and curious travellers. He unfolded his creased and battered photograph to show to the Kiwi working the bar. As the Aucklander poured a perfect shamrock on the top of his pint Hunter wearily recited his routine. The barman examined it casually then, shouting above the piped Irish music, beckoned over one of the girls walking the main room to join them.

'She's from KL. If anyone knows where Frank Cassatto is, she should. They were a bit of a thing once, but not so much recently, if you know what I mean?'

The woman who joined them at the bar was a little older than the rest of the girls and wore her plastic nametag and green and white uniform a degree more carefully.

'This is Maya,' the barman said before leaving them to attend to a fresh order.

'What can I get you? Do you need to see a menu?' Maya glanced at the Guinness on the bar by Hunter's elbow. 'You okay for a drink?' she added professionally masking any confusion.

'I think you know this man?'

Maya looked at the photograph Hunter handed her and then at Hunter.

'I know him, yes,' she said raising her chin proudly.

'Do you know where I might find him?'

'Why?'

'I'd like to talk to him.'

'So would a great many people, including me. Who are you? Why should I tell you where he is? You're not American.'

'No. I'm from London. I work for one of the papers, we're chasing a story, thought Frank might be able to help us, for a fee, of course.'

'Which paper?'

'London Evening Standard.'

This seemed to satisfy the inquisitive Maya, who reached into her apron and withdrew a pen and order pad. She lent on the bar and with a flurry wrote out an address. 'You see him, you tell him Maya still works here.' She tore the sheet from its book and handed it to Hunter. 'You tell him he should come and see Maya.'

'I will,' said Hunter, 'and thank you.'

Hunter consulted the map he'd picked up at the hotel before heading up and into Kowloon Park, out past the public swimming pool and north towards Mong Kok and the last sighting of his quarry. His shirt was sticking to his back in the thick afternoon heat and he was reeling from the jet lag and humidity as he waited to cross Austin Road and enter Jordan. Dodging red and white cabs he crossed the road and ducked into an open-air café, pointing at the first dish he saw on the laminated board the waitress held up for him. Ten minutes later the diminutive Chinese woman running the place returned, much to the amusement of a pair of giggling young girls at a neighbouring table, carrying a dish of darkly red chillies with a scratch of meat beneath. Each mouthful burned Hunter's lips and tongue terribly, but he was so hungry he forced down the meat. Only partially restored he continued north before finally arriving in the sweltering heat of Mong Kok's covered market. Movement through the tarpaulin shrouded streets was almost impossible. The heat and the overpowering smell of hot sticky bodies threatening to overwhelm him.

Mong Kok market, the pinnacle of imitation and deception. Stall after stall of cheaply made fakes. Hunter was feeling strangely at home. Everything around him was Western in its origin, but with a Chinese twist. All the most recent children's toys slavishly reproduced, but at a fraction of the cost. Pots, souvenirs, bells and good luck charms, pieces of jade, possibly. They were selling China like a box of confectioneries. A pick and mix. A handful of this culture, a sprinkling of that. Hunter paid little attention to any of it. He was not there to buy trinkets and keepsakes.

He fought his way through the stalls and tried to find his bearings. The address Maya had given him was one street back from the main thoroughfare. As he moved away from the market and the crowds began to thin he realised that, in amongst the sea of hair salons, barbershop's poles and eleven stories of glass were the apartments he'd been looking for. Seven flights of stairs later and feeling as though he'd been pursued every step of the way by the pungent aroma of open drains and fish sauce Hunter arrived tired and panting outside Frank Cassatto's flat. The American stood in his doorway, barring admittance with one long broad arm. From what little Hunter could see of the apartment's interior, it made his tiny flat in Harrow seem positively palatial. A shunned television set flickered on the floor in the hall, State National News competing with any number of whining air conditioning units, their cables trailing this way and that over a sallow collection of cheap and cracked floor tiles, the foot of a single bed poking out from behind a wall.

Cassatto was about thirty years older than his photograph, in faded green cargo shorts that appeared never to have been washed, a pale blue shirt which appeared never to have met an iron but hid a drinker's paunch, and a pair of sweat-stained deck shoes which were quietly giving way at the soles. His eyes were still keen and intelligent but shot through and yellowing and the once thick dark hair which appeared in his photograph was now thinning and sickly. His nose was red and mapped by years of abuse, his skin bloated and cracked from the sun. Hunter imagined there had never been less than a week's stubble on his chin.

'Can I help you?' Cassatto's overblown Brooklyn accent stepped straight off a film set. Direct, jabbing and confrontational, cutting through the thick humid air and, like all good counter punchers, following up before Hunter could reply, 'You the Brit who's been asking questions about me? Maya warned me you was on your way. What the hell do you want?' Cassatto's mouth puckered into a sneer, his brow knotted as he peered at Hunter. 'I don't forget a face, especially not one I owe money to. I don't owe you money, do I?'

'No.'

'And you sure as shit don't owe me nothing,' he laughed, 'I'd remember that too, so what d'ya want, kid?'

'I want to talk to you about someone.'

'You want to talk to me about someone? Well ain't that lovely? Who do I look like, Johnny Carson? I'm busy, kid.'

'Really?' Hunter said edging forward and insinuating his foot in the door, 'Doing what exactly?'

'Huh?' The American seemed genuinely taken aback by Hunter's forthright approach and so he continued.

'What are you so busy doing? I mean, I've just flown six thousand miles to talk to you, I think the least you can do is tell me what's quite so pressing you can't spare me a couple of minutes of your time?'

'Who do you wanna talk about?'

'You were in London recently, am I right?'

'Uh-huh,' Cassatto muttered looking over Hunter's shoulder into the empty stairwell behind him. 'Okay. You want to talk, sure, let's talk. I know a nice quiet little place. You're buying, am I right?'

'Fine. Where are we going?'

'I'll meet you Hong Kong side, Saint John's Cathedral, off Garden Road. You know it?'

'I can find it.'

'Fine. Eight-thirty. The walk'll do you good. They give a kid like you an expenses account?'

'Uh-huh.'

'Great. Bring it with you,' he laughed, 'you're going to need it. Now get lost, I got some work to take care of.' Then the door to Frank Cassatto's apartment was slamming in Hunter's face. He turned and was about to start down the winding stairs when he heard the door behind him open again. 'Hey, kid!'

Hunter spun round.

'You got anything a little smarter with you, you know like a jacket or such?'

'I'll see what I can do,' he replied.

***

That evening, and wearing a hurriedly purchased linen jacket over his T-shirt, Hunter took the Star Ferry across the harbour. A floating one stop bus service facilitating commuters from outlying islands and tourists from around the world. Following the handover of Hong Kong in '97 the ferry still wore its *Made in Liverpool* plaque but now with an awkwardness, the housewarming guest who stubbornly refuses to leave having outstayed their welcome, unwilling or possibly unable to navigate their way home. Hunter sat on the long wooden swing benches and tried to take in the dizzying array of skyscrapers and neon which made up Hong Kong Island. The crossing was quick and uneventful and then Hunter was walking and climbing towards The Peak. He stood and waited outside Saint John's Cathedral for almost an hour and was just about to call it a night and head back across the water, all the while cursing Frank Cassatto and Michael Healy and anyone else he could think of, when the overweight American finally showed up.

'What's the big story the Standard's chasing down?' Cassatto began without any apology, gesturing for Hunter to follow him. He'd thrown on a badly creased jacket and poured himself into an odd pair of trousers. 'They've got guys out here. None of them handle it? Pete Austin, Peter Austin, used to drink in Mes Amis before they shut it down, he's their guy in the Far East isn't he? I checked. Why can't he take it?'

'I really have no idea.'

'But you'd know him, right? Pete,' Cassatto continued breathlessly as they started to climb their way up Albert Road, 'from The Standard?'

'Can't say I do,' Hunter replied, 'How long's he been out here?'

'Oh, years.'

'Then he probably left the UK before I even got the job.'

'Yeah, probably. Why they got to send a kid though? What's the story? Jesus, couldn't they at least have sent someone old enough to buy a round of drinks? Have you got an angle on the protests?'

Hunter was reeling under Cassatto's relentless questioning, the American not pausing long enough to allow him to answer.

'It's an old story,' he put in quickly. 'They wanted a different perspective.'

'Well come on kid, you going to keep me hanging, standing there yanking my chain all day? What's the deal? You said you were looking for somebody.'

'Ewen Connolly.'

Cassatto never broke his stride. 'Nope, sorry.'

'Or Henderson, or Hoffstetter?'

'Sorry, kid,' Cassatto said again, sounding as though he genuinely meant it. Unless it was the prospect of a drink slipping from his fingers which was upsetting the American. Hunter tried to remember his meeting with Healy. He had never said that Cassatto had provided the name Connolly, just that he might know where to find him. It was conceivable that he knew him by a completely different name altogether. Then there was that bloody number. If he failed to get anywhere with Cassatto, where would he try next? One last roll of the dice.

'Does Landslide mean anything to you?'

The older man stopped to catch his breath and consider the answer.

'Landslide? Nope, can't say it does.'

But it was too hasty, too quick a denial.

'You're quite sure?'

'Yeah I'm sure, you heard me.' Cassatto was moving again, angrily talking over his shoulder. '*Landslide*. I mean it ain't much to go on.'

'No. I suppose it isn't. My information must have been wrong then.'

Cassatto nodded. 'I guess so, kid.'

'It's just I'd been told you were making your own enquiries about Landslide, recently, in London.'

Cassatto ignored him. 'And that's all you got? One word?'

'And a number, yes.'

'What number?' he stopped again, allowing Hunter to catch up. 'You never mentioned a number.'

'24172738'

'Well Christ that could be anything from your boyfriend's telephone number to last night's winning lottery ticket.'

'I know.'

The number had been troubling Hunter ever since he'd first heard it. His mind was a whirl with the possibilities, all of them mathematical and most of them highly improbable.

'Who'd you say you work for, kid?'

'London.'

'Yeah right, London. Okay, here's what's gonna happen.

We're gonna go in here and have a couple of drinks or three until I can remember whatever it was I forgot about Landslide. But before we do, a couple of points of order. First off, they don't take cash here, in fact they don't even let guests *buy* drinks, so ain't you the lucky one? Second, turn your cell off. It's not open to discussion, kid. You want in? You want to talk to me about Landslide or anything else for that matter, then no cellphone. Remember, they ain't my rules, they're the house rules.'

Somewhat reluctantly Hunter found his mobile and switched it to silent.

'Switch it off,' Cassatto repeated uncompromisingly.

Hunter switched it off.

The Foreign Correspondents' Club with its alternating bands of red low-rise and white stucco bricks was quintessentially neoclassical and colonial. With the letters FCC in white prominently above the door, Hunter thought the old dairy farm depot looked like a forgetful cinema which had mislaid its upper storey. 'Right, Simon Frost, follow me.'

Watching Frank Cassatto enter the Foreign Correspondents Club Hunter suddenly saw a man totally at ease with his surroundings. Immediately he crossed the threshold and was greeted by an affable young man who needlessly directed him towards the bar, the American's prickly demeanour began to waver and wane. With each step he took into the club Hunter observed a softening in him, in his body language, the rough edges drifting away as he shed his thick outer carapace. And when he eased through the double doors and into the main bar, Hunter even thought he saw him smile. Patrons turned to greet him, enquire as to his wellbeing. Hunter began to suspect that Frank Cassatto felt more at home here than in his cramped apartment in Mong Kok. Once at the front of the queue the American turned to face him.

'Whatcha drinking, kid?'

'Whisky. No ice. Large.'

Cassatto raised an eyebrow and ordered himself a vodka and tonic. The drinks appeared quickly. A single highland malt for Hunter who instinctively reached for his wallet.

'Remember, kid. You're my guest, so put that away.'

Hunter had never been in a place quite like this. The barman smiled politely as he replaced his wallet, having seen this performance many times before and turned to the American.

'It's Mr Cassatto, isn't it?'

Frank nodded.

'Good to see you again, sir. One whisky and one vodka and tonic,' the barman continued, scribbling in his ledger.

'You wanna put a slice a lime in there?' Cassatto barked over the bar.

The barman smiled dutifully and quickly returned with some freshly cut lime. 'And perhaps we might discuss the matter of your tab before the evening is out,' he added before nodding politely and moving off and around the bar to another patron.

'Some place,' Hunter said.

'I like it, yeah,' Cassatto said staring into his drink. 'Let's find somewhere a little quieter we can talk.

'Listen Kid, are you sure about this? I mean, you're young, you get the chance to come out here, nice big cheque book, blow the lid on a juicy story like Landslide, okay, I get it. Good for you. You go home the big scoop, maybe get moved up a rung or two.'

'You do know something then?'

'Sure, I know something. It just may not turn out to be the

something you're after. So, I'm going to ask you again, are you quite sure you want to get into this?'

'Get into what? I don't follow you.'

'Ever occur to you that people could, you know, people might get hurt... by this story of yours? That ever occur to you?'

It had never occurred to Hunter that as a consequence of his crazy trip to Hong Kong any harm might befall someone. He didn't know anything about Landslide, just what Michael Healy had told him, that no one had wanted to talk much about it. But that had been twenty years ago. Surely there wouldn't be any recriminations now, not after all that time? This was just... Well what was it? Why was he here, halfway around the world with little or no clue about an operation the service had launched all those years ago and had suddenly only now rediscovered an interest in?

'I was told you weren't really that bothered who you sold your story to – just as long as you got a piece of the action. Was I wrong?'

Now Cassatto seemed to remember who he was. 'Sure, sure, that's me.'

'Landslide. What happened?'

Cassatto threw back his vodka tonic and signalled to the barman he'd like another. 'Don't fuck about with the next one, drown the bitch, and get the kid another whisky, straight up.'

'Yes, sir.'

Hunter waited patiently whilst their drinks were poured and recorded. They arrived on fresh, white coasters and the American quickly took a long, hard draw on his. 'Okay. You seem to know what you want, but I don't have that.'

'What do you mean?'

'I can't give you Landslide.'

After everything. After the chase across Hong Kong and Kowloon only to be told his one and only lead had nothing. Well, Healy had said the Yank was an unreliable shit.

'I can't, it's complicated. But I can put you in touch with a man who can.'

'Explain.'

'I met him in here, the man who I think can help you. He stood right where you're standing now. He called himself Alex Cameron then. I figured he was just like everyone else in here. He had that look about him. See the people in this joint, look at them, they're here for the story, do you know what I mean?'

Hunter understood that he should have but didn't, so decided to allow Cassatto to talk, which he did freely.

'There's two types of guy who drink in here. Look around you. This guy here,' Cassatto nodded across the bar at a lonely looking individual nursing a glass of red wine. 'Ten'll get you twenty that guy's got a story burning away inside of him, he's just looking for the right guy to share it with. He's been in prison, he's broken out of prison, I don't know, maybe he owns the fuckin' prison. This guy,' Cassatto gestured to a man sitting quietly in a corner. 'Jesus, will you look at this guy. He murdered his wife, chopped her into tiny little pieces and fed her to the cat just so he could run off with the help, but then he murders her as well, buried her out on Turtle Cove Beach. Fuck I don't know, but every other guy in here has a tale to tell. They want to be recorded for posterity, made into a film or something so their big trip out here isn't just a complete waste of everyone's time. See someday that guy and that guy and that guy there, they're all gonna go home, or at least somewhere deep down they'd like to think of as home, and you know what you can't do when you go home? You can't appear to have spent the last however many years sitting out here on your big fat fanny doing fuck nothing, see? And then there's me, and him and him,' he sticks out a finger jabbing it around the bar, 'the guys who come in here looking for that story, do you see? That's where we come in, kid.'

'What happened? Who did you meet?'

'Guy about my age, Brit, like you. He's in here all washed up and my God was he drunk. First off he starts bawling on about what he's up to in Hong Kong. Yawn, yawn. Usual shady bullshit I've heard a million times before. Bunch of half-truths and tall stories designed to impress. Get rich quick schemes mostly, that kind of thing. Hong Kong runs on that sort of crap. If you're a white face with a clean shirt on, you can talk your way into pretty much anything here. So, he's telling me some sob story about moving money out of Macao. It's okay, but I've heard it a hundred times. I can't use it, you see, so I dig a little deeper. What's he doing in here in the first place? Why's he so drunk? There's always a reason and quite often I can get a story out of it, you know, the real angle. So, I start probing a bit. What did he do before he came out to Honkers, what was his line of business, how did he get here? Well that's when he really starts to clam up on me. The bourbon's flowing by now you know, I got us a bottle on the bar, but suddenly he's not talking, just watching his drink go down.'

'*And*,' Hunter pressed.

'And then he says one word. Literally, one word. *Landslide*. And that was that, like I'm supposed to know what the fuck he's talking about. Don't get me wrong I had an idea or two of my own by then, and once we went our separate ways I did do a little digging, but nothing. Just one brick wall after another. It was like this guy didn't exist.'

'And then the next time you were in London, you thought you'd dig a little deeper?'

'Oh yeah, you heard about that. So? I had a hunch. There was just something about the guy. I wanted to push it by some old pals on the South Bank.'

'Spooks?'

'You tell me, Simon Frost.'

'Anything come of it?'

'You've got to be kidding. They had even less to say than he did. Didn't exactly buy me a ticket straight home, but they sure as hell would have helped me find a cab to the airport.'

'The man you met, in the bar, here, what happened to him?'

Cassatto ordered two more drinks.

'By the time I got back he'd moved on. I tried a little to find him, but not too hard. I got the distinct impression that, if he didn't want to be found, that was him, he'd just disappear.'

'Could he still be on Hong Kong?'

'Not a chance.'

'So I'm screwed then.'

'Not necessarily. Before we got to his dim and distant past and he lost the ability to speak, you remember I said he told me about some of the scams he used to run. All based here and, I'm guessing, all closed down a long time ago. All but one. He said he was involved with a retired Chinese General. God knows how he'd run into him, in here probably. I remember because it was one of the few things he told me I could actually have made some copy out of. He never said as much, but he implied they were running guns taken from army stores, sent on to a semi-legit company in China and then out of the country to, well your guess is as good as mine, but I'd imagine somewhere in Africa. There's generally a war going on out there and people are always looking for cheap weapons and don't care too much where they come from.'

'Where's the General now?'

Cassatto laughed quietly and Hunter realised how preposterous tracking down and questioning a Chinese General in Hong Kong would be.

'I'm sorry, kid. There's not a chance.'

Another dead end. Cassatto flicked his hand at the barman and a fresh vodka sat up next to Hunter's whisky.

'But the guy you're after, he'll take a dram of the golden stuff.'

'What do you mean?'

'He's Scottish.'

'You're sure?'

'Sure, I'm sure. I know what you're thinking. Dumb bloody Yank, thinks we're all related to the Queen and live in a palace. But I do know the difference between Connery and Moore, okay?'

'Okay.'

'You ever been to Scotland, kid? It's a nice spot,' Cassatto said nodding to himself.

'I believe the Scottish prefer to think of it as more of a country than a spot.'

'Oh yeah? Well, whatever. Now, time to pay the piper, kid.' Cassatto got the attention of one of the bar staff. 'I'd like to settle my tab with you, in full please. This young gentleman will be paying. By the way, kid, you never did tell me which desk you're flying at The Standard?'

'No, I didn't, did I.'

Cassatto watched with barely concealed glee as Hunter counted out eight hundred in American dollars.

'The General, he have a name?'

'Song Shicheng.'

'Thank you, Mr Cassatto,' Hunter said, laying the money down on the bar.

'You got it.'

It wasn't quite what Hunter had been hoping for, but it was a start and along with the name Cameron he felt that he was making slow but steady progress towards understanding Landslide. He also knew the man he was looking for was Scottish and as shady as they came. Hunter thanked Cassatto for his time, clinked his glass and headed for the door, eager to sober up and get on. He'd walk back down to Central, hope the fresh night air might clear his head and that he hadn't missed the last ferry to Kowloon.

As he weaved down Wyndham Street, surrounded by towering skyscrapers, home to many of the world's most powerful banks, the Hong Kong and Shanghai Banking Corporation; stripped back functionality, the Hang Seng Bank; separate and austere and, presiding over it all the Bank of China; the knife in the heart of Hong Kong, something in Hunter's mind clicked. All the training he'd received from Williams was fighting to overcome the whisky he'd drunk. Someone was following him. Very slowly he opened his stride and started to search for an escape route. The sound of footsteps behind him quickened to match his own. Hunter prepared himself. He could feel his heartrate rising, the adrenalin pumping through his veins, the butterflies building in his stomach, just the way Williams had said they would. The secret now would be to channel these emotions in readiness for the attack the way he'd been taught. He crossed the narrow road and tried to think sober thoughts, all the while wondering who might be following him and when they might make their move. Hunter concentrated all his senses on the footsteps behind him. They crossed the road too. He was straining to hear, for the slightest clue as to the identity of his pursuer. Their step was confident and masculine he decided. Leather soled shoes and not trainers, so possibly not a young man. As Wyndham Street dipped down towards Central, the ferry terminal and Hunter hoped, safety, the footsteps behind him quickened again. From between sky-scrappers a glimpse of jewellery shops and ferries criss-crossing the harbour, lit up like children's toys. If he could just make it a little further, down towards the still bustling Queen's Road he might be able to shake the man off. Another glimpse of the harbour and then the feet behind him were running. Hunter braced himself, hoping to use his attacker's strengths against him. He felt in his jeans' pockets for anything he could use as a weapon. His hand found the metal key fob from the hotel. He slipped it from his pocket, holding it firmly in his right hand, the metal edge exposed between fingers. It could be enough. It could be enough to catch the man unawares, stun him enough for Hunter to run the remainder of the way to the Queen's Road and safety. The running footsteps were almost upon him now. Hunter shifted his weight onto his front foot and stopped abruptly, preparing for the blow that would follow. He looked up the street back the way he had come just in time to see a tiny Chinese businessman carrying a leather briefcase streak past him.

Hunter breathed easy. More than likely the man was doing

exactly what he was doing, trying to catch the last boat home. He let his shoulders slump forward and replaced the key fob in his pocket. He allowed the adrenaline to peak and subside. His breathing began slowly to return to normal and he let himself laugh with the relief. He was thousands of miles from home and paranoid as hell, but in that brief moment, as he watched the running man disappear behind a building shrouded in bamboo poles and netting, and for the first time in a long while, Scott Hunter felt strangely content. Sure, he hadn't made a huge amount of progress, but he was feeling just a little closer to Landslide and Ewen Connolly. And that was when he felt the dull tip of a knife in his back.

'Thanks for the drink, kid, but now I want my story. Who the fuck are you and who are you working for, really?'

Hunter recognised Cassatto's voice immediately. The Yank was drunk, he'd been drunk at the club, but the difference now was the knife he held in the small of Hunter's back. Hunter let his knees sag forward, taking the sting out of the weapon's tip whilst, in the same movement, spinning to his right. His arm swung round in a tight blocking curve and he easily deflected Cassatto's hand. It was a small serrated fruit knife which their waiter had used to cut the American's lime. Nice touch Frank, Hunter thought. With his open left hand he delivered a healthy slap across Cassatto's right ear. Not hard enough to leave a mark, just firm enough to disorientate the man. Then Hunter's hands encircled Cassatto's wrist. The knife flew clear and, using the larger man's weight, Hunter quickly had him on his back. Then he stood above him as Williams had taught, controlling the American's body with the smallest twist of his wrist, each tweak and turn eliciting a fresh Brooklyn yelp of pain. Hunter flicked

Cassatto over onto his front and lent a knee heavily on the man's outstretched triceps, effectively pinning him to the ground.

'Now you're going to tell me everything *you* know or I'm going to break your wrist and pop your elbow right out of its fucking socket. How about we start with the name and location of that nasty old import-export company?'

7

Shekou Industrial Zone, Shenzhen, Guangdong Province, China

Still travelling under the name Frost, Hunter took a short one-hour flight north and into China. The address Frank Cassatto had given him turned out to be bogus but the name of the company was not and so, after several excruciating and lengthy conversations with any number of increasingly disgruntled Chinese Government officials at the local Port Authority in Guangzhou, Hunter had traced the company to the Shekou district of Shenzhen. Following a miserable two-and-a-half-hour bus journey south, he stood on a dusty street corner in an unlovely district of the city and wondered just how much business the company opposite him really did. The words *Heavy Truck Import and Export Co.* dominated the front of the block in large, blunt red letters, once perhaps imposing and impressive but now tired and coated in the same mix of cement dust which covered everything and required the local population to wear facemasks The imposing double-fronted doors were firmly secured and appeared to have been so for some time, a thick chain padlocked uncompromisingly through their handles. Were it not for the sounds of machinery coming from within, Hunter could easily have supposed the place had long been abandoned, left to fall apart from neglect or be subsumed by the omnipresent cement like some improbable Egyptian temple. Hunter needed another way in. He walked around the front of the building and then turned and continued down a gravel path and along its side. At the far end he came upon a tall security fence topped off with razor wire and watched as a forklift turned and disappeared, its loading prongs empty, its capped driver shouting to another unseen man before drawing heavily on his cigarette.

Hunter spotted his way in. An entry gate with a camera trained on it and an intercom. But now that he was here he had no idea what he was going to say. He was looking for someone. So what? If he was going to be successful, he would need some form of leverage or the people who owned *Heavy Truck Import and Export* would never allow him admittance.

'I'd like to speak to someone, urgently.'

'Who are you?'

'I don't think you understand,' Hunter said with more than a hint of exasperation, 'I need to speak with your boss and I need to speak to him now. Tony Ding sent me,' he continued remembering the name of the helpful bellhop at his hotel in Kowloon. 'I need to speak to your boss about an order that's gone missing. Mr Ding is not happy.'

The intercom crackled and buzzed and then the electronic click of an interested and, Hunter hoped, concerned party.

The gate swung open and he walked into the loading bay area at the rear. The first thing which caught his eye as he rounded the corner following the path the forklift had taken, were a pair of Chinese guards, each carrying an AK47 slung over his shoulder. The one nudged the other and the man nearest Hunter raised his rifle and began shouting angrily at him. Hunter did the only thing he could under the circumstances and apologetically raised his hands. The man pointing the AK drew nearer and pushed the tip of the weapon into Hunter's stomach. Hunter could smell his breath, rich with ginger and fish sauce, rotten with cigarette smoke. He was barking at him in Mandarin whilst simultaneously gesturing with the machine gun. Hunter considered snatching the AK from him and turning it on them as Williams had demonstrated, but then the guard's partner would just as likely gun him down first.

'Tony Ding,' said Hunter repeating the man's name over the shouting until finally the intonation seemed to get through. The guard turned to his friend and conferred noisily before sweeping the gun behind Hunter and ushering him towards the huge loading bay doors at the rear of the building, whilst his friend barked Mandarin over his walkie-talkie.

As' Hunter made his way deeper into the warehouse he noticed palletized goods piled high awaiting forward delivery. Packing crates and cases with American, Asian, African and European stamps and at the far end of the warehouse, casting a huge shadow over a pile of water fountain bottles and everything else in its proximity, a vast metal shipping container with what Hunter could only suppose was a giant Chinese symbol spray painted on its side and presumably destined for the back of a cargo ship and the high seas. The forklift returned, its operator puffing immutable clouds of thick grey smoke. Then, as Hunter approached the front of the building a sharply dressed Chinese man in his forties appeared to greet him.

'You must forgive my men. They are under used and lazy, and this one,' he gestured to the man who had first challenged Hunter, 'is as stupid as a dog. I only employ him because he is married to my cousin.' The man laughed at his own joke and pushed a business card at Hunter.

'Bill Guo, I'm the owner of *Heavy Truck*. And you would be?'

'Simon Frost.'

'I am happy to meet you, Mr Frost. As you can see, we do not receive many guests of any sort, and very few from?'

'London, England.'

'How may I assist you? We are a big company dealing with many thousands of orders from around the globe, so you will forgive me if I do not recognise the name... Tony Ding?'

Hunter made great play of making sure that they were alone, conspiratorially ushering Guo into a darkened corner. 'Mr Ding and I have been working with General Song Shicheng. I didn't want to have to mention his name in front of your men. The General and I are most concerned that a former employee of ours has been behaving less than honourably.'

'I see,' Guo said nodding his head sagely, understanding the gravity of what Hunter was suggesting. 'That is most serious, yes I do see. And you mention General Song Shicheng. How is it that a Mr Frost from London, England knows the General?'

'I'm helping General Shicheng with a shipment. It has come to our attention that someone may have been stealing from him.'

'That would be most,' Guo, who's English was flawless, took a moment whilst he carefully considered his next word, 'unwise of them.' He smiled broadly, satisfied with the choice.

'I'm looking for a man. I believe he may have worked here. All I want is an address and then I'll go. The General and I will take care of him ourselves.'

'Please come, come into my office. If I am able to help you I shall. Please, the man's name?'

Bill Guo stood next to a desk piled high with paperwork, chits, receipts, an outmoded computer and the company's intercom.

'Connolly,' Hunter said.

'Connolly? I see,' Guo replied. 'No, I don't believe I employ anyone of that name.'

Hunter watched the man's face carefully. 'Cameron then or Hoffstetter?'

'Mr Frost, just how many men are you looking for, one, two or three?'

'Cameron. Alex Cameron.'

Guo looked down at the desk in front of him.

'I'm sorry, Mr Frost,' he replied surveying the confusion and idly repositioning a stapler, 'but I don't know anyone by the name Cameron, or Connolly or Hoffstetter for that matter. All the men we employ here are Chinese and I know every one of them personally.'

That brief hesitation though, particularly from a man Hunter had already identified as one who didn't suffer fools and never wavered.

'But you do recognise the name,' he probed.

'No, I don't believe so,' Guo continued rearranging some

papers. 'Perhaps there is some other way I may be able to assist you?'

Hunter was far from convinced that Bill Guo was being straight with him, but he decided to press on with the only other piece of information he possessed.

'Does the number 24172738 mean anything to you?'

Bill Guo thought for a moment before shaking his head. 'I can't say that it does. Is it a telephone number? Perhaps if you were able to tell me what it was in connection with? Could it be for an order form?' This hadn't occurred to Hunter. Another avenue to explore. The chances of ever finding Connolly or Cameron seemed to be dwindling with every enquiry.

'I suppose it could be an order number,' he heard himself say a little weakly.

'Yet you are looking for a man?'

'Yes.'

'We trade in a very many different commodities Mr Frost but I am glad to say that people are not one of them,' Guo said permitting himself another smile.

'Would you mind if I looked through your records?' Hunter asked.

'As I said. I don't recognise the names or the number and I cannot see how allowing you to look through my records would be of any benefit to either of us. I'm sorry Mr Frost and please don't think me discourteous, but rarely do I let anyone inspect my papers, Government officials, even trusted members of the family, and certainly not men I have just met and who arrive unannounced. You must forgive me, I am terribly busy. It has been a great pleasure to meet you, now one of my men will show you out.'

Hunter smelt the forklift driver before he felt his hand on his shoulder. He thanked Bill Guo for his time and after having been escorted from the complex with a degree more graciousness than he had anticipated, found a hotel for the night, determined to return and examine the contents of the businessman's office at his own leisure. Bill Guo had been hiding something, that was clear. Hunter understood a company's reluctance to share its paperwork, particularly a company like the *Heavy Truck Import and Export Co* which was obviously sailing tight and close to the wind, but he was convinced there was something there to connect Guo with Ewen Connolly. Once everything was quiet he popped some nicotine gum, slipped on a pair of dark jeans, a black T-shirt and hoodie and returned to the warehouse.

Hunter retraced his steps along the side of the building, stopping just short of the entry gate which would take him into the main compound. He waited for the leaden plod of the night watchman. As the man approached Hunter placed his hand high on the wall and pretended to urinate. As the guard's figure filled the gate, Hunter groaned loudly, zipped up his fly and, continuing his act, withdrew a battered packet of cigarettes from the back pocket of his jeans. Then he was staggering towards the fence, a cheery gweilo who'd had too much to drink and lost his way and his matches. As the watchman shouted and swore at him Hunter observed the dull glint of gun metal slung over his shoulder.

'Got a light?'

The guard stared back blankly at him through the fence, his arm above his head, playing the beam of a flashlight over Hunter's face, ordering him to leave. Hunter continued with his routine. As he reached the gate, his arm outstretched, his hand offering up the unlit cigarette, he stumbled and fell. The guard continued to berate him, but Hunter lay where he had fallen, on his side with his back to the fence, the cigarette lying next to him where it had landed. He did not stir. The guard considered leaving this unwanted drunken visitor, but gradually his voice grew quieter, losing its aggressive edge until, after Hunter had remained motionless for two minutes or more, the guard's tone became positively conciliatory. Hunter couldn't understand *what* was being said, but he understood *how* it was being said.

Then, as he lay in the gravel, he heard a key turn in the gate. The guard never stopped talking, enquiring. Then the man was standing over him, Hunter saw his ragged plastic footwear, his burnt and cracked feet. As he bent to see if Hunter were dead or alive, one swollen foot almost at his armpit, Hunter sprang. He hooked his left foot behind the guard's ankle, his right leg snapping back and forward, the sole of his desert boot connecting firmly just below the guard's knee and then he was falling backwards. Hunter had to act quickly, flipping the man over whilst simultaneously placing him in a naked choke as Williams had instructed. The man's body was limp before he hit the ground. Hunter gathered up the guard's flashlight and moved to the open gate. He edged into the compound, finding a camera trained on the rear entry point. The guard would no doubt identify him later, but for now there was no need for his image to be recorded unnecessarily. He took the gum from his mouth and pressed it over the camera's lens. Next the security door. A numeric keypad barred his entry. When he had been there in the afternoon the huge loading bay doors had been open and there had been no need for him to use the security door. But at night Hunter imagined the entire complex would be locked up with guards only required to patrol the perimeter. He shone the torch at the keypad. There were two small bulbs. The red one flashing stubbornly whilst the green remained inactive and unaccommodating. Beneath them twelve square buttons, old and worn like the rest of the building. All the numbers running through from 1 to 0 and a star and a hash. Providing the numbers alone were used that would still mean a possible 10,000 combinations and he'd just knocked out the only person around who might have known the correct one. Hunter had read a paper at university about data genetics and so he could hope to get those odds down considerably. He knew he was looking for a 4 digit code and that some combinations of numbers were statistically more likely than others. He started with the most common; 1-2-3-4. Nothing. Then he tried 1-7-9-3 and 0-0-0-0 all possible combinations used by lazy employees or simply left as the factory default. A few more efforts. He even tried a consolidation of the numbers Healy had shared with him, but none of them lit the tiny green light or produced the satisfying click he was hoping for. Hunter began to think there was a danger the keypad would lock him out permanently if he continued to guess incorrectly and he couldn't afford for that to happen. There was also the very real chance that a remote alarm might be triggered, if it hadn't been already. He went back to the guard, but the man was still out cold. Hunter swore quietly to himself. If he hadn't knocked the guard out he could easily have extracted the necessary information using one of the many techniques Williams had taught him, but the Chinese man splayed out awkwardly on the ground at his feet was going to be of no use to him what-so-ever.

The Chinese man. Hunter paused, thinking. Perhaps he'd been too hasty, perhaps he'd been approaching the problem from completely the wrong angle, from too Western a perspective. Assuming the keypad had been reprogrammed since leaving the factory it would have been done by someone Chinese and not an English maths graduate from Cambridge. Hunter knew that some cultures considered particular numbers both lucky and unlucky. The idea had often struck him as irrational and absurd. How many of the architects in America, for instance, who refused to acknowledge the thirteenth floor were regular church goers or could even name the other twelve apostles? The Japanese he knew held the number nine in particularly low regard because it sounded so similar to the word for pain or suffering, similarly the Cantonese for four sounded much like the word for death, so he could discount that too. Hunter stopped to think. What were they trying to achieve at Bill Guo's *Heavy Truck Import and Export Co?* On the surface of it they were in the business of shipping questionable merchandise around the world, but Hunter understood that that was only the means to an altogether more rapacious end, the making of money. He also knew that in China the number eight was inextricably linked with the attainment of wealth and prosperity. Hunter rushed back to the secure door, keyed in 8-8-8-8 and was pleased to see the little red light blink out and the green one flicker obligingly on. There was a gratifying click as the lock snapped open and he was in.

He retraced his steps from that morning. The space was at rest, quiet and dark now, familiar shapes given fresh resonance by their shifting shadows. A pair of lumbering forklifts, abandoned and inert. Hunter flicked on the flashlight he'd lifted from the guard and played its beam up and down the rows of crates and packing cases. He was sure there had to be a link to Landslide somewhere within these walls and that Bill Guo had been hiding something from him in his office. That was where he would start. Cautiously he nudged the door open, flicked on the lights and went straight to the desk. Guo had moved a pile of documents when Hunter had brought up Cameron's name and that number. He pulled back the owner's swivel chair and sat down. It was too much to hope that Guo had left the papers where they were. That afternoon the desk had been chaotic, strewn with packing orders, receipts, travel permits and carnets. Since Hunter's unexpected visit it had been reorganised and tidied. Where there had been contracts and affidavits, now sat a clean and lonely ashtray, a much-used telephone, a stapler and a jade handled letter opener. Hunter opened the desk's drawers. Nothing of any interest save perhaps for a bottle of Vietnam's finest Scotch which briefly caught his eye.

Lined up against the backwall were three imposing filing cabinets. Hunter quickly discounted the righthand cabinet nearest Guo's desk, it opened easily and was full of workaday stationery. The other two cabinets were locked and consequently of more interest. Hunter found a paperclip and set to work on the first of the two. After a brief struggle he had the three drawers open. The top one was crammed with what appeared to be government registration forms and was almost exclusively in Chinese. Hunter didn't have time to waste and moved down to the second, documents for the fleet of trucks Guo owned. 24172738 could be a specific vehicle he supposed, but then, on closer inspection, each vehicle number began and ended with a Chinese character, so Hunter moved on to the bottom drawer. Orders and receipts. These carried an 8 digit number stamped in red on the top right corner of each page. Hunter withdrew the first file and flicked through it. They were arranged sequentially and so he moved to the last sheet in the file, then he removed several more until he was confident he'd located the one containing order number 24172738. He spread the thin copy pages out over Guo's desk looking for the receipt. Page after page covered in incomprehensible Chinese text. For the life of him Hunter couldn't imagine why he'd been sent. Surely there was someone with a background in Mandarin or Cantonese who would have been much better suited to this assignment. He had no knowledge of Landslide either – whatever that proved to be. Deep down though Hunter knew there would be a reason he and not someone else had been selected. These people, Healy, Wiseman, Lazarus, were nothing if not meticulous. He turned over another order sheet. Occasionally he would see a name or an address. Guo was sending goods worldwide; across Europe, Northern Africa and America. Hunter looked at a batch of diabetes medicines and anabolic steroids bound for Palm Desert in California. Was this what Landslide was about? A smuggling operation? Counterfeit drugs? Was Song Shicheng moving phoney medicines out of China and across the globe? It would certainly go some way to account for the high level of security surrounding the place. But for every entry that was headed to the other side of the world another was bound much closer. There were washing machines to Shanghai, air conditioning units destined for Nanning, car parts moved to Linyi. Hunter was nearly at receipt number 24172738. He flicked back the page. The exhaust mufflers that were to be delivered to Linyi. There was an address and then, beneath the address, the name of the delivery's recipient. Cameron. He took the sheet of paper and folded it away in his pocket. Quickly he found the order he'd been looking for; a shipment of counterfeit children's toys, ripped off MP3 players and ersatz wireless headphones bound for Tucson, Arizona. He was no further on with the mysterious number, but now he had an address for the man Cassatto had suggest he contact. He would have to get himself to Linyi, wherever the hell that was. He closed the file and returned it to the cabinet's bottom drawer. It was as he was closing the drawer that he realised he was no longer alone. Bill Guo stood in the doorway.

'General Song Shicheng, you say?'

'He told me to straighten out business here, said he was losing confidence in your abilities to run the operation. But as you seem reluctant to help, I decided to help myself. General Song Shicheng is not a man to be kept waiting.'

Guo inclined his head slowly and smiled.

'I quite agree, Mr Frost. You are absolutely correct, General Shicheng is certainly not someone you kept waiting. But, well perhaps I have become, what is the word you would use, blasé, because General Shicheng does not frighten me anymore. I no longer worry about keeping the good General waiting you see,' Guo continued 'because General Song Shicheng, is dead. He died some months ago. His body was found in the back of an abandoned car at the bottom of the Dongyin Canal. He'd been beaten to death,' Guo said moving towards his desk. Hunter backed away weighing up his options.

'And as a result, I'm afraid we don't have much need for an inquisitive young Englishman who asks too many difficult questions,' Guo continued, picking up the jade handled letter opener. 'I wonder how many people even know you are here, Mr Frost, and how many of those people will miss you when you are suddenly no longer here?'

Hunter was forced to wonder the same.

'I see,' Guo continued yawning complacently. Hunter was going to have to act quickly if Guo wasn't about to make him disappear like one of his packing cases. He desperately tried to remember his training, to recall each and every pithy word Williams had uttered whilst simultaneously assessing his situation. Should he cross that line into violence as Frank Cassatto had forced him to or see if he could in some way placate the advancing man?

Hunter extended what he hoped was a conciliatory hand.

'Let me try and explain,' he said.

But Bill Guo ignored his overtures and slashed at Hunter, catching him just below the elbow, the tip of the letter opener easily slicing through his clothing and tearing through his forearm.

Guo continued his attack as Hunter instinctively clutched at the wound. He would have to cross Williams's chalk line. As Guo raised the knife to strike again, Hunter seized his opportunity. As Guo's arm flashed through the air he moved in close, spinning his assailant round. One hand quickly extended Guo's arm whilst with the other he delivered a debilitating blow to his kidneys. Guo let out an agonised grunt as Hunter completed the move, yanking his arm hard up against his back as Williams had instructed, sending the letter opener clattering to the floor.

'Enough,' Hunter shouted.

'Who are you?'

'I'm no one Mr Guo,' Hunter said, kicking the letter opener under his desk and struggling to ignore the searing pain in his arm. 'My advice to you is just pretend you never met me,' he concluded, pushing him away.

Bill Guo made one last exhausted lunge at him, but Hunter caught him firmly with a straight jab that even Williams would have been proud of. This final blow seemed to have the desired effect. Guo's body language suddenly became that of resigned capitulation.

'What are you going to do now?'

'That shipping container,' Hunter said pointing behind him, 'you're going to get in it.'

Hunter pulled the huge metal door open and nodded into its gloomy interior, one thin shaft of light cutting down from a hole in the roof where years of seawater and rust had eventually won out.

'What? But I'll...'

'Just get in will you. I don't want to hurt you, but don't think I can't.'

Reluctantly Bill Guo traipsed into the metal box and Hunter padlocked its door.

He turned back towards Guo's office. Blood was soaking through his shirt and dripping from the ends of his fingers. He found Guo's jade knife and cut the sleeve from his top, exposing a long diagonal gash running across his forearm. Ideally the cut would require stitches, but that was out of the question. The first thing was to stop the bleeding. He wound the material from his top into a cord and wrapped it into a tourniquet just above the wound, then he took a pen from Guo's desk and, jamming it beneath the material he began to twist the cord tight until it became so constricted he worried he would lose all feeling in his hand. Then he opened the drawer in Guo's desk and took out the

Vietnamese whisky. Unscrewing the lid he downed a healthy slug for himself before pouring half the bottle over his arm. The fiery pain was excruciating, but now the wound was clean and had stopped bleeding he needed something to dress it with. Hunter flicked through the papers on Guo's desk. He'd seen a manifest of medical supplies which were to be flown out to Mwanza in Tanzania.

Hunter cautiously opened the shipping container. Bill Guo was sat in its farthest corner sulking, an unpleasant yellowing purple semi-circle developing beneath his eye.

'Are you going to kill me?' he asked not looking up. 'If you kill me my family will come after you Mr Frost. All of them.'

'I need to know where this shipment is?' Hunter said shoving the paperwork under Guo's nose.

'I hurt you then. Good.'

Guo looked away from the brittle piece of paper Hunter was holding.

'What day is it today, please remind me?' Hunter asked.

Guo looked up at him from his position on the floor but said nothing.

'Okay,' Hunter continued, 'I'll help you out. It's just turned Saturday. Once I've locked you in here and moved you somewhere quiet where they'll never find you, even in ideal conditions, you've got three days to survive without water tops. But my guess is you'll probably freeze to death before you die of dehydration. Either way, not much fun.'

Hunter waved the paperwork in front of Guo again and this time when he looked up Hunter was sure he would tell him where the medical supplies were.

He locked up the container for a second time and followed

Guo's directions to the far corner of the warehouse. After a cursory search he found a palette wrapped in clear plastic with a matching reference number and destined for East Africa. His arm hurt him terribly as he tore off the plastic and smashed open the wooden crate. More boxes, but eventually he found what he'd been looking for. Surgical pads bound for the operating theatre, but as long as they helped to protect the wound, Hunter didn't care. He grabbed a handful of the sterile packets and back in Guo's office secured them with packing tape. Hearing his return Guo started beating on the container's door and so Hunter opened it again and threw in as many bottles of water as his injured arm would allow. Then he said his goodbyes, locked up and left.

8

When Scott's mother, riddled with the guilt of a survivor, had taken her own life, David Hunter had known, he'd known the moment he'd found her, why she had felt so unable to carry on. He'd understood better than she'd ever credited him how much the guilt of her father's actions in Hitler's death camps had eroded her spirit and consumed her soul. After all, she hadn't been the first. But then, David had a young son to look after and protect. People were talking, neighbours had been witness to some of their all too public arguments. A name caught erroneously on the wind.

This is all that bitch Pat King's fault! shouted at David's retreating back, as he, for the sake of their reputation, pretended to go to a job he no longer held. It wasn't taking people long to put two and two together and come up with five. There had been another woman, that had been the obvious yet wholly incorrect assumption. Then news started to seep out that, not only was David Hunter having an affair, he had lost his mysterious job too and that was why his poor lovely wife had hanged herself. And so

David had let them believe what they seemed so desperate to believe, it was just one more lie in a lifetime's worth. Better to let his son think that too, rather than the truth. He packed up any lingering trace of her father the Nazi war criminal, sealed them in a cardboard box and hid them in the attic together with all his other secrets, unable to completely sever the link with his beloved wife. He took the clock, smashed as she had fallen to her death and wrapped that up too. Then he'd tried to get on with his new life as a single father with no job. The service had come good in the end. They'd settled on a healthy pension, and paid off his mortgage, but after a while David had decided, with the neighbours still rebuffing him and the cost of living in London only rising, to sell up, downsize and take his son out to the country and what he hoped would be a fresh beginning for them both.

Initially the move had proven successful. Scott had enjoyed the open spaces, the tractors and harvesters, the horses in their paddocks down the lane. But then, unable to find new friends he had taken to long, lonely walks through the countryside. The brooding teenager had heard the whispers behind his back, just as his father had.

His mum killed herself because the old man was doing it with someone else.

He eventually summoned up the courage to confront his father, and when David did nothing to deny the stories, Scott started on his terrible descent into a full nervous breakdown. The lie already told, his father decided to let the truth simmer dangerously in their attic, the answers to all of Scott's questions lying in a dusty box. David, reasoning enough damage had been done and not wishing to further upset his emotionally fragile son would let the truth remain where it was, untouched.

Slowly, and no thanks to the medication Scott had initially been prescribed, they had come to an uneasy truce. Scott became obsessed with codes and code breaking and David was pleased to see, developed a rare gift for mathematics. Their relationship bumped along, Scott never feeling completely able to trust the man he believed responsible for his mother's death. University coming as a welcome reprieve for both father and son.

Linyi, Shandong Province, China

The following day and Hunter found himself on a flight from Shenzhen in the south to Linyi, a little north of Shanghai. He was astonished by the drop in temperature, a cold blast of wind whipping through the plane the instant the door had been opened. He took a bus into the city, arriving under a thick blanket of smog which he felt would never lift, in much the same way he felt he would never find Ewen Connolly. As he sat at the rear of the K201 and tried to breath over the overwhelming smell of cordite and ozone he wondered if he would ever understand those eight enigmatic figures, ever get to the bottom of Landslide. He wondered how much more time he was destined to spend in the pursuit of what seemed like lost causes.

They passed over another frozen river, the sky a solid dirty white, local people struggling along the pavement hidden behind facemasks as silent electric mopeds gracefully avoided one another in a ballet of traffic. Even the wintry trees with their white painted socks were struggling it seemed.

It didn't take long for Hunter to discover the whereabouts of *Linyi Global Auto Parts.* A whole quarter of the city was devoted to the production of car parts and little else, with block after block of cramped aluminium cabins cranking out everything from manifolds to spark plugs, their produce often spilling out onto the busy streets. Hunter still had the sheet he'd taken from Guo's in Shenzhen. He showed it to the owner of the first parts shop he came to, pointing at the address. A disinterested shake of the head the man's only response. The next shop was only steps away. Perhaps he would fare better there? He found the owner, a toothless chain-smoking mechanic who took the sheet from Hunter, pulled a collection of discouraging faces and then withdrew to consult with a younger man who was noisily working over a lathe. After a minute's shouting and considered debate both men confronted him. The younger of the pair jabbed his finger enthusiastically at the address and pointed up the street and away from the direction Hunter had come, then raised the five fingers of his left hand. Five blocks? Five minutes? Five miles? Hunter didn't know but now at least he knew in which direction he must head.

He followed the younger man's advice. It was lunchtime and he had to negotiate squatting shop owners preparing to cook or eat by the side of the road. Hopefully he looked at the fifth shop along, but the name bore no relation and so he pressed on. Then, after about five minutes he found it. In no way significantly different from any of the other car part shops along the street, with wound up shutters, boxes of tools, lathes and jack stands, cordless drills and torque wrenches. At the rear of the shop a tiny office space where a young Chinese girl was studiously inputting data into an outmoded computer, its keyboard protected from the endemic grime by a flexible rubber cover. Hunter was briefly intrigued by the machine but then, remembering the purpose of his visit, withdrew the oil stained sheet from his rear pocket.

'Is this Global Auto Parts?' he asked, pointing at the name and address on the order form. The girl nodded enthusiastically, perhaps thinking there was business in the offing. She continued to nod as she pointed to a long banner running at head height on the opposite wall with the name of the shop and under it the slogan *Great Quality @ Affordable Prices*. Hunter's fingers traced down the page to below the address and the name.

'Could I speak to Mr Cameron, I think he might be the owner?'

The girl's eyes widened and she looked between the order form and Hunter several times before replying in slow, halting English, 'He is not here.'

'He does work here then?'

'No,' she thought for a second, checking the words in her head, 'No, he does not work here. He is not here.'

'When will he be back?'

'He does not work here,' she said again, shaking her head.

'I understand. Do you know him?'

'No, I do not know him.' She seemed to be growing in confidence. 'I have never met,' she pointed at the name on the form, 'Alex Cameron,' she said stumbling slightly over the pronunciation.

'But he is down as the delivery contact for this shop.'

The girl stared back blankly.

'He worked here, but not now. I work here now, my name is Lilly. I am new. He does not work here.'

Hunter thanked Lilly and retrieved the order form, but he

wasn't convinced. Perhaps the girl was telling the truth and there was simply a misunderstanding caused by the language, but he hadn't come this far to give up quite so easily. As he left the shop he heard Lilly lift the receiver and commence a rapid conversation. Hunter was prepared to bet the person on the other end of the line was Alex Cameron. He crossed the road, found a wall to prop up which provided him with some shade and waited. Shortly after Lilly appeared at the front of the shop and hurried off and away up the road. Hunter fell in step behind her on the opposite side of the street.

Across a busy junction she disappeared from sight and Hunter momentarily worried he'd lost her. He ran the lights and caught her back as she turned into a collection of rickety single storey houses. Above the alleyway the girl had taken hung a brown and white sign. A Hutong. Hunter had read about them; narrow alleys and courtyards packed with houses and dating back as far as the Yuan dynasty. He knew they had been the source of much controversy, with many of the neighbourhoods demolished to make way for new roads. The fronts of the buildings each extravagantly decorated in a mixture of dark, communist red and traditional gold script. The roofs all the same distinctive dark grey tile, small yet practical in design. As he struggled to keep the girl in his sights an elderly man shot past on a motorized trike almost knocking him off his feet. Lilly emerged from behind an oddly bent and gnarled tree, its stump whitewashed to protect its tender young bark. Then he watched as she disappeared into one of the tiny houses. Hunter followed uncertain of what action he should take once he'd arrived at the house.

The door was ajar and so he quietly elbowed his way inside. The house had been appointed by a westerner, there was no question. The furniture was a curious combination of ornamental Chinese, bought he supposed for its aesthetic appeal, and purely functional European furniture which could have come from any number of catalogues or online stores. At its rear a curtain slung up separating the main room in which he stood from the kitchen.

All the signs of a very western life, and a recently abandoned one too. Next to a tyre iron and greasy rag, a cup of English breakfast tea sat steaming on the table, shelves brimming with treats sent from home to ease western taste buds in a foreign land, a week-old newspaper open at the sports pages. As Hunter took in the scene, developing a picture of the man who lived there, something else came to mind. Hunter was suddenly quite certain he was not alone. The faintest noise. A stifled cough, but not a man's deep cough. Hunter moved around the table at the centre of the room, picking up odd items as he progressed, eager to appear casual; a heavy round coin representing the universe, a square hole, depicting China at its centre, a small bell attached to glistening red silken cord, a glossy car magazine and a dirty plate. Hunter was at the curtains leading to the kitchen. His right hand swept the heavy material to one side and in the same movement he grabbed the young girl from the shop around her neck, quickly standing behind her.

'I don't like being spied on.'

She struggled, but only a little, Hunter being careful this time not to exert a full choke.

'You are not such a nice man I don't think.'

The girl's English seemed to have improved leaps and bounds since he had last spoken to her.

'Why did you lie to me?'

'He does not like strangers, Mr Cameron, that is why he stays away from the shop. He said, anyone comes asking questions I should call him, straight away.'

'I know, I saw you. What did he tell you to do next?'

The girl was suddenly sulkily silent and so Hunter tightened his grip around her neck. 'What did he tell you to do next?' he whispered coarsely in her ear.

'He say to come here, so I can tell him all about you. What you say, what you look like, everything.'

'So, where is he now?'

As Hunter exerted a little more pressure, Lilly raised her foot and brought it down sharply on his toe, shocking him into letting her go. She leapt across the living room grabbing the tyre iron and putting the low coffee table between them.

'You not nice man! He is gone. You never find him!' she shrieked, shaking the tyre iron at Hunter and looking out of the kitchen through the open door into the jumbled backstreets of the Hutong. Hunter had no choice but to agree, Alex Cameron could be anywhere by now.

'Your English isn't so lousy, is it?'

Hunter moved to cover the opening into the kitchen, preventing her escape. If she turned and tried to flee through the door behind her, by the time she'd unbolted it, he could grab her again.

'And is this how he does business with everyone who comes to buy car parts from him?'

The girl slashed at the air with the tyre iron, forcing Hunter to back off.

'You never say you wanted to buy anything earlier, just you were looking for Mr Alex.'

'Well, I'm telling you now. I want to place an order and you can tell Mr Alex it's likely to be a substantial one, but I will have to meet with him first, like it or not. Does he have a cell phone?'

The girl nodded, 'But he will only speak to me.'

'Phone him then. Tell him I want to meet him tomorrow morning, I'll be at the parts shop. Ten o'clock sound okay?'

The girl stopped brandishing the tyre iron and nodded.

'Phone him please.'

Lilly Chen stood in the middle of Cameron's tiny living room and made the call, scowling at Hunter the whole time. She broke off from a steady flow of Cantonese to ask one question.

'Mr Cameron, he wants to know, your name?'

'Simon Frost'

***

David Hunter had not been an active field agent for many years. He had instead raised, and lost, a son. But, even though the years had dimmed his sight, muffled his hearing, slowed his once sharp reflexes, he still knew when he was being watched. Immediately on his ignominious departure from the service he had been followed relentlessly, his previous employers eager to establish that he hadn't developed any noisy habits and wasn't looking for fresh and, in their eyes, less savoury employ elsewhere. David had no such intentions. He hadn't enjoyed the nature of his leaving, but he had understood it and, if he'd been asked, which of course he wasn't, wouldn't have hesitated to pledge his allegiance to flag and country all over again.

Gradually then, over time, his followers had either tired or become sufficiently convinced of his loyalties and, as David had known they would, moved to more pressing and urgent matters, so that when he returned late from the village pub there were fewer and fewer cars parked under dark trees along his lane. Cars which, on seeing him approach, often snapped on their headlights and disappeared. There had been a brief period, when his surveillance had all but stopped, and David had missed the attention. But he had a teenage boy to bring up singlehandedly and so the cars and their enigmatic occupants were quickly and gratefully forgotten. The craft, the signs, the tells, the indicators that he was under scrutiny never left him however and now he knew, after so many years of blissful ignominy, that someone was taking an interest in him once more. What David Hunter couldn't fathom, was why. There'd been the unpleasant episode with Frederick Sinclair which had ended with a long stay in hospital and the loss of his spleen, but that was ancient history, done and dusted. And in any case, he had been dragged into it by his son as something of an innocent bystander. These people who sat in their car outside his house seemed interested in him and him alone. They could, he supposed, be waiting for Scott to return, but that seemed a wasteful and illogical use of manpower and as such out of character with the service he knew, and so he was left with the inescapable conclusion that *he* was the object of their unsolicited attentions. Another aspect of their presence confused him. If they were in fact from the service, they seemed unusually inept at their job. It crossed his mind, as it often did when he watched the news or listened to modern music, that things just weren't the same, standards had slipped, nothing was quite as good as it had been in *his* day *et cetera et cetera*, but then he pulled himself up for such lazy thinking. He had caught regular looks at the passenger, not so the driver who was more expert in his work, but the pretty young girl who accompanied him wasn't quite the finished article, not yet. The driver remained the biggest mystery and so David had concocted a need to be along the lane. He'd exited his garden using the broken down back gate and, plastic bag in hand, had approached the car unseen. The man in the driver's seat was considerably older than his female companion. Father and daughter? No one was buying that. The strangest thing was that David thought he recognised the man, had seen him before and not just when he'd been staking out his house. But then, once he'd returned home, empty bag in hand, he'd reflected; didn't they all, and he reluctantly had to include himself, didn't they all have that same hunted, world weary look about them, the men who stuck it out that was. Perhaps it simply was he had identified a type. His own kind, like looking in a mirror, at a tired and greying middle aged man, carrying a few extra pounds and performing a largely thankless and utterly unrewarding and sedentary task. That was probably it, David Hunter thought. That or he was completely wrong and the access to his house was being used by some grubby old man as a lover's lane.

***

The following morning Hunter returned to the parts shop in Linyi, arriving just before ten o'clock. Lilly scowled at him as he entered. He glanced at his mobile and then at the young girl. 'It's time, where is he?'

'He's not coming. He said he wanted to ask a few questions before he sat down with Simon Frost.'

'I'll wait.'

'No,' the girl continued, 'he thinks you are from the British Government, sent here to arrest him for smuggling.'

'I'm not, although I would like to talk to him about what he's selling.'

Cautiously she walked towards Hunter and handed him a small book of matches. On a black background and slightly embossed, the fierce head of a snarling gold dragon.

'Amber's. You'll find him there.'

Hunter flipped the book over. The Golden Dragon Bar and an address.

'Be there at eight.'

***

Finding the Golden Dragon was one thing but getting in proved quite another. Either side of the narrow, lacquered doorway stood two enormous dragons, and in their shadows, two equally huge bouncers with shaven heads and ill-fitting jackets. Hunter drew himself up to his full height and took a deep breath. As he approached the two men squared up to meet him. He'd been lucky up to this point, but he could see his luck was about to run out. He was never going to tackle the doormen and come away with anything other than a significant stay in a Chinese hospital.

'I'm supposed to be meeting someone here, at eight,' he said unapologetically.

The bouncers looked at one another and then back at Hunter. Nothing was said, but one of the men folded his arms in a way that was not encouraging.

'I'm to meet Alex Cameron, here, at eight.'

Now the second man folded his arms, aping the first.

Hunter was about to concede defeat when he felt the book of matches in his jeans pocket. He examined them ruefully, another dead end. But the instant the doormen caught sight of the black and gold dragon they parted, as if Hunter had produced a magical key. Arms were outstretched in welcome and Hunter found himself being graciously ushered inside.

Dark sloping corridors, floors flickering with neon and strip lighting, the noise from the club rising and rising the deeper Hunter went. The techno bass line irresistibly rising up through his feet. Then the shocking mixture of cigarette smoke and flashing, swirling lights. Hunter was about to step onto the dance floor, already scouring the tables for western faces, when a firm hand grabbed his wounded elbow and he was being frogmarched towards an empty table.

'Let's have a little chat, Mr Frost.'

Hunter tried turning his head to catch a look at the man behind him, but every time he moved the vicelike grip on his bandaged forearm tightened until finally he gave up.

'It's been a while since I've had my arse felt by Her Majesty's Customs and Excise. What do you want?'

'Car parts,' Hunter managed over the pain and the relentless backbeat. 'I'm nothing to do with customs, I'm trying to buy car parts. I was told you could do me a deal.'

They reached a table and Hunter was unceremoniously dumped into a chair. The man who sat down next to him was about his father's age, his face burnished from the cold Chinese winds, craggy and tired, whilst at the same time curiously prepossessing. He wore jeans and a smart open necked shirt, his hair cropped short. The older man looked at Hunter properly for the first time. His brow furrowed suspiciously and Hunter thought he saw the briefest flicker of consternation but then just as quickly he was gesturing for service and the moment had passed.

'Alex Cameron,' he said without proffering a hand.

Hunter was just about to introduce himself when the owner of The Golden Dragon arrived. A busy Chinese woman in a yellow pantsuit that wouldn't have looked out of place in the 1970s and wearing thick black-framed glasses, who, after taking his jacket introduced herself as Amber. She handed Hunter an already opened bottle of Zhujiang beer and suddenly Hunter was back in Sam's claustrophobic flat in North London with Michael Healy standing over him prodding him in the face with the business end of what he now knew to be a supressed Walther PPK.

'Would you mind very much bringing me a fresh one,' he asked, 'and a bottle opener?'

She looked quizzically at Cameron who smiled and nodded approvingly.

'He doesn't trust us Amber. And he's probably right not to. Put it on my tab. So, you want to get into the import-export business do you? I can probably do you a deal on air filters, although I only have Citroen and Peugeot right now. If it's brake pads you're after they'll be a little more. I can do you for Mercedes or BMW just now or you can come back in a month or two and we can talk again. Spark plugs, anything small like that, I'd send by courier as samples so you don't pay the tax.'

'That all sounds excellent,' Hunter said.

'It would do wouldn't it, if any of it were true. I've heard some crap in my time, Mr Frost, but you're just full of it. You're not here to buy car parts. You're not even from the HMRC, are you? You're even worse than that bunch of blood sucking bastards. Oh, try not to look so surprised. We do have the internet here you know?'

Hunter's heart was racing. Cameron had already shown himself to be powerful but even if he could outrun him there were the two gorillas on the door to contend with.

'You're a bloody journalist.'

Hunter breathed a little easier.

'The lowest of the low. Nothing more than a piss-ridden bunch of masturbating chimps.'

He bowed his head in acknowledgement of his crime.

'What I can't imagine is why a journalist should want to talk to me. Nobody's paid the slightest interest in me for years,' Cameron continued, letting a touch of regret show through his bluff Scottish exterior, then, catching himself, 'and that's the way I've come to prefer it, so what the hell do you want?'

'I'm looking for someone. Ewen Connolly.'

'Really? Good Lord, well I'm sorry to have to tell you, son, but you're wasting your time.'

'How's that?'

'Ewen Connolly's dead.'

This came as less of a shock to Hunter than it might have. It had always been at the back of his mind that he'd been chasing shadows.

'When?'

'A few years ago now.'

'How?'

'Does it matter?'

'Not to me,' Hunter said shaking his head and lighting a

cigarette, 'but there are people, friends of mine, who will want to know.'

Amber returns with another bottle, unopened and hands Hunter a waiter's friend.

'Thanks, Amber,' Cameron said not bothering to make eye contact or waiting for her to leave before producing a small clear bottle with a red cap from inside his jacket pocket. He unscrewed the lid and offered the bottle to his guest.

'What is it?'

'Local brandy. Makes the beer taste a little less disgusting.'

Hunter acquiesced and Alex Cameron splashed two large measures into waiting glasses.

'Does this mean you trust me now?'

'Possibly.'

'Good, now, indulge an old fool will you? It's been a while since I've had a drinking partner.'

Hunter realised Cameron was holding up his brandy and so raised his by turn.

'I take this glass into my hand and drink to all that's here,

For we don't know where we shall be this time another year,'

Cameron fixed Hunter's eye, determined he should share the full profundity of the toast.

'We may be dead,

We may be slain,

We may be laying low,'

And then, quite without thinking Hunter found himself joining in,

'We may be in a foreign land and not know where to go.

Slange Var.'

Both men threw their drinks back, Cameron surprised and

delighted by Hunter's rendition as Hunter's insides burnt with the dark syrupy liquor.

'Now, take your beer,' Cameron prompted paternally, grinning from ear to ear. Hunter felt the spirit burn through him, gnawing at his stomach and greedily swallowed down the foul-tasting mixture of barley and chemicals.

'Cheers.'

'Where did a young Englishman learn that, if I may ask?'

'My father used to say it, every Christmas Day, without fail. He hasn't for years though, mostly drinks wine these days.'

'Does he?'

'So?'

'So what?'

'So how did he die, Ewen Connolly?'

'Contracted a fever. Local thing, highly unpleasant. Gone in a day, no longer.'

'I'll need proof.'

'For your friends?'

'Exactly.'

'At the paper? I'll see what I can do.'

Hunter took another slug of his beer.

'How well did you know him?'

'Well enough. Fellow Scot, you see. Birds of a feather and all that shite.'

'Where did you meet him?'

'I forget. In here I expect.' Cameron took another pull on his beer, 'And just what was so important that you went to all the trouble of coming out here to talk to poor old Ewen Connolly about, if I may ask?'

Hunter chugged on his beer and thought on Cameron's

request. One word. One silly word he was never going to understand the significance of and a bunch of numbers and if Cameron was telling the truth and Connolly really was dead there was no harm in telling him.

'Landslide.'

'Landslide?' the Scot repeated.

'Mean anything to you?'

'No,' Cameron said shaking his head and laughing, 'why would it? Landslide?'

'I don't know, you knew Connolly, I wondered if he ever mentioned it?'

'I don't believe he ever did.'

'Not even when he'd been drinking?'

'No, I don't think so. And that's all you've been sent out here with, one word and good taste in prosaic drinking toasts?'

'That and a bunch of numbers. 24172738. None of it means a damn thing to me,' Hunter said suddenly defeated. And that was that. He'd finally admitted it not only to himself but to a perfect stranger. He was out of his depth, a failure.

'And your friends wanted to talk to him about... Landslide?'

Hunter nodded.

'They must think it's pretty damn important, to send you all this way?'

'I guess they must.'

'So what is it, or do you not know?'

'Nobody seems to know. Listen, can you help me or not?'

'I'm sorry, but I think your friends are going to be disappointed.'

'What makes you say that?'

But before Cameron could answer Amber had turned the

music up to an unhealthy level. The Chinese girls who had been coming and going with unstinting regularity since Hunter's arrival withdrew to gather together by the bar, the room suddenly alive with the buzz of expectation.

'You've come just in time to witness Amber's son do his thing. It's what passes for entertainment around these parts,' Cameron shouts over the deafening Chinese pop music and then, as the lighting changes, Hunter watched in astonishment as the owner's son, waiting for the music to reach its climax, makes his entrance. Hunter guessed he must have been at least six feet tall, although it was impossible to say, as he wore a significant pair of sparkling silver high heels, around his broad shoulders a pure white fur coat which stopped just above the floor and on his head a set of enormous red curved horns. He stretched his legs, shaven and oiled, from beneath the fur and gracefully made his way in time with the music across the dance floor to a table at the centre of the room and crowded with drinks. Hunter was impressed to see him leap up onto the table without disturbing a single glass, then he began pirouetting languidly in time with the music, his fur coat rising higher and higher, displaying more and more of his long shaven legs. Then in one fluid movement he undid the coat, sending it flying across the bar towards the shrieking girls, revealing a shimmering red posing pouch. The male patrons gathered around the table, whooping and cheering in terrified delight as he proceeds to thrust his pelvis towards each of them in turn. Identifying his first victim, a terrified looking businessman in a suit and crooked tie, he runs a languorous arm over the drunk man's chest, a glistening leg extended provocatively, his twitching crotch next to the man's face provoking more shouting and the flashes of mobile phone cameras.

Cameron looks on impassively and then pours two more large brandies from his private supply.

The owner's son, spotting the movement and having bored of the businessmen, floats across the room towards them. So much, Hunter thought, for keeping a low profile.

A beautifully manicured hand slid across Hunter's back, but the cabaret act only has eyes for Alex Cameron, seeming intent upon obtaining a reaction from the older of the two men. As his hand grazed Cameron's shirt the Scotsman seized his fingers, bending them fiercely back and causing the ladyboy to yelp in pain.

'Fuck off someplace else,' he hissed, 'and quickly.' Cameron released his grip and shot the owner a fierce look. The music came to an abrupt halt and the table of businessmen who had been looking their way quickly find somewhere else to stare and return to their drinks.

'Sorry about that,' Cameron said quietly.

Amber was with them in seconds. 'Mr Cameron, I'm so sorry. So sorry. I will talk with the boy. He is not to bother you again.'

Cameron flashes her a reassuring smile.

'Don't worry Amber, although we are going to need a little privacy here.'

'Of course, Alex. It will be my pleasure,' Amber says graciously, closing her eyes and dipping her head. Cameron slaps down a wad of RMB on the table.

'That ought to cover it.'

Amber throws up her hands in indignation. 'No, no Mr Cameron. You are a good customer. It will be my pleasure to entertain you and your friend. Would you like I send some of the girls over?'

'That won't be necessary Amber, we simply need somewhere a little quieter, where we can talk properly.'

Amber nods enthusiastically and gestures for them to follow her to a secluded area at the back of the club where there are booths full of high-class Chinese hookers and call girls. 'So sorry. I will speak to the boy later. Please, please you follow me.' She shoos the girls away and waves across to one of the waiters to come and clean up the table and then when he approaches instructs him that whatever Mr Cameron and his guest want to drink is on the house. Once Amber has stopped fussing and the waiter has brought over two more beers, Cameron stands on a chair and unscrews a light bulb, plunging the already gloomy booth into almost complete darkness. Then, happy they will not be disturbed and to Hunter's complete amazement Alex Cameron starts taking off his shirt.

'When I was a young lad, well younger than you anyway, and growing up in the North East of Scotland, there wasn't a whole hell of a lot for us. There was the oil business I suppose, down the road in Aberdeen, but it wasn't quite the oil capital of Europe it is now.'

Cameron continues to unbutton his shirt.

'I worked the rigs for a couple of months straight out of school, but I couldn't see a future in it. With hindsight I probably should have stuck it out, but, you know, when you're young you do what you do. So I moved down to Glasgow. Thought I might get some work at one of the shipyards, but I couldn't have timed it any worse. It was the early eighties and Thatcher. Scotstoun were dismantling their cranes and you could see the writing was on the wall for most of the yards so, after a long afternoon cruising Sauchiehall Street's finest establishments, I found myself joining up.'

Another button and then another.

'After some basic training and all that shite I did a stint with the Trogs in Northern Ireland. Rickshaws, cabs and taxis was what they called us. That would have been 1982? Not a fun time to be a red arse in Belfast I can assure you of that Junior. There were the hunger strikes, people were being murdered in front of their families, Jesus the IRA were even killing their own. Personally, I saw fuck all. People'll tell you about the horror stories. Only horror story I ever saw was a Drill Sergeant called Pendleton.'

Cameron undid the last of his shirt buttons and starts to pull it from his belt.

'Pendleton was a complete prick. Scouser. Hated me too. Can't think why. Anyway, after a night out in Belfast chasing girls and drinking whiskey, I get back to the barracks and a bit of an altercation breaks out, if you get me? I landed a couple of punches, he landed a couple back, nothing serious you understand? The next day I get woken up by a pair of MPs with murder on their mind. From what they said, you'd think I'd killed the tosser. Wound up in pokey for two weeks on a charge of aggravated GBH, and that's where they found me.'

'Who?'

'Our mutual friends. Same people that found you, I'm guessing.'

'I'm not sure I follow you.'

Cameron finished removing his shirt and turned his side to face Hunter. Just below his shoulder blade, squarely in the centre of what Hunter was impressed to see was a surprisingly well-honed bicep, the tattoo of a military insignia. The crown above an eight-pointed star, at its centre the Queen's moniker, and swirling beneath that, in a band of yellowy gold, Royal Corps of Transport. But what really caught Hunter's eye wasn't the centre piece, it wasn't the semi-circle above that in blue black which read Op Banner, it was the sequence of numbers which ran below. The same eight numbers Hunter had been told on leaving the UK.

'24172738' he heard himself say.

'That's me. 24172738 Private Connolly, Sah!'

Ewen Connolly turned to face Hunter, already slipping his shirt back on. 'We need to have a serious talk, son.'

Hunter agreed about that. 'But first I need to do one thing,' he said.

He found his mobile phone, scrolled through the variety of apps until he found his email account and left a message in his drafts as he'd been instructed.

I'm with a man calling himself Ewen Connolly. Now what?

Connolly had tucked his shirt back into his jeans and was taking a seat. Hunter pulled up a chair, placed his mobile phone on the table between them and sat down.

'So, I guess you want to know about Landslide?'

Hunter shook his head.

'No. I had to find you and that's what I've done.'

'Believe me, you *need* to know about Landslide.'

Against all the odds Hunter had gone first to Hong Kong and then mainland China and found a man who could just as likely have been dead.

'It's not my problem. I had to find you and I found you.'

'Perhaps you're right? Perhaps it's for the best. Landslide

would only put you in more danger.' Connolly thought for a moment. 'How did you find me, by the way?'

'I heard a story about someone selling arms out of China into Africa.'

'I never sold weapons,' Connolly corrected him quickly.

'That wasn't the impression they were under.'

'Well impressions can be misleading. I moved some crates for Song Shicheng, but I had no idea what was in them. Then, when I found out...'

'He said they found the General's body in the boot of his car...'

'How unfortunate.'

'At the bottom of a canal. My understanding, he'd been struck once, quite expertly, on the back of the head with a blunt instrument.'

'Really? Fascinating.'

'A spanner, Guo seemed to think, or wrench, something like that?'

Connolly had nothing more to add.

'The sort of thing you'd easily find lying around in a garage. No connection, I suppose,' Hunter continued.

'I can see I shall have to have a word with Lilly,' Connolly joked. 'You were telling me how it is you find yourself in Linyi?'

'Well after a little gentle persuasion Frank managed to remember the name of the import-export company and the city it was based in. I did the rest.'

'I heard there'd been a spot of trouble in Shenzhen. No connection I suppose?'

'If you say so,' Hunter replied taking another drink.

'How did you get from Shenzhen to Linyi?'

'I saw the name Cameron on an old order form.'

'Ah, that was careless. But that still doesn't explain how you found me. You said something about Frank?'

'Cassatto.'

'That old drunk? But I never told him anything, well nothing worth speaking of. He didn't even know my name.'

'He said you mentioned Landslide,' Connolly's head snapped towards Hunter, 'when you were drunk. He said that that was all you'd said, but that when he was in London he brought it up but just in the wrong company. Sounded like you could have cut the air with the proverbial. Anyway, you know Frank, once he got the sniff of a story there was no stopping him. He came tearing back to Hong Kong, but the trail had gone cold. He said he must have just missed you.'

Connolly smiled and took a slug of his beer.

'The irony is, just as you caught up with me, this is the first time in years I've been on the level, totally legit, well as legit as any other businessman in China. Linyi isn't great, in fact the air pollution's bloody terrible, but people here leave me alone to get on with my business. Lilly's a good kid, knows the trade better than I do now, and whilst I'm not rich, I'm pretty happy. Amber keeps me entertained and sends a bottle of this crap my way every once in a while,' Connolly held up the brandy, 'so by and large, life's pretty okay.'

'I'm sorry,' Hunter said. There was a part of him which envied Ewen Connolly and his simple life thousands of miles from home.

'Why are you sorry, son?'

'For finding you.'

'Why?'

'Because it looks like you've got a good thing going here.'

'I have, but you're worried that that will all come to end once your phone buzzes with your next instruction, am I right?'

Hunter shrugged. 'I've done my bit.'

'Have you, Scott?'

Hunter took a long pull on his beer, buying himself time to think.

'My name's Simon Frost,' he said as calmly as he could.

'Aye. Of course it is.' Connolly nodded to himself, his head on one side, as if trying to look at Hunter through a different angle would help him understand. 'How's David?'

'I'm sorry, I don't know what you're talking about? I don't know anyone called David.'

What the hell was happening? How did this man, this man who up until very recently had been a total stranger, seem to know so much about him? Another one of Michael Healy's tests?

'And your mother, Scott, how's Jane?'

'My mother killed herself,' Hunter said, unsure who he was saying it to.

'Oh Scott, I'm so sorry, I had no idea. Oh dear God, how's David?'

'I don't understand. How do you know them? How do you know my parents? Who are you?'

'You really don't recognise me, do you?'

Why would he recognise this man? He'd been given no photograph, that had very much been the problem hadn't it? He travelled all of that way and the one consistent thing which had nagged at Hunter the whole time was, how should I recognise this man.

'Your parents are,' but Connolly couldn't continue and

corrected himself, 'your parents were my friends and you Scott, you're my godson, I knew it the moment I saw you.'

'I don't remember,' Hunter said, suddenly feeling quite lost.

'You were very young.'

Both men stared out into the swirling chaos of the club and tried to recollect a time long passed. Hunter was the first to speak.

'You brought me things...'

'That's right,' Connolly laughed, 'when I was able to. Children love chocolates.'

'That's right, chocolates. I remember,' Hunter said five years old again, 'and you read to me?'

'I loved that, Scott, more than anything.'

'But then you stopped coming. Why was that? No one would talk to me.'

'I suspect once you understand why I had to leave, you may well understand what you are doing here.'

Hunter looked at his godfather, encouraging him to complete the sentiment, but Connolly picked up his beer and pointedly looked away so Hunter closed his eyes and sank back deeper into his own past.

'My mother, she was upset, very upset. Had you something to do with that?'

'No, Scott, I'm afraid not.'

Hunter nodded quietly, knowing the truth, but unwilling perhaps to accept it.

'For years I thought my father had had an affair with somebody from his work, and that had been why my mum had... but last year I discovered the truth. He'd been protecting me all that time.'

'That sounds like David.'

'I remember there was a big bust up just before Mum died. There were a lot of arguments and then Dad lost his job and then not long after, well...'

'I'm so sorry, Scott.'

'It was a long time ago now, and anyway there's nothing you could have done.'

'But Scott, I'm the man who betrayed your father. He wasn't having an affair, he would never have done that to Jane. He loved your mother far too much. I was the one having the affair, or trying to. I thought I was doing the right thing at the time. I was trying to protect someone, someone who meant a great deal to me, but by doing what I did, I hurt your father very badly. I'm the reason he lost his job. I should never have run away, I should have stayed and faced the music, but I was scared and running for my life.'

'From who?'

'Landslide.'

'I thought that was an op that went bad years ago?'

'Partly true. Landslide was a man, a very powerful man with connections and equally powerful friends reaching far and wide.'

'And you what, pissed him off somehow?'

'No. No, I never met him and I don't suppose he ever knew who I was.'

'I don't understand then. Unless you weren't worried about Landslide, but about his friends?'

Connolly shot Hunter that pained expression again and swiftly changed the subject.

'What's the plan then? Put me in handcuffs, sling me in the

jump seat and take me home to Auntie so I can explain myself. I'm not going back.'

'What do I tell Healy?'

'Who's Healy?'

'My boss.'

'Never heard of him. Tell him to go fuck himself, that's what I'd do. Go fuck yourself, whoever you are,' Connolly laughed. 'Tell him you did all you could, but I'm a stubborn old bastard who won't be told. Better still, tell him you couldn't find me at all.'

'It's a bit late for that,' Hunter said gesturing at his phone.

'Well if they want me that badly they can come out here themselves, the food's not that awful.'

'Would you come back and see my dad?'

Connolly laughed to himself. 'You're not going to give up easily, are you Scotty?'

'Why don't you see him? Tell him you're sorry, you might be surprised. He forgave me.'

'He's a good man, your father, but what I did, the way that I left him, it was unforgivable, even by him.'

'Get the flight with me tomorrow and tell him why. Explain to him about Landslide.'

'I can't. I'd have to answer to Alperton and that arsehole Sandy Harper. I can't do it.'

'You know he's not well, my father.' Hunter knew what he was doing was wrong, using one lie against another, but then doing wrong, lying, that was the name of the game, wasn't it? 'If you don't try and see him soon you may never have the opportunity.'

'What's the matter with him? Cancer?'

'It was my fault. He was shot,' another white lie, 'lost his spleen. There've been all sorts of complications, he might not make it to Christmas, none of us know.'

'That's a tough break, but I'm sorry son, I'm still not coming. Tell him, tell him I'm sorry, especially about Jane. I loved her almost as much as your father did.'

'I will,' Hunter nodded.

The mobile on the table in front of them buzzed silently. Hunter and Connolly looked at it.

'Are you going to get that?' the Scotsman suggested.

'I suppose I should.'

Scott Hunter picked up the phone, input his pin and opened his email account.

Well done. Now kill him.

9

Moscow, 1999

To the casual observer John Alperton's hotel room would have looked no different from any other tourist's. His camel jacket hung from a hook behind the door, its pockets filled with the litter of authenticity; a yellow Paris metro ticket, the stub from a concert of Mozart and Shostakovich, coins, both Russian and French and a receipt for some ham he'd bought in a charming little *charcuterie* on the Rue Montorgueil. Hanging alongside his jacket, his camera which, had anyone bothered to examine it revealed nothing more interesting than a monotonous stream of unremarkable photographs. A couple of establishing shots taken in Paris. A cat patrolling "his flat", a view over rooftops, the Seine lit up at night. Then the plane he had rather bumpily arrived on, a shot of clouds over a shimmering silver wing-tip. Moscow, but only the safe, sanitized side of Moscow. Red Square, tiles from the underground and The Kremlin, but taken from a distance and no different from the photographs hundreds of other tourists would take, or from the postcards you could buy from the state authorized kiosks. Alperton's other camera was considerably less conspicuous. The Tessina 35 he'd taken such great care to hide beneath a loose slat in the hotel's wardrobe. The rest of the room was largely empty. A couple of French guidebooks on Moscow lay by his bed, corners folded over, particular pages intentionally well-thumbed, another metro stub acting as a placeholder and next to them a map the concierge had given him, with obligingly circled places of interest and a restaurant he simply must try. At the foot of his bed the hotel had helpfully provided a wooden folding luggage rack which supported his sagging tartan suitcase. Alperton had dutifully shaken, then ironed, then lovingly hung up his shirts and trousers, his shoes lay in a neat polished row next to the door. Underwear and socks were squared away in the dresser beneath the mirror. In the bathroom, on the glass shelf above the sink, an orderly row of shaving products and balms from Galeries Lafayette at the rear of The Opera. The only items remaining in his suitcase; a purloined cotton laundry bag embroidered with the name of a five-star hotel in Madrid and cementing his credentials as the travelling man he purported to be, a recently opened carton of Marlboro cigarettes bought from the duty free at Charles de Gaulle and a copy of *Lui*. He had been forced to hand in his passport at the hotel's reception.

Alperton checked and rechecked the room, making absolutely certain any information acquired by an over inquisitive chambermaid, or worse, was the information he was happy to share and not an indication as to the true purpose of his visit. He straightened out his cable-knit sweater, pulled on his heavy jacket and set out for the theatre two stops away on Moscow's famous underground.

At Teatralnaya station he paused by a newspaper kiosk, wary that he was already being followed, and bought a three-day old copy of *Le Figaro*. Alperton smoked a cigarette whilst he busied himself with the headlines and then, happy he hadn't picked up an unwanted shadow proceeded to descend into Moscow's grandiose underground system.

Ten minutes later and Alperton caught himself in the freezing cold blast which hit him as he reached the top of Mayakovskaya Metro station. He knew that people regularly froze to death in Moscow's winter months, but even in April the wind had cut him to the core and he wondered if he would ever feel warm again.

At thirty-five and the son of an East End fishmonger, he hadn't taken the conventional route into the service. A knock about upbringing in a variety of Newham's poorer Catholic schools after which, having begged to take the eleven-plus, seven years of stability and learning by rote at Finchley Grammar School, where with his muscular physique he'd quickly established himself as a star of the school's rugby team. Then, with exam results and a report which wholly endorsed his decision to attend the school he left for university to study French Literature. Following in his socialist father's footsteps he'd been at a student's and workers' union meeting when a lofty individual had approached him and suggested there might be a way in which he could help his country. How would he feel about regularly attending these meetings and maybe some others too, getting to know one or two people and then simply recounting their conversations? Initially reluctant, the individual had suggested he think on it a while and they meet for a chat a few days later. After some drinks and a little light conversation the individual brought more pressure to bear on Alperton, suggesting that the people he would be observing, never spying on - that was made quite clear - might not have the nation's best interests at heart.

I would never insult you by offering to buy your allegiance the man had said lighting a cigar. Alperton's moral and ethical code sufficiently stroked he'd agreed. All low-level stuff, and exactly as his handler had said it would be. But after two months of reporting nothing of any great significance, the man had suggested he might enjoy a short trip to Paris. The young Alperton had needed little persuading, the lure of bright lights, pretty French girls and fine food being more than enough. Here was a train ticket. All he need do, enjoy himself. *Go to a few museums, why not give Rodin's a look,* the man had said, *I hear it's fascinating. The parks are always splendid at this time of year, oh and would you mind meeting a friend of mine in a cheeky little wine bar on the South Bank and bringing something back for me?*

It had been every bit as straight forward as his mentor had suggested and Alperton had even managed a fleeting but very real romance in the time he'd been away. They'd met at the boating lake in Luxembourg Gardens, Alperton gallantly stepping in to free her boat when it had become entangled with another. She was American, bright, young and attractive and extremely happy to be shown the sites of Paris by a handsome Englishman who took great care over his appearance and spoke the language like a native. John Alperton wined and dined her around the 11th arrondissement, all on the stipend the funny cigar smoking gent had given him, even insisting she join him at his rendezvous in the wine bar on the Seine. It would be fun, he'd said, and hardly take up any of their precious time together. And he'd been right. The foreign gentleman they'd met, briefly, had pushed a small cardboard container not much larger than a matchbox into his hand and that had been that. Later Alperton was told just how impressed the man they'd met had been. Two charming tourists sharing a bottle of wine together with eyes only for one another, the perfect cover. For his part John Alperton was delighted, the only fly in the ointment when he had had to return to London. Everyone seemed pleased enough with him. Everyone except the man who had asked him to go in the first place. Very politely, but quite firmly George Wiseman had set him straight. He was pleased to see John was enjoying himself, but cautioned that, in the future he might like to be a little more careful. This woman, what did he really know about her? She could have been anyone. In the future try not to let your attentions wander like that again. Alperton had protested both his and the girl's innocence but, once he had had time to reflect on Wiseman's words, he'd privately conceded that he was probably right. The magnitude of the work he was becoming embroiled in striking him only then.

Despite this minor set back Alperton had commenced his slow and steady rise through the ranks, until now, at nearly forty he was about to meet a Russian woman called Viktorija and receive intelligence information from an asset thought to be cruising in the Federal Assembly's upper echelons. He pulled his jacket tight around him and searched for his gloves.

In the foyer of the tiny theatre were a small group of bent and humbled women clutching yellow and red cleaning cloths and diligently polishing anything wooden, brass or glass. One of them raised their head as Alperton entered and half spoke, half sang something to her friends in that conspiratorial music of tired and put-upon housewives. Her friends followed her gaze and gave a throaty laugh on seeing the tall young foreigner in their midst. Alperton's Russian wasn't a match for his French but he understood enough. He was happy for them to have their joke at his expense, after all these were not the women he had come to see. He found the small entrance at the bottom of the stairs, loosened his jacket and opened the door. It made into a small yet functional office space; typewriters, a filing cabinet and, perched behind a desk, a pretty young woman perhaps a little older than himself. Slim and tall, in a tailored dark green velvet jacket with what appeared to be gold buttons, her straight strawberry blonde hair falling in curls as it reached her shoulders, a defiantly proud look about her.

'I was wondering if you might be able to help me,' he asked in French, 'are there any tickets left for this evening's concert?'

'That depends,' the young woman replied, her French almost on a par with his, 'How many tickets will you require?'

'I was meant to be bringing a friend, but they're ill, so it's just me.'

'That's a shame,' the girl said, reaching for her coat which lay over the back of a chair.

'Unless you'd care to join me?' A break from their script, but Alperton hadn't been able to help himself. The girl replied with a stern look and produced a small postcard sized envelope.

'Just one then.'

'Yes, thank you.'

She tore a ticket from its roll and handed it to Alperton along with the envelope.

'Thank you,' he said pushing it deep into an inside pocket,

suddenly embarrassed by his lapse in professionalism. 'Will you be at the concert this evening?'

'No,' she replied softly.

'I should very much like to buy you a drink, to say thank you for the ticket.'

'You know where to find me.'

'And what should I call you?'

'Viktorija.'

'It was a pleasure meeting you, Viktorija. My name is Henry, Henry Lazarus. I hope to see you again soon.'

'As do I, Monsieur Lazarus.'

The following day he returned to the theatre hoping he'd guessed the time the box office would close for the evening correctly. He hadn't and waited an hour and a half only for a short, poorly dressed man, wearing moon-rimmed spectacles, an ushanka-hat tied severely beneath his chin, and smoking earnestly to emerge from the tiny room. It crossed his mind to ask the man if he knew Viktorija's whereabouts, but he understood he was already flouting so many service protocols so he returned to the previous week's copy of *Le Figaro* he had been clutching and decided to come back another day. Two more failed attempts to see her and then, as he stood on the opposite side of the road trying not to freeze to death in the harsh Moscow night air he saw the doors open and the distinctive head of pure blonde flash briefly under the theatre's lights before Viktorija, for he was certain it was her, hunched her shoulders against the fierce wind which tore up and down the streets and headed south towards Tverskaya station. Alperton scampered cross the road and took her elbow. She spun to face him, seething in her native tongue, then seeing his face beneath the streetlight admonishing him in French.

'What the hell are you doing?'

'I thought I'd like to buy you that drink.'

'Have you completely lost your mind? Get your hands off me.'

'I had to see you.'

'There is a procedure, or are you unaware of this?'

'You know that's not what I mean.'

'If we are seen together, like this people will ask questions.'

'People will see a handsome young couple out for an evening's stroll together.'

'You have clearly spent little time in Russia, Monsieur Lazarus.'

Alperton had to concede that that was true, although he did detect a thawing in Viktorija. He still held her elbow, but now she let him slip his arm into hers and they walked a little easier.

'Let us suppose that I agree. Where do you intend to take me for this drink?'

'I'm always happy to bow to local knowledge, Viktorija.'

'I might know a little place not far from here where we may not be disturbed.'

Alperton let her guide him through the back streets of Moscow's Meatpacking District and to Bar Mishka. They spent an enchanting evening together, talking and drinking and then, when the owner of the bar had suggested as tactfully as he could, that seeing as how everyone else had left some time ago, he too might like to retire for the evening and shut up shop, they'd found themselves out on the pavement in the freezing cold again. He had offered to walk her home. She had smiled but shaken her head. He had lent in to kiss her. She had turned away.

The next time they met was in a Georgian restaurant on Bolotny Island opposite the Kremlin where the Lobio was good but the Khinkali was better. To anyone watching they were just a couple having lunch together. The restaurant boasted its own band playing traditional music and a tree which sprouted from the centre of the dining area and disappeared up and through the building's roof. Alperton ordered a bottle of Georgian white wine but quickly abandoned it in favour of the vodka which had been left at the table. The band played and he was able to discreetly quiz his beautiful companion as to the source of her information. Despite the vodka and the numerous toasts, Viktorija remained tight lipped. She, she informed him, was simply the go between, another layer of security. Don't forget, she scolded him, it is not uncommon to see defected ex-members of Britain's so called secret service drunkenly wandering the streets of Moscow.

Alperton politely thanked her for reminding him of his employer's shortcomings.

At the end of the meal, once their transaction was complete and he had offered to pay and she had accepted, she thanked him, and, leaning in close, kissed him on the cheeks three times in the French way, whilst squeezing his hand. He knew he was playing a dangerous game, but he also knew, which she did not, that his time in Moscow was coming to an end. A date for his extraction had already been set.

'When can I see you again?' he'd asked. He was free for dinner he'd joked, almost every night.

She would contact him. She would leave a message for him at the front desk of his hotel.

'When?' he'd wanted to know, unsurprised that she knew where he was staying.

'You must be patient, Henry. It will be soon.' Then she'd smiled, given his hand another firmer squeeze, turned and walked away.

Days passed and then a week before Alperton next heard from Viktorija. He had not long returned to his hotel off Ilyinka Street after a long and lonely lunch when there was a telephone call from reception.

'Monsieur Lazarus?'

'Yes.'

'A Miss Viktorija would like to see you.'

He understood and asked where and when she would like to meet him.

'She is downstairs, Monsieur, waiting for you in the lobby.'

Alperton suffered a sudden and quite curious mix of emotions. She should never be seen to make contact so openly, there were protocols for such things, the same protocols he'd flaunted so blatantly. But on the other hand she was standing in the foyer of his hotel asking to see him, this beautiful woman he was so strongly attracted to. He raced downstairs to greet her. What was she doing here?

'There is no need for alarm,' she said steering him away to a quieter corner. 'I was passing and I wanted to see you. And give you this of course.' She planted the object firmly in his hand and just as quickly it disappeared inside a pocket. 'I thought you might like to take me for lunch?' she purred.

Alperton explained he'd not long returned from lunch himself.

'Then perhaps you might like to take me to bed?'

Alperton was still supposed to be considering just how much or how little the service should trust Viktorija and her source, but this changed everything.

That afternoon they became lovers. As Viktorija lay smoking and watching him, Alperton photographed the information she had brought. It would be sent back to London in a diplomatic pouch with a message saying he needed more time before he could be sure about her.

'Please don't go.'

'You know that I have to,' she said kissing his forehead.

'Why?'

A sigh, a raised eyebrow.

'Because. I don't want to get caught here, with you. It would be awkward, very awkward, for both of us.'

Alperton knew he was breaking all his own rules and if Wiseman ever found out he could only imagine the scene. 'Please stay. I shall be sad if you leave.'

She looked up at him, her head on his chest. He was playing the hurt little boy, his accent slipping slightly as he adopted the persona.

'You will be fine,' she said, chiding him a little, 'and in any case, you know what we Russians say when we hear that an Englishman is sad? You are an Englishman are you not Mr Lazarus?'

He kissed her.

'Tell me,' he continued in French, 'what do you Russians say about the sad English?'

'We say that when the English are sad, we are very sad. And that when the English are very sad, we are very, very sad.'

He smiled at her now, sensing the pay off.

'And that when the English are very, very sad,' she kissed him playfully, making him wait, 'we are very, very happy.'

They laughed and Alperton grabbed her round her slender waist, determined to keep her in his bed just a little while longer.

'So, you're trying to make me sad?'

'Am I succeeding?'

'Only if you leave.'

'I have to.'

He let her go, not knowing when he might see her again.

Following that first afternoon together they met almost daily, but with Viktorija insisting they take more care than they had done. Alperton checked them into a succession of hotels across Moscow. Often they would arrive together, enjoying playing the married couple. Sometimes one would show up before the other and elaborate ruses were concocted. John Alperton realized that, perhaps for the first time in his life, he was falling in love, and that, to the best of his knowledge his beautiful Russian companion with the flawless French and connections which appeared to run deep within the Kremlin felt the same way too.

On the first of May they'd agreed to meet at the Patriarch's Ponds. Alperton had waved down a succession of private taxis to get him there. The first took him across town from his hotel to Arbat Street under the pretense that he was going to see Pushkin's Monument. Soon after he flagged down a second heading almost straight back the way that he'd come. The driver dropped him off outside the Bulgakov Museum and then, like the devil before him, he entered the park. They had arranged to meet in an open area surrounded by benches overlooking the water. Alperton was early and sat anxiously, smoking and watching the pigeons scavenge for scraps of food.

Then he saw her. He thought she looked more beautiful than ever, in a short summer frock. She floated across the chequered flagstones towards him, the red fabric hugging her body where it ought to and shimmering and swaying elegantly everywhere else. Her hand came to rest on his shoulder with a concert pianist's lightness of touch. He stood, their bodies close and she kissed him without speaking. Then she took him by the hand and led him past the huge manmade lake and out of the park. Nothing could have prepared John Alperton for the joy he experienced at that moment. She was the most beautiful woman he had ever seen and she appeared to love him very much. He wanted to stop her, to halt her in her tracks and tell her just how much he cared, how much he loved her. He wanted more than anything, to tell her his real name so that the next time she spoke to him she would know, really know, exactly who she was talking to. Not a spook from Paris with a cat he'd never met and a pocket load of metro tickets he'd been given by a man he barely knew in a flat in Aldgate, but a real living man, with a real name, a real history, a home and an exhausting father and somewhere a medal he would show her from a rugby tournament he'd won when he was sixteen. Even the knowledge that this would never happen, that he would never properly share his life with her, that her name was almost certainly not Viktorija, could not diminish the joy he felt as she took his hand in the golden sunlight and led him from the park. He tried to ask her where they were going, but today she was full of fun and surprises and he would let her have her fun. Every time he tried to ask she would stop and kiss him ardently and then laugh and giggle and take him by the hand again and lead him down another street, until eventually they arrived at a hotel.

'I thought it would be nice,' she said a little shyly.

John Alperton followed her inside. He didn't like or want to know where the money for such an elegant suite had come from.

They made love all afternoon and into the evening.

'Do you not have to go,' he'd asked.

'No, my love.'

'Do you never think about it?'

'What?'

'The work we do, the information you're passing?'

'Never. Why would I? It's nothing to do with me, and I would advise you to do the same. It's our job, Henry, it's just our job. I try not to think about it like I try not to think too much about you, and how you're not really Henry Lazarus from Paris, and how there's probably a Mademoiselle waiting at home somewhere wondering where you are and what you're doing.'

'There isn't.'

'Don't. It doesn't make any difference. Better we enjoy what we have whilst we have it.'

'And you're not concerned where your country's secrets might be headed?'

'I'm the delivery girl, Henry, nothing more. I have the utmost faith in the man who sent me.'

'Why?'

'Because I have to. You see, I've already entrusted everything I have to him.'

***

Hyde Park, London, 2017

These lads were pretty decent with a ball. Pakistani from the odd shouted phrase of Pashto he'd heard. They were certainly enjoying the sun and even though the fielding team seemed only to have nine players, the standard was high. From what little Wiseman had seen, the chap at the striker's end had a fine cover drive but looked susceptible to the short ball. George thought the leggy lad in jeans and adidas T-shirt who was regularly banging them in on a line and length almost certainly had one of those in his locker. In he came again, thundering through the little patch of Hyde Park they'd chosen, firmly planting his leading leg where they'd agreed the crease could be. Everything about the young man giving the impression he would fizz one down towards his friend. But no, not this time. He aims to deceive, this tall youth with the darkest of hair and the beginnings of a moustache. His fingers spread around the ball, when his arm swings through its rapid arc, the ball follows more slowly, appearing to be one thing, but in fact quite another. A natural bounce followed by the most beautiful sound in the world. The batsman, picking the slower delivery but not tempted to lash out, pushes forward, steering the ball firmly into the ground and then out past the bowler to what might have been long off.

Wiseman's eyesight was failing him now, his peripheral vision particularly poor, but the small five and a half ounces of cork and highly polished leather was tearing across the recently mown grass directly toward him. In a bygone era he would have run to the ball, dropped to one knee, as his gymnastics' teacher had instructed, thus preventing the boundary. Then he would have sprung to his feet and returned it with interest. Now all he is able to do is stick out a foot. The ball caught the middle of his brogue with a satisfying thud and, with great determination and no little effort, Wiseman stooped and retrieved it, bruised and battered from many happy hours at the park, the gold maker's name now all but illegible. Some of the stitching looked in danger of unravelling and the whole ball could not, strictly speaking, be considered spherical. Wiseman held it up like a religious artefact. He'd have loved to have tossed it nonchalantly into the air just once, perhaps with a subtle flick of the hand to add a touch of spin but didn't trust himself.

The two batsmen had stopped in the middle of their imagined wicket. *That was a four,* the body language said.

One, the non-striker, turns George's way, enquiring after their ball.

A young Asian boy was slowing his run towards the boundary. Fifteen or sixteen George imagined. How he envied him his vitality. The boy beamed an open, honest smile, his head tilting infinitesimally, scrutinizing the old man. *Yes, you may have your ball back.*

It was time. A time for the finishing of things. For the conclusion of people, operations and lives. A time, once and for all, to tie up loose ends. As Wiseman raised his arm to throw the ball back he felt the file beneath his overcoat. As his arm reached the extent of its parabola, Wiseman opened his ancient hand and released the small leather ball. It looped up into the warm spring air and was gone. Wiseman thought the boy nodded a thank you and then he too turned and was gone. He was going to miss all this.

He struck on as boldly as his legs would allow towards The Serpentine, Peter Pan and Sir John Alperton.

From this distance he could make out a blurry grey figure and an occasional puff of smoke sat on the bench where they'd agreed to meet. That had been kind of John, to arrange somewhere so close to his apartment. Well, one act of kindness deserved another. Alperton had chosen this moment to be rid of Frederick Sinclair once and for all, and Wiseman was not going to blame him for that.

But there was more in the firm grey file which encumbered the old man's stride. It was time. Time he shared this piece of the jigsaw with his protégé and friend. Had they ever truly been friends? Wiseman wondered. Regardless, John Alperton had done great things in George's name. Achieved a level of distinction and paid the price for that achievement, for his loyalty. Wiseman owed him this one last morsel before the end. Viktorija had caused him so much pain. It was time for Sir John Alperton to understand Aleksei's true identity, and that of the man Aleksei had recruited all those years before.

10

Sarratt, Hertfordshire

David Hunter was just about to change into his pyjamas when he heard it. A bottle. Probably he reflected with a reluctant grin, a wine bottle, being knocked over. He went to the drawer by his bed, quickly found what he was looking for, removed his shoes and turned off the light.

David had not seen the man standing in his kitchen amidst the half-light and the empty bottles for almost twenty years, but he didn't think twice before pressing the muzzle of his pistol into the base of the man's neck.

'Hands. Let me see your hands.'

'It's me, you silly old fool.'

'I know it's you, that's why I'd like to see your hands.'

'Put that thing away and get some glasses.'

'Give me one good reason why I shouldn't shoot you?' David said already relaxing his grip.

'My godson a good enough reason?'

David Hunter let the pistol drop and in the brittle darkness of his kitchen, Ewen Connolly turned to face him. 'Seems he's as bad at following orders as his old man was. Hello, David. It's been a long time.'

David Hunter was still pointing the gun at Connolly's midriff.

'Christ sake, put that bloody thing away will you? You never were much of a shot, even at this range.'

'You bastard,' David smiled.

Connolly held out a hand and took the gun from him. 'Now, how about that drink?'

'What are you doing here, Ewen?'

'Bumped into your lad. Seems he may have been sent to kill me.'

David wasn't surprised. A little disappointed perhaps, but not surprised.

'Appears he has a problem doing what he's told. Not unlike his father.'

'Is he okay, Scott?'

'Of course he is, Jesus you don't think I'd let any harm come to him do you?'

'Where is he then?'

'I'm his godfather, David, not his bloody keeper. Last time I saw him he was queuing up to get on the flight before me.'

'Scotch?' David held up a bottle and two glasses.

'Anything's fine.'

He flicked on the kitchen lights and gestured to his guest to take a seat.

'Mind if smoke?'

Grudgingly his host waved him off.

'Good of you. Filthy habit. Thought I'd kicked it for good, but started again out there.'

By *out there* David could only assume he meant wherever he'd been hiding for the last twenty years. Ewen drew long and hard on the cigarette before looking at David meaningly. It had been so long since David had smoked he'd almost forgotten. He found an old saucer and placed it between them.

'Sure that's okay?' Ewen asked, eyeing the dish.

'Last in a set. No one's going to miss it.'

'Aye, Scott told me about Jane. I'm so sorry, David. I had no idea.'

'No, of course you didn't. How could you, from the other side of the world?'

In a drawer full of old batteries and rubber bands David found a notepad and pencil.

'What *are* you doing here then?' he said throwing them down in front of Connolly.

'Thought I'd drop in and see an old friend.'

'Little overdue, wouldn't you say?'

'I've been busy, David, but yes, a little perhaps.'

'Where did you go, Ewen?'

'Oh, you know, here, there, bloody everywhere.'

'You know what I mean. After Istanbul, where did you go, up through the Ukraine and into Belarus?'

'No actually. South into Armenia, then Azerbaijan, Iraq and Tajikistan.'

'The old garlic trail.'

Connolly nodded.

'Picked up an Alevi guide in East Turkey and then on horseback through the Alborz mountains.'

'You had your own reasons for avoiding Russia as I remember, not to mention Chechnya. But even so Ewen, Iran? That was pretty ballsy.'

'Wound up in Kazakhstan. Holed up in Almaty for six months. You ever been?'

'Can't say I have.'

'Can't say I blame you.'

'When?'

'End of '99 into 2000. Good time to be there. Lots of Yankie greenbacks kicking around. Rich pickings for yours truly.'

'Until?'

'Until I had to move on. Profile getting a little too high, if you follow me? Met a Maoist who took me through the Tian Shan mountains and then into China.'

'Maoists?'

'Don't be naïve, David. The CIA's been running Maoists to get them into the Xinjiang province since the sixties.'

'Then what?'

'Hong Kong eventually, just the same as all the other refugees. Thought it might make sense to be somewhere the old British Passport was a help rather than a hinderance.'

'How did you get as far as you did? Aliases?'

'Three. Most of the way through Iran and into Kazakhstan as a Swiss businessman, but then when that got sticky in Almaty I burnt Hoffstetter and played possum for a while.'

'And all the way across China?'

'Rode my luck. There's a trainline which goes from Turpan to Lanzhou. Once I'd made up my mind to go to Hong Kong it only took me a few days to get down to Shenzhen. Next stop Honkers.'

'In 2000 no one was going straight in or out of Hong Kong,' David said suspiciously, 'especially not a British citizen with a folder on him an inch thick at Six. How'd you manage it?'

'I did the only thing I could, I swam for it, in the South China Sea.'

'You're having me on?'

'No. Across Deep Bay to Lau Fau Shan. Got picked up by a junk and ended up on Lamma Island. Stayed put there for a while, keeping my head down until the money ran out.'

'Anyone corroborate that?'

'Just fifty thousand jelly fish and a shitload of sharks. What do you mean? I didn't join a bloody swim club.'

'All I'm saying is that story might raise a few eyebrows?'

'I thought you were retired?'

'Just looking out for the boy. Then what?' David asked.

'I did favours for people.'

'Which people?'

'Started out with some door-work, then got into the palm tree scam. Huge areas of Hong Kong and Kowloon were being gentrified; The Peak, Stanley, from the tennis club all the way down to Admiralty. Palm trees need time to grow, so we'd dig them up in the middle of the night, load them on to a flatbed and find someone rich to flog them to. Trees go in easy, especially with a team of locals doing the humping. Twenty-four hours later, once everyone's been paid, it's nice and dark and the owner's in bed, you pop back, wheech out the trees and on you go to the next guy. Some of the clever gangs would sell the same trees back to the same people over and over.'

'You?'

'No need. After a while we got a nice cosy thing going robbing out rebar from building contractors and replacing it with, well with any old crap really. Then, when that was done I met a bent copper in an Irish Pub down by the harbour. Ex-Hong Kong Police. Used to walk the border fences. Horrible fat little man. He knew every God damn trick in the book, even a few I'd never considered. If he hadn't been so busy drinking himself to death I'd have thought he was one of your lot. Anyway, over a Guinness he tells me he's got some friends who might like to meet me. Bad people, real nasty types. But when you're on the run, what are you going to do, right?'

'If you say so.'

'Fuck you, David. So, he takes me out, buys me a cheap suit from a third-floor backstreet tailors near Kowloon Park and a fresh pair of shoes. Once I look half decent we head over the water to Hong Kong and The Foreign Correspondents Club. Ever been?'

'Can't say I have.'

'Fifty thousand types of journalistic arsehole all crammed under the one fan, fighting to get to the bloody bar.'

'Sounds fun.'

'It wasn't. Every bugger wants to tell you their life story. Introduces me to the only Chinese guy in the joint. Seems he's a Mr Fix-it for some wealthy bad guys working out of mainland China.'

'Triad?'

'I don't think he said.'

'Drugs?'

'I don't do the drugs thing, okay?'

'Okay. What then?'

'Money laundering, through Macao.'

'So, low on funds, you decided to...'

'Jesus David, I know it's been a while, but just because I've been out the country I didn't grow into a complete idiot. You rip off the Triad they find your arms in Kowloon, your legs in Hong Kong and your head bobbing up and down in the harbour somewhere in between.'

'What happened then?'

'The smooth little Mr Fix-it in the Correspondents Club explains to me they're washing cash out of mainland China. No one wants Chinese RMB, not even the Chinese, so they bring it into Honkers and fly it out to the casinos in Macao. Sky above Hong Kong harbour's buzzing with tiny little black helicopters full of dodgy cash. God forbid they should crash into one another, the entire local economy'd be fucked. They fly the stuff out to Macao, the casinos clean it for us and take a filthy great percentage into the bargain.'

'How filthy?'

'As much as fifty percent. Depends on who's doing the selling, and who's doing the buying, but either way, fifty percent of a fuck of a lot of cash, is still...'

'A fuck of a lot of cash,' David said smiling.

'Exactly.'

'And your role in all this? Bag man?'

'Please. Well, initially yes, but then once they'd cottoned on I could open doors in a couple of languages they moved me up to meet and greet.'

'Explain.'

'My job, to make sure the deal goes well. Everyone's happy. Once the money's come in from the Island, it was over to me, you see? The guy wants a girl, I buy him a girl. The guy wants some coke, well, you get the picture?'

'Until?'

'Until all did not go smoothly. Nothing to do with me I hasten to add. I was bloody good at my job by the way, but one over enthusiastic client, that's all it takes. Guy turns up with over a hundred million in Chinese RMB and expensive tastes to match. Next thing, I'm looking at a dead Malay prostitute and a shit load of un-snorted coke. My boss gets in his nice shiny black helicopter with his briefcase full of freshly laundered greenbacks and fucks off into the deep blue yonder, leaving yours truly here holding the baby.'

'So?'

'That's when I went. Vanished for good this time. Left everything and everybody behind.'

'Everybody?'

'Yes, everybody. Never went back to Kowloon, never can. And I've been minding my own business ever since. Still would be if Junior hadn't found me.'

'Money?'

'What about it?'

'How did you get by, if you never went back?'

'You take a little slice here and a little slice there.'

'No. No one steals from the Triads, not even little slices. You're not sharing, Ewen.'

'I suppose it doesn't matter. SARs?'

'Outbreak in 2003. Potentially fatal epidemic of severe acute respiratory syndrome or avian flu. Covered most of the Far East as far as I recall and even made it to parts of Europe. Government here started shitting itself round about May time. Never came to anything.'

'In February 2003 Hong Kong Island was the epicentre for bird flu. People panicked. I mean big time. Everyone and Uncle Ho starts selling up and fucking off in all directions. I'd saved up a little cash, so I moved in, bought up a couple of flats under my Swiss alias, waited for everything to blow over, which it duly did. Made a tidy sum, thank you very much.'

'Mind if I take you back a couple of steps? Some of this is sounding a little routine if you'll forgive me for saying?'

'You've got to be joking right?'

'All this crap about SARs and making a killing on the property market. I don't ever recall you having the first idea about bricks and mortar.'

'Charles Merry and Sons.'

'What about them?'

'Solicitors I used. Check them out. I'd give you my bank details if I thought you were still in the service, but as this is supposed to be a nice cosy social call and you tell me you're not, frankly you can kiss my arse.'

'I am going to want *some* details, Ewen.'

Connolly took up the pencil David had left him and quickly scrawled two addresses in block caps.

'How much of this is true?'

'Enough.'

'Enough for who?'

'For you probably, for Six definitely.'

'Names?'

'What?'

'The hotels?'

'The Grand in Macau.'

'And the one you flew from?'

'The Peninsula. Want the name of the pilot?'

'What about your passport? How did you get out of China?'

'Amazing who you meet in Wan Chai when you're flying millions of dollars in dodgy cash around. Similar background I think, if we'd cared to look, which we didn't. A Chinese firm'll employ you simply to sit in their office, drink tea and look white. They seem to think it lends their business a certain degree of kudos. In the home of capitalism no one gives a toss as long as your credit's good and your business card's clean.'

'Your contact in Wan Chai?' David gently reminded his guest.

'Used to drink in the White Hart. I didn't like to ask too much, but he let it slip he could get me a nice new shiny passport any time.'

'Let it slip the way we might let it slip?'

'Exactly.'

'Name?'

'David, come on.'

'*Name?*'

'Mark Stephenson.'

'Cover?'

'I expect so with a name like that, don't you?'

'Even worth checking him out?'

'I wouldn't waste your energy. Anytime he said. Just had to turn up at the correct address.'

David Hunter turned a fresh page of his notepad and licked the end of his pencil in anticipation.

'The Belmont Hotel, Queen's Road, Wan Chai, alright?'

'Ever go and check it out?'

'Never felt the need.'

'Bollocks.'

'Twenty-five rooms in three stories of hell all in the shadow of some of the most expensive real estate in the world.'

'Which brings us all rather neatly to the here and now. What are you doing here? Life too comfortable for you?'

'I like it here. Plus, your boy makes a compelling argument,' Connolly said almost laughing.

'I don't buy it.'

'Not my problem, David. Last time I checked this was just one pal come halfway round the world to check in on his godson and have a wee drink with his sick old friend. Which reminds me,' Ewen said dragging the bottle across the table, 'I take this glass into my hand!'

Ah, how many times had David heard this toast?

'and drink to all that's here,'

and never quite the same way twice. The irregularities of the years all part of its faded charm.

'Slange Var.'

'Why are you here, Ewen?'

'To make things right, David. To make Istanbul right, okay, is that what you want me to say?'

'Landslide?'

'Perhaps.'

'Tell me. What did happen? I've always imagined it was King who went to the bazaar and not you?'

'Aye.'

'And?'

'She was boxed. Professional job too, from what she told me.

Couple of young guns, Turks probably, trying to drag her this way and that. *You have husband, boyfriend back home, you come, buy kilim for your boyfriend* that kind of rubbish.'

The events of Istanbul rushing back to David as if mere days and not years have passed.

'She should have been there earlier, walking the place,' he says abruptly.

'I told you she was inexperienced.'

'And?'

'And there may have been a man.'

'That's what I told Sandy. Jesus.'

'So, she's running late...'

'Hot and flustered after an afternoon in the sack?' David put in angrily.

'Says you. She's running late, she gets to the bazaar and no sooner is she looking for the apothecary, than two or three guys are grabbing her.'

'Which is it?'

'Which is what?'

'Two or three?'

'Two or three. Her words. Real professional. Just the right side of charming not to get a slap.'

'And she misses Landslide by?'

'Minutes. Moments. Fuck, I don't know. Does it matter?'

'I suppose not. What do *you* think happened?'

'Four-man team. Snatch squad. That's what I'd have done, same as you. Landslide gets where he's going and there's someone already there waiting for him. Our gal gets suitably waylaid by the carpet salesmen, and that's it, it's all over. Our asset disappears off the face of the earth, never to be seen or heard from again. Or at least that's how it appears.'

'What do you mean by that?'

'Unable to answer any questions, name any names, point any fingers,' Connolly concludes.

'Ewen, what the hell are you driving at?'

Connolly splashes some more Scotch into his glass and thinks about lighting another cigarette.

'As soon as Pat came back I went straight there to see. There were no signs in the back room. A good team could have cleaned up in that time I suppose, but... I scoured the area, David. There was no blood, no signs of a struggle, everything as it should be. Whatever had happened we were blown, so I came back and sent the flash.'

'You didn't think to consult King first?'

'She'd have only tried to talk me out of it. No point. Once the flash was sent I went and packed my bags and waited for London to send someone. I just never thought it would be you.'

'And your little sightseeing trip down by the river?'

'All bollocks to buy me some time. Never happened.'

'You never went?'

'No.'

'But you can see how bad it looked?'

'Aye. Better than coming back here to a public thrashing and watching you lot finally put the blame on Pat's shoulders.'

'Listen to yourself man. She *was* to blame.'

'David, I've had twenty-something years of wondering whether I did the right thing. You don't think I've been round this?'

'There's more though, isn't there?'

'I never bought it. Any of it. Not then, not now,' Ewen said draining his glass and holding it out for David to re-fill. 'Are *you* going to tell me who Landslide really was?'

'I'm not sure I need to. You already know,' David said looking at his friend in astonishment.

'I've a pretty good idea, yeah,' Connolly replied nodding.

'Asset. Hot one, according to Sandy. Straight out of Russia. Lots of goodies and happy to share, that's what I was told,' David replies.

'That's what I thought too. So, why send me and the girl?'

'Because it ought to have been a routine pick up and debrief.'

'Sure. Even if I believed that, which I don't by the way, how did it go so wrong? There was a team waiting, in Istanbul. How? They knew where to be and when.'

'What are you saying? The Russians? Turkish SIP?'

'Bit out of their league.' Ewen sipped at his drink. 'One of ours?'

'Not to my knowledge. And anyway...'

'Who knew Pat was going to that meeting? Who gave the order?'

'You were there, Sandy Harper.'

'Come on, David. Who really gave the order? Sandy's just a nasty little queen with an eye for the dramatic. Who gave him the nod?'

'Alperton?'

'I don't buy it. He was fresh back from Moscow and so screwed up he wasn't in a fit state to do anything. And anyway, he had no idea who Landslide was, trust me.'

'Higher?'

'George?'

'I hope not for your sake. He died last year.'

'So I heard. Gray then? Sandy was always beholden to him. Alperton never entertained the man. And the idea that Alperton would use Sandy is laughable.'

'Why?'

'Because if Landslide is who I think he is, I'm guessing he had something on Gray that Toby would rather he kept to himself.'

'That's strong stuff Ewen. Something bad enough to kill for?'

'Bad enough for me to disappear halfway round the world for, yes.'

'If only King had been straight with everyone.'

'I'm not certain she'd have made it onto the plane home. Same goes for me.'

'Slash and burn?'

'Exactly.'

'How did she survive it then?'

'Friends in low places.'

'That would've been my guess. Sandy?'

'Possibly.'

'Gray?'

'Probably. They were sleeping together, weren't they?'

'And you decided to play the fall guy? Did you love her?'

'Who?'

'The Mother bloody Teresa, who do you think? Were you in love with Pat King?'

Connolly laughs nervously. 'Don't be ridiculous, David.'

'Christ Ewen. Really?'

'You asked. I'm telling you.'

'Tell her?'

'No. What would have been the point?'

'You're saying she never knew?'

'That's a different question altogether. You'd have to ask her. I was in love with her, David, alright?'

'You gallantly fall on your sword and King walks away. Then what the hell happened?'

'They wanted a scape goat.'

'Which should have been you.'

'Aye.'

'But it seems they wanted more than that. A head on a pole to parade around Westminster. Visible proof that someone has been a naughty boy.'

'Or girl.'

'Quite. When you decided to do your midnight flit, the service finds itself minus one head.'

'Agreed.'

'You buggered off playing Marco Polo and I got left to carry the can. Hung out to dry by the service, early retirement, spending more time tending my garden and all that type of crap, followed by public humiliation and disgrace, for letting Ewen Connolly, the reliable traitor slip quite so easily through my fingers.'

'I had no idea, David. I thought I could make it disappear. I thought I could make it all just go away. I never thought it would end like that.'

'King leaves a couple of years later, promoted sideways no doubt into the civil service and no one's any the wiser. And in the middle of it all, Landslide. Everything keeps coming back to Landslide. What do you know, Ewen?

'I never told you about Moscow, what really happened, I

mean. I was never allowed to. They were looking for someone who'd keep an eye on Alperton's girl you see, someone who wasn't screwing her naturally and who could follow her back to her source.'

'Who's they Ewen?'

'Harper and Gray. Sandy Harper sent me, Alperton never knew. He had other things on his mind. Sandy said I was to be as quiet as the proverbial. It wasn't difficult keeping track of Viktorija, after all everyone down to the char boy had worked out they were sleeping together. But Landslide, he was different. He went to great lengths not to be identified. Their dead-drop took me days to figure out. Instead of one location at the same time every day, they had seven, dotted about Moscow, so when you were trailing her, you never knew where the hell you were going next. Anyway, by day eight I'd realised I was back where I started. I took a punt and showed up nice and early for the following day's drop. Funny little man Landslide, not what I'd been expecting at all. Quite short, with a bit of a pot and receding hair. He must have had terrible eyesight too judging by the glasses he wore. I clocked him third time around, having a fag as he checked the place out. He always had a fag on the go, I remember that. And then an hour or so later Alperton's squeeze turns up. The next day I did as Sandy asked and followed him.'

'You know who he was?'

Ewen nodded, but David knew better than to ask.

'He was hot shit, David. High up, I mean really fucking high up. I was terrified once I got onto him. If I'd been made we certainly wouldn't be having this conversation now and I think I would have simply vanished off the face of the earth.'

'So why cut him free? Why walk away from someone so powerful who was sending us such good stuff?'

'I'm getting to that. I've spent the last twenty years wondering who cut him loose and why. But first you need to know what happened two days after I made him. It was awful, David. I don't know who reported her, at that time it could have been almost anyone from a greedy taxi driver to the cook at the hotel. I'm sat outside one of their favourite haunts, a little Uzbek restaurant in Kitay-Gorod, when a car pulls up. As Alperton and the girl go to leave, out jumps Aleksei.'

'Aleksei?'

'Kadnikov, deputy head of the SVR.'

'Jesus.' David immediately pours himself another stiff drink.

'Bad scene, David. I mean a really bad scene. Kadnikov starts bawling and shouting at the girl, virtually strong-arms her into his car and that was pretty much the last time I saw Viktorija. But you know the strangest thing? Once she was in the car he went and spoke to Alperton. I couldn't hear what was being said of course, but there was a lot of finger pointing and I could see John protesting, but the Russian was having none of it.'

'And yet when you were interviewed by Sandy after the op was wound down you neglected to mention any of this?'

'Alperton swore me to secrecy. You'd have probably done the same in the circumstances. Said it was imperative London never know he'd met the Russian face to face. Said I could tell them anything I wanted to about him screwing around, all of that kind of stuff, but I must never mention that I'd seen him with Kadnikov.'

'And what do you think about Viktorija? Was she a honey trap designed to get one of ours out in the open?'

Ewen shook his head. 'Sadly not. She was found where she shouldn't have been, in bed with a questionable foreign national. The tragedy is, if I'm right about who Landslide was, he could have stepped in to save her, but chose not to.'

'Really? You told Sandy she cracked her head at the hotel. You told Sandy you followed them back there. You never clocked the muscle and then you arrived too late to save her after she fell.'

Ewen Connolly shook his head and David Hunter watched as a trembling hand reached for his tumbler.

'All bull, cooked up by Alperton at the safehouse. I knew she was being followed, but Sandy had said on no account was I to get involved. I wasn't far behind her you see, but I got to the hotel just too late.'

'She was dead?'

'No. I arrived just as they were dragging her off. One of them had put John Alperton flat on his back, that was the sort of muscle we were up against and that was the last time either of us saw her, alive at any rate. After that Alperton spent days trying to find her. He hardly slept. I did what I could but John broke every damned rule in the book. I really believe he loved her you know. It was enough to make you weep, David.'

'What happened?'

Connolly poured himself another Scotch and lit another cigarette. 'They'd tied her up and beaten her to death. John found her. An abandoned warehouse in the Podolsk district, about a half-hour south of the city. He never forgave Landslide for that, for not trying to help her, and God knows he could have. Her death destroyed him for a good while. He came back from Moscow a very different man, you see? Started taking those bloody elocution lessons, determined to get to the top at any cost.

That's why Sandy and he never got along. They'd both got their eyes on the prize.'

'And the question that no one wanted to answer at the time was how the hell did the Russians know exactly where she would be?' David shot Ewen a look. 'I thought you said they followed her?'

'Someone did. But I'd never seen these guys before. These guys were hired muscle, not FSB, and definitely not SVR. Whoever was paying them, wasn't from the Russian Secret Service, I'm sure of it.'

'How can you be?'

'Because I found them, David. Whilst John was turning Moscow upside down looking for his girlfriend I went and did a bit of investigating of my own.'

David looked at his old friend. He'd seldom seen him wear such a grim expression. 'Am I going to need a drink for this?'

'A large one, I'd say.'

'Who were they then?'

'I don't know for sure, they weren't big on small talk if you follow me?'

'Ewen.'

'Honestly, I don't. I can't give you names, that's what I mean, but what I can tell you is, they weren't Chechen.'

'How do you know?'

'I threw that in to muddy the waters. I also did some rooting around, found them two days later in a bar, still drunk.'

'And?'

'Initially they weren't too keen to talk, but I managed to persuade one of them.' David could only imagine. 'They were

Russian, David. GRU, David. GR fucking U, Putin's own private band of arseholes.'

Connolly slapped his glass down on the table and David quickly topped it up.

'They step up to the mark, kidnap the girl and drag her off for some one on one time, never really knowing who she is. Once they've beaten the colours of the flag out of her I'm guessing she tells them who her stepdad is and that's when the fun really begins. She assumes that telling them daddy is the deputy director of the SVR will be enough to make them let her go, but instead...'

'It gets her killed.'

'Exactly.'

'Dear God. So, the girl that Alperton was sleeping with, her father was...'

'Step-father,' Connolly interjects, correcting him 'was Aleksei Kadnikov, yes.'

'And all that time she was working for Landslide?'

'That's right. But Kadnikov, Landslide, don't you see it yet? And you, the one I thought saw everything. They're one and the same, David, they're one and the same.'

'Who knew?'

'Me, Pat, now you and Toby Gray.'

'John?'

Ewen shook his head.

'I'm afraid that's not the worst of it though.'

David had assumed as much.

'After a little more digging I was able to ascertain who'd been paying the goons from the GRU.'

'Go on.'

'This whole sordid little escapade was being funded by us, David. The money was coming direct from the British Embassy.'

David Hunter looked up to the ancient ceiling in his tiny cottage in Sarratt. He shouldn't know it was true, but he did. He shouldn't believe Ewen Connolly, but he had to. He'd always known, hadn't he, that something had been deeply flawed with that operation in Moscow? He put his head in his hands and rubbed his eyes. After all, he'd been there, hadn't he? At that fateful de-brief. He'd watched impassively from behind the glass in 15c as Ewen and John Alperton had gone through their pitiful charade. He'd had his finger on the record button as Ewen Connolly had been briefed before being ordered to Istanbul, never to return.

'We sanctioned it, David,' Ewen concluded, tapping the table firmly with his finger to emphasise each and every word. 'Right here. Us.'

If he knows that, how much more does he know, or thinks he knows, David is forced to wonder. He mutters some words of profound astonishment and displeasure and reaches for another drink.

'And where,' David finally asks his oldest friend whilst already knowing the answer, 'did their information come from? If they were working for London,' he takes another healthy slug of Scotch, 'where were they getting their intelligence from?'

'Listen old pal, the information may have come from me, but I didn't pull the trigger.' David reached for the bottle and refilled Ewen's glass. 'Believe me, once I'd joined the dots there was nobody felt sicker about it than I did.'

'Do you know who gave the order from London?' David

asked, not wishing to hear the answer but aware he must discover just how much Ewen knows.

'I don't. Could have been Sandy? He hated the whole idea of the op from the start. I figure he thought he should have been next in line, you see? Once George Wiseman moved on he thought he should have had the top job, not Toby Gray. Then Gray puts this cracking little informer, who just happens to be the deputy director of the fuckin' SVR on the table and with intel to die for and suddenly Sandy's all washed up and yesterday's news. Perhaps he didn't think it would play out quite the way it did but... If he felt he could fuck up his operation and leave the blame on John Alperton's shoulders, well it would have been a win-win scenario as far as he was concerned?'

'And Turkey? Alperton takes revenge by gifting Landslide to the Turks, they saw him into tiny little pieces and chuck him for the fish to feed on? You, me, Pat, we're all just collateral damage as part of some petty little vendetta?' David says, knowing it's a lie.

'No. I don't like Alperton. He's the worst type of English arsehole, but even he wouldn't stoop that low. And anyway, he didn't know who Landslide was, trust me. As far as Alperton's concerned he was just another asset.'

'That only leaves Toby Gray. Why would Toby burn his best asset?'

'You're forgetting. I don't think he was burnt. The body they found bobbing around in the Bosphorus? I've seen Kadnikov with my own eyes remember, I'm one of the few who could identity him. And I can tell you for nothing, head or no head, the body they pulled out of the water was not his. No way.'

'None of that's any use without some proof, Ewen. Did Alperton know about Aleksei?'

'No. His point of contact was Viktorija. To the best of my knowledge he had no idea who was passing her the intel and I don't believe he had the first idea when Kadnikov approached him outside the restaurant that he was actually looking at the source. He swears me to secrecy because he's terrified of what'll happen when he has to tell Wiseman he's had his arse felt by his opposite number, not to mention the girl.'

'None of that's any use without something to back it up with,' David put in.

'You don't seriously think that I'd just bugger off without leaving some form of insurance do you? But then if you do, that can only mean one thing,' Connolly said stabbing out a cigarette in the saucer David had provided him, 'that George Wiseman now has the file.'

'And George is dead, remember?'

'In which case, we're properly screwed.'

'I'll phone Scott and get him to come over tomorrow morning.'

'Good,' Connolly smiled for the first time in a while, 'it'll be nice to see the sneaky little shit again.'

11

By nature a light sleeper David Hunter relished his mornings in Sarratt, the sun's rays washing through the kitchen window sending the night's shadows scampering for cover.

As the espresso machine's primer clicked on, announcing the next step in his daily ritual, David thought about the man who had broken into his house the previous evening. This most unexpected of guests. What did Ewen want and why had he made the journey, the exceptional journey, not to see Sandy Harper, or John Alperton, nor Toby Gray, or even Patricia Hedley-King, née Pat King of the Home Office and subject of his misguided affections all those many years ago. No, Ewen Connolly had made that extraordinary journey to see him and him alone.

David understood the guilt Ewen clearly felt at the fallout from his actions, but then, by understanding David had also forgiven him, guilt being an emotion he understood almost professionally. He poured some coffee beans into the burr grinder which sat next to the sink and did his best to concentrate over the incessant noise of the machine. Much water had passed under the bridge since Istanbul. David's life had eventually settled down following his removal from the service and he had adapted. He'd had to. Following his wife's suicide he'd become a single parent and so, whilst he missed the service, the work and some but not all of the people, when his beautiful Jane had taken her life, his own existence had been thrown into stark relief. He had found himself wholly responsible for another human being. Any help he might have received from Scott's godfather, a long way away.

He tamped down the finely ground coffee into the machine's metal basket, twisted the walnut portafilter handle into place and flicked on the pump. As he stared out of the kitchen window overlooking his garden and listened to the steady drip, drip, drip of thick Italian coffee a thought came to him. Perhaps his unexpected guest had not come to see him after all. Had he flown all this way in order to finally support his godson? If, as Ewen claimed, there was a rotten apple in the service's barrel, it was entirely conceivable Scott would have come into contact with them. Had Ewen come to protect him from this wrongdoer further up what Sandy Harper would have lazily referred to as "the food chain"? Was it possible that Ewen knew with some degree of certainty that that was indeed the case? A gift to David and Jane, his long dead wife from their all too absent, oft supposed deceased, godparent.

David resolved it was time to have it out with Ewen Connolly. It was time they cut out all the crap and just for once were completely honest with one another. He too had things he wished to say, burdens of guilt he wished to share. As he placed his espresso cup in the sink there was a knock at the front door.

'Scott, come in. Sorry, I'm not dressed, bit of a late night,'

David said more than a little sheepishly. 'We were just about to sit and have breakfast.'

'He's here then? After everything he said in China, he's here?'

'Upstairs. I'll give him a shout, we can have breakfast together and then, I don't know, take a walk? Maybe lunch at the pub. There's plenty we need to talk about, I think that's clear.'

Scott began scouring his father's kitchen for plates and cutlery leaving his father to rouse their unexpected guest, but even as David's foot planted on the first stair he already suspected what he would find when he reached the top. He had, thanks to the whisky they'd imbibed, slept soundly through the night and so wasn't surprised when, after knocking several times and then tentatively pushing open the door to his seldom occupied guest bedroom, he found it empty, the bed still made. Ewen had done what he'd become so famous for and run away, again. David swore silently under his breath several times and then, still cursing his errant friend returned downstairs to see if Ewen had at least left him his aged Volvo, or whether that too had disappeared in the middle of the night. Seeing the rusting estate languishing in his driveway David found himself thrown back several years. He was standing not at his own front door, nor the door to his guest room, but to room 1205 of the Marmara Hotel, Istanbul, his head in his hands as he stared in disbelief at the long abandoned bed in Ewen Connolly's room. But this time the situation was subtly different. He wouldn't have to explain anything to Sandy Harper or the service for one thing, and perhaps more importantly he knew where Connolly was, or at least where he was headed. He wouldn't be there just yet, the journey would take almost a day, but David Hunter was confident. As he closed his eyes to the morning sun he saw the exact spot where his friend was bound. Ewen had taken him there many, many years before. Momentarily it crossed his mind that he should follow him, but this was work for a younger man. A job to be undertaken by the next generation, by David's son, Ewen's godson and the real reason the Scotsman had returned.

'He's gone, Scott, and you need to get after him and bring him back.'

'*Again*?'

'Again. You talked him round once before. He'll listen to you, I know he will.'

'Why bother, Dad?' Scott asked a trifle petulantly.

'Because we were all wrong. I assumed that Ewen went rogue to protect Pat King, in the same way we assumed he'd been brought back to dish the dirt on her. The service assumed that he'd just gone bad and buggered off to sell his soul to the Russians. We were all wrong. He'd long since worked out that she wasn't involved. Someone wanted him dead because he knew who Landslide was, not because he was in bed with him. He isn't here to blow the whistle on Hedley-King, he's here to expose whoever set her up. If Landslide's a Russian asset, Ewen knows who they were and more importantly, who was in their pocket.'

'He didn't tell you last night?'

'Even after all this time, he's terrified. Added to which he's probably trying to protect me, and you.'

'How was Landslide's intel brought out of Russia, do you know?'

'It could have been any number of ways. Microfilm predominantly, but then copies of the originals and even, on one occasion I'm told, the original material itself.'

'Who did the carrying?'

'That's where it gets interesting. John Alperton was a young agent back then, sent out posing as a French tourist.'

'Are you saying Alperton's double crossed us?'

'There was a scene, with a girl. It didn't end well. The girl died. Alperton's story was always that some thugs followed him back to his hotel, found him and the girl together. There was some pushing and shoving, she went over, cracked her head and died. It was an accident.'

'How was Ewen involved?'

'He was supposed to be keeping an eye on things. He told us that he turned up just in time to see the muscle leave and John Alperton kneeling over the body of a dead Russian national.'

'*He told us*? You don't sound very convinced, Dad?'

'I never was. Too many things just weren't right. For one, can you imagine a scenario where Ewen Connolly just sat back and did nothing? He was always the first to the scene of a fight, that was one of the reasons we recruited him.'

'And?'

'And he and Alperton never quite got their stories straight. There were always inconsistences. For instance, after the girl died, if she died in the way Ewen described it, the pair of them should have been beating down the doors at the British Embassy. Ewen said they went to a safe house he knew. Not a bad call given the circumstances, but not procedure and not by a long way. Then, once they're there, Ewen said they never left the place, but then Alperton tells us Ewen slipped out for some bread and booze. I remember thinking at the time that I'd never heard such a load of rubbish. And the really extraordinary thing, how none of this was questioned at the time. Alperton went to recuperate in Paris and they sent Ewen off to Istanbul, and we all know what happened there,' David said with a wry smile. 'But last night, when we got talking, Ewen told me that not only was he not out at the local supermarket buying bread and sticky buns, but that the girl didn't die in the hotel but was dragged off. He also said that Alperton tore up half of Moscow looking for her, and when he did eventually track her down she'd been beaten to death. Sounded like she was tortured and then killed. Ewen found the men responsible and traced them back to their employers.'

'Who were?'

'He wouldn't say.'

'Where is he then?'

'A warm Sunday in May? I've a pretty fair idea. I don't think we ever took you to Brora, did we? I'd lend you my car but I'm not sure it would make it.'

Hunter's phone pinged with a fresh text message from Michael Healy.

Hope you've had a nice holiday, see you at the gym tomorrow, 8am and don't be late.

'Your lord and master?' his father asked.

Ignoring him, Scott quickly replied.

Sorry, have to go to Inverness to catch up with a long lost relative.

He didn't have long to wait for Healy's reply.

Sounds important. Anything I can do to help?

A car would be good. Scott typed quickly. *Preferably four-wheel drive.*

Again Michael Healy's reply came back surprisingly swiftly.

There'll be a jeep waiting for you outside the Royal Hotel,

Inverness. Keys under the driver side wheel-arch and a room booked for Mr Frost.

'Seems as though I'm going to Scotland,' Scott said to his father.

David drove his son around the M25 to Watford Junction and the railway station, where tickets were waiting in his name. He settled back in his seat. The journey up the east coast to Edinburgh and then on and north to Inverness would take most of the day, and all to do a job he'd already done once. His godfather was proving to be an evasive character, but this time, providing the information his father had given him was correct, he knew where to find Ewen Connolly.

***

The first thing Hunter saw on leaving Inverness Station was The Royal Highland Hotel and opposite that, as Healy had promised, a small green Toyota 4x4 with a parking ticket stuck to its windscreen. Hunter removed the ticket and threw it and his overnight bag onto the passenger seat. Healy had said to trust no one, so Hunter decided to pass up the offer of a room in the name of Mr Frost and strike on and up the coast. By his reckoning and assuming the information his father had supplied proved correct, he still had the best part of an hour's drive ahead of him.

The A9 wound up the east coast, hugging the shoreline when it wasn't crossing bridges. Hunter was enjoying the drive. The scenery was breathtaking and there was always the chance that he might see a seal bobbing languorously in the Moray Firth. He even found a serene beauty in the partially constructed oilrigs which were being towed out to sea, their stanchions covered with twinkling lights, like giant floating Christmas decorations.

Small towns and villages came and went. Dingwall, Invergordon and Tain, until his mobile phone informed him that he had reached Golspie. He swung the car off the main road and onto a single track which immediately broke away and headed for the hills. His phone said he would reach his destination in approximately half-an-hour. It was half-past nine but with the sun finally beginning to set and Hunter unable to imagine anyone out on the hills after dark, he elected to turn back and find somewhere to sleep for the night. On the opposite side of the road he'd just left, a small town boasting a bar, a distillery and a beleaguered row of boarded up shops.

The Rob Roy Hotel wasn't wasting a square inch in paying tribute to its titular patron. The entry hall was carpeted in a rich red tartan, stags' heads and life-size murals of the Jacobite hero in any number of threatening poses lined the walls. Hunter secured himself a room for the night, popped a couple of Healy's little pink tablets and slept.

***

The following morning, after a hearty Scottish breakfast, he thanked the owner, threw his few belongings into the back of the jeep and retraced his route of the previous evening to where his phone showed a path which struck off from the main road and up into the hills. After a quarter of a mile and with the jeep's wheels skidding and slipping on the loose shale, Hunter was forced to stop. A quick consultation of the jeep's handbook and he discovered a smaller lever next to the handbrake, which, with a little cajoling threw the jeep into four-wheel drive.

The path he was crawling up must have been a logging route, Hunter decided. Signs of fresh timber being hauled away were scattered everywhere. Large open tracks which he imagined had been home to Scots pine or Douglas fir now nakedly surrounded the car. A little further on and he was forced to jump from the jeep to open a gate. The path, which had barely been adequate now all but completely disappeared. And all the time Hunter was climbing and with no end in sight. A white chested Osprey briefly circled overhead perhaps searching for its mate, gliding effortlessly on magical currents before sweeping majestically low over the car and disappearing off towards the opposite side of the hill.

Hunter followed the direction the bird had taken up the long winding track until eventually as he knew it must, it came to an abrupt and ignominious end. The path, such as it was, ceased to be altogether and so Hunter was finally forced to abandon the jeep. The owner of the pub had been good enough to lend him a pair of binoculars he kept for deer stalking. Hunter threw the leather strap over his neck and struck out towards the top of the hill.

He lay on the warm damp moss and let the sun caress his back. The lip of the hill, before the gentle descent to the loch, had been tough going, stones sliding beneath his feet as he struggled for grip. Then cresting the hill he had been faced with the most extraordinary sight. Dark green mountains, their tops still wearing the last of the winter's snow lay in front of him, before disappearing off into a hazy horizon. In the volcanic pit beneath him, nature had created a perfect basin full of rippling blue-green water. Between Hunter and the glassy loch an undulating hill of smooth mosses and heathers descending to a pebbly beach at the end of which perched a single lonely hut. Too big to be a shed, too small to properly be called a boathouse, although Hunter surmised, that was clearly its purpose. A 15ft wooden clinker gliding serenely across the heart of the loch, a rope trailing hopefully from its ring towards the glistening water.

Hunter had his father back and now there was this man from his childhood, his godparent, bobbing about happily in his boat at the centre of a remote loch and looking so content and peaceful in his surroundings. Hunter's father had explained that this was where Ewen came to think and now he saw him patiently flicking his line at small eddies in the water it made such total sense. Hunter could imagine him as a young man, an attentive father by his side, helping with flies and knots, then demonstrating the complicated cast, handing down his knowledge to the next generation of Scottish fly fisherman and the pleasure that that would have given him.

On the water there was a brief flurry of activity. Hunter watched as Connolly delicately shifted his balance in the tiny vessel as it slapped and swayed lightly beneath him, speculating as to the reason for such a sudden movement. Then a concentric ring of circles broke to the left of the boat and he saw the hump of a fish crest and disappear. The object of his godfather's attentions. His arm went back in one sharp fluid motion and then flicked as quickly forward presenting his fly a foot or so beyond the rising fish. Then... nothing.

Hunter, who had never seen anyone fish before felt an acute pang of disappointment for his godfather and was wondering if *he* would have the patience to stand in all weathers on the off-chance he might catch something, when there was another burst of activity. Through his binoculars he saw the mouth of the trout suck in the fly, flash its tail clear of the water and then plunge deep into the loch's murky depths. And as it did this, a tremendous curve appeared in Ewen's rod. Hunter repositioned his binoculars to better see his godfather who was allowing line to stream from the reel. Then, as the rod's curve diminished, he began to take control of the line and of the fish on the other end. Hunter was fascinated to see how Connolly guided his prey, playing it away from a patch of reeds, gently discouraging it from diving under the boat, and finally persuading it to the surface. Twice it made a valiant attempt to break from its captor, but Connolly's control was inexorable. With the fish gasping for air on the top of the water Connolly bent, reaching for his landing net. Calmly he slid it under the trout and carefully brought his catch back in. Hunter watched him unhook and quickly dispatch the fish and then, as Connolly examined his fly to cast again, Hunter reached his decision. He would not trouble his godparent, at least not straight away. He would allow him this peaceful moment of reflection. Once he was done, whenever that might be, Hunter would approach him and try, for a second time, to convince him to head south and talk to persons unknown about Landslide.

The decision made, Hunter smiled and placed the binoculars on the ground in front of him. And that was when he heard the pop and whizz as a bullet raced past his head.

***

Ewen Connolly, once of Six, part time gunrunner, money

launderer and occasional godfather pinched the small tuft of duck's feather between thumb and forefinger. It had been an age since he'd fished these waters. Following some advice in the local pub the previous evening he had decided on the smaller size 16 hook today, brown trout being a more selective quarry than their brutish rainbow cousins.

After so many years, this felt like a very real and intensely personal homecoming. He threaded the hook in his gently swaying boat and took in the mountains which surrounded the small loch he had chosen, steeped in heather their purples and lilacs built an intense carpet of colours. This was home. *He* was home.

As was so often the way with fishing and fishermen, the simple act of being there, at one with nature, far outweighed the actual catching of any fish. Ewen understood better than most how tricky wild brownies could be, he'd fished this loch and its neighbours as a child, enthralled by his father's taciturn adventures. His unerring ability to flick a dry fly onto the nose of a rising fish. As a small boy he'd learnt that this was where his father came to think, to clear his mind. And now it was where he had come.

He checked his knot and applied a dab of gink to the line. Perhaps this change would be the one, the killer fly. He stripped out a good length, *not too much* his father would have cautioned, *there's no need*. He visualised where he wanted his fly to land and flicked the boat rod back. The line swished behind him and then, feeling the power in the cane, he drew his hand quickly back, level with his ear and the line shot forward followed by the tiny blob of grey duck's feather wrapped around the shank of a barbless size 16.

What was he to do? He'd unburdened himself considerably at David Hunter's house. Was that enough, or ought he to see this business through to its bitter end? Should he act on his suspicions or was that simply too dangerous? Wasn't he obliged to do something? Obligation. His life had been one long obligation. Was it now out of the question to contact Pat? He knew she'd married, had had and lost a family. But none of that mattered. Did he want to see her and how would she relish the idea of a long dead spy turning up on her doorstep and telling her what he should have told her so many years before?

Not more than a foot from his offering a trout rose, breaking the surface and sucking down a fly. Ewen smiled and swore, quietly. Quickly he stripped in the line. One false cast and then he attempted to cover the fish as his father would have done.

The memories came flooding back. Twenty years of memories. Of waiting anxiously for his unrequited love to return, for Pat King to return from her first assignment, the assignment he had briefed her for so carefully. An assignment he had walked her through on several occasions to be sure that nothing should go wrong. Taking her hand in the bazaar, kidding on, despite the age difference, that they were a couple of giddy honeymooners. Sipping the sweet apple tea together at strategically positioned tables so she might scope the place out, all the while wishing he were able to rest his hand on her knee, stroke her hair. Then he had sent her on her way, as ready and prepared as was possible, and he had waited, pacing in his hotel room and wishing he'd still smoked. When she had finally returned, her eyes puffy and red with tears, her cheeks blackened with mascara, he'd wanted to take her in his arms and tell her everything would be alright but hadn't dared to, instead electing to sit at a discreet distance, at the other end of his bed.

Tell me everything, he had said, and she had. A huge outpouring of emotions, of failure and despair. And he had been what, furious, disappointed? No. He, Ewen Connolly, ex-army, good with his fists and a gun had been terrified, his mind filling with the immutable truth of their situation. There had been so few options available to him. He had felt blinkered, like one of Sandy's dumb bloody horses. And that was when he had taken the decision which would shape the rest of his life. He had gone to the bathroom and found the file on Aleksei Kadnikov which he'd hidden there and he'd insisted she take it. She, he'd told her firmly, would know what to do with it if and when the time ever came. And then he'd given her all the money he could spare and made her promise to get back to England as quickly as she possibly could. People would be coming, sent from London, to hold them to account. Better she was not there. He would do the talking, make sure she was alright. He'd tutored her through the story again and again until she was hoarse from repeating it and then he'd told her an address in London NW3. A safe house and the people she was to speak to and the people she was not to speak to. As soon as you land, he had said, you are to phone George Wiseman on this number and no other or David Hunter on this number and no other. They will make sure you are looked after. There had been tears in her eyes as she had begun to understand exactly what he was doing for her. She had started to understand that this man, Ewen Connolly, a man she knew a little and respected a lot, was about to sacrifice everything for her. But why was he doing this, she had wanted to know. And he had spun her a tale, told her the buck stopped with him, she was not to blame. He'd even reassured her, even though she knew he was never coming back, that he would see her again soon, once the dust had settled. Take the file he had insisted. You are to give it to George Wiseman and George Wiseman alone. A man that he had met once before and then only briefly, but a man who came with the highest of personal recommendations. His friend, his drinking partner, the man who had asked him to be godfather to his only son, David Hunter spoke only great things of Wiseman, and if Wiseman was good enough for David, Ewen would entrust this, his most valued piece of information and the life of his most precious friend, Pat King, into his hands. You are to find George Wiseman as soon as you are able and give him this, and he had managed a smile at that and she had almost returned his smile. And she had cried and cried until he had become cross and angry. Go and pack your bags, there will be a plane home first thing, you must be ready to leave the hotel and take that plane. Do not hesitate. Never look back.

Other memories fogged his mind. A young boy, his godson, and a bear, a red bear with small white polka-dot spots that they had christened, what? Too many years had passed and he had forgotten, but he still remembered his English friend and his lost wife. The bear though, what had been the name of that bear? He recalled buying it. He'd been in Berlin, working of course, but had found the time to visit a Christmas market. He had always found time for the boy, until Istanbul. Until Landslide.

Ewen heard the crack and in that instant he knew, because it was a sound he knew all too well. A sound he'd heard often as it had reverberated through reticent subterranean tunnels buried deep beneath a neglected Victorian railway bridge near Clapham, SW4. A sound he'd grown to love, the snap of the

SA80. And suddenly there wasn't time to think about the consequences of the noise, there wasn't time for regret, reflection, sorrow, or sadness of any kind. There was just the moment of falling and then darkness.

Aloysius.

***

Hunter watched in horror as his godfather's head snapped back. His body crumpled under its own weight and the rod slipped from his hands, clattering to the bottom of the boat. He fell in slow motion, his knees folding, arms unnaturally by his sides. There was no need to call for help, to examine the body. Ewen Connolly, David Hunter's long-estranged friend, Scott's godfather and one of the few people to know the true identity of the man they called Landslide, was dead.

Fighting every instinct to run, Hunter kept his head down, pressed deep into the thick gorse. If the shooter had seen him he might well be his next target. He resolved to lie as still as he could, measure his breathing and when he thought enough time had passed, get as far away from the loch as possible.

When he did eventually look up, Hunter was surprised to see just how far the boat had drifted. The only sign of Connolly, the tip of his boat rod poking over the side. The boat had been blown by a slight breeze to the other side of the loch, where it bumped and jostled in the bed of reeds which might once have provided sanctuary for Connolly's catch, but were now, along with fifteen feet of tangled drogue, his final resting place.

The shot had come from behind Hunter, from where he'd left the jeep. Foolish to turn and head straight back the way he had come. Cautiously he retrieved his binoculars, swung them around his neck and, crouching, ran down to the bank. From there he moved as quickly as he thought prudent around the loch, away from the boat and to a new position. Looking up he made out an outcrop of boulders to the west. If he could just make it there, they would provide enough cover whilst he reconnoitred the track on the other side to the jeep. He beat a path up and through the heather and quickly flattened himself at the base of the boulders, then, taking the hotel manager's binoculars he inched his way around the sandy base of the rocks to where he could see better. Nothing moved and so Hunter swept the binoculars down and along in hope of spotting the jeep.

From where he lay only the roof of the vehicle was visible and so he crawled out from his cover and slowly moved down, keeping parallel with the track. Now he was exposed and if the shooter were still present it would be easy work to pick him off. A broom bush sat blowing imperiously in the wind twenty feet away. The sharp shards of slate and shale were digging painfully into his knees and elbows. Gorse was whipping at his face making his cheeks sting and burn. But once at the broom he was able to relax a little. He put the binoculars to his eyes again. The jeep was clearly visible now but was not alone. Stood next to it, an elderly gentleman. Hunter doubted he could be the shooter. This man was either the local ghillie-cum-gamekeeper or a well-to-do landowner. He wore rough Harris tweed trousers, a thick fleece and expensive looking Wellington boots, on his head a deerstalker covered in salmon flies and propped up by Hunter's jeep a hazel walking stick with a ram's horn handle. As Hunter adjusted the binoculars, cleaning up the image, the ghillie turned. He had been making a phone call. When Hunter saw what was resting on the passenger's seat of the jeep, the nature of the phone call became immediately apparent. Resting on its stock an Enfield SA80, complete with telescopic sight. At once Hunter knew several things with complete confidence. This was the gun which had killed Ewen Connolly, and this was almost certainly the gun he had trained with in the service's damp and claustrophobic dungeon in Clapham. He didn't need to be able to see the deep gouge running down one side of its stock, he knew how these people worked. And he knew he was being set up.

Hunter had to get to civilisation and as quickly as possible, but the GPS on his phone had chosen this moment to drop out. Someone was winding up Landslide and that meant they would be coming for anyone who'd been a part of the operation. Ewen Connolly, was just the tip of the iceberg. Hunter thought of all the other people who might join his godfather, and then it struck him. His own father must surely be in danger. As he observed the farmer and his jeep another vehicle approached. A police car, certainly from the nearby town and presumably at the behest of the farmer. Hunter would have to find another way. The main road was out, like his GPS, but he could just see the tip of nearby headland before it broke, heading down towards the sea. As long as he kept the sea to his left, he would be heading south and sooner or later he was bound to come upon a coastal village or town where he would... what? Hitch a lift? Steal a car? For the time being that decision would have to wait. But now, and not for the first time in his brief life he had to get as far away from the police as he could.

12

Having travelled through the night, Hunter retraced his steps to West Norwood and easily found Boden Road. Halfway along and on the opposite side of the road, that was where he remembered Williams's house being. Hunter checked down both sides of the street. There was no sign of his yellow fiesta. He peered up the path at the olive-green front door, chipped and cracking. Half a dozen swift strides and Hunter planted the base of his right foot squarely next to the lock. The wood, old and rotting on either side, splintered, and the door sagged. Another firmer kick and the lock tore from its mountings and the door swung open. Hunter reached behind him and withdrew the Glock from the top of his trousers. Sweeping the pistol across the empty hallway as Williams had taught him he moved into the house. No sound came from upstairs and he shouldered his way into the sitting room following the Glock, any element of surprise already stolen by his size tens. He hadn't been sure what to expect; a three-piece suite perhaps and television? Williams himself? But the room was empty, completely bare, no people, no furniture, no pictures or paintings. Nothing. And in that instant Hunter understood. He would clear the rest of the house, but only through a strange compulsion that would not let him leave the job unfinished, but he already suspected what he would find and that would be more nothing. Gary Williams had never lived there, not in the true sense of the word. It was a safe house. There might be a table in the kitchen, a bed in one of the rooms upstairs, but that would probably be all, just like Harrow.

And then he smelt it, a strange mixture of tobacco and vanilla. Hunter followed the smell, moved to the end of the lounge and the door leading into the kitchen. Increasingly certain he already knew who was on the other side he checked his gun and twisted the doorknob.

'Hello, Scott.' Sat at the kitchen table, an e-cigarette clutched reluctantly in one hand, the owner of the BMW and the expensive suits who had helped Hunter once upon a time. 'How are you?'

'Where's Williams?'

'Why?'

'I'm going to kill him,' and then, as something of an afterthought 'And who are you?'

'My name is Sir John Alperton, and I'm your boss. You might do well to remember that, Scott.'

'You helped me once when I needed to get to my father's.'

'I have known your father for many years, Scott,' Alperton continued with a smile. 'He is a truly incredible man.'

Hunter wasn't certain how to take this fresh piece of information so decided to press on.

'And now you're here to what, arrest me?'

'God no. Why on earth would I want to do that?'

'I've just watched Ewen Connolly get shot in the head.'

'I know,' Alperton replied coolly.

'And I'm pretty sure whoever did it is trying to set me up.'

'Yes, I expect you're probably right, Scott. But what makes you think I would have anything to do with that?'

'I know you've always wanted Ewen dead.'

'And where did that misguided idea come from?'

'He told me.'

The older man sighed. 'There was a time, yes, when I'd have been quite happy for Ewen Connolly to quietly disappear, but with the years has come fresh information.'

'About Landslide?'

'Landslide is the key to everything, Scott.'

'But now Ewen's dead you'll never know who he was, will you?'

'That is also not quite true. There is a lady, and I use the word advisedly, who lives in Chiswick, West London...'

'Miss White?'

'Indeed. Right now, Michael Healy is sat outside her house, as I believe you should be. I want you and Michael to go and introduce yourselves and ask her to attend a little gathering I have arranged.'

'Where?'

'You've certainly inherited your father's directness, I like that. Obfuscation is such a boring trait. The Traitors Gate Public house in Bermondsey.'

'Alright.'

'Thank you, Scott. But before you go, one last thing. I shall expect you to pay for the damage incurred to the front door, do you understand? Now Michael will be waiting. Off you go.'

***

Hunter walked from Turnham Green Tube, across a desolate strip of parkland, towards South Acton and Radnor Road. At the end of a line of silver birch and anonymous semis he paused, acutely aware that all was not quite right with the world. Upon reflection he couldn't be sure Williams had shot Connolly and John Alperton had certainly done little to confirm or deny it. That only left Michael Healy and if he'd been responsible for setting him up Hunter was going to have to tread extremely carefully. He felt the butt of the Glock resting reassuringly at the base of his spine. There was White's house, quiet at the moment.

Five past eight.

There was the blacked-out Audi, Michael Healy at the wheel. A small huddle of commuters walked past and so Hunter tagged along behind, putting them between himself and the car. Then, once he was alongside the passenger door of the A4 he stopped, withdrew the Glock and tapped it on the window. The door unlocked and he swung into the passenger seat.

'What the hell are you doing here?' Healy barked at him, 'and put that bloody thing away.'

'No. Not until I get some answers.'

'But you shouldn't be here. Did I text you?'

'No. Alperton sent me.'

Hunter jabbed the Glock into Healy's stomach.

'What are you doing? What's going on?' Healy asked ignoring the gun.

'I should be asking you. The rifle in my car? Your idea I presume. Ewen Conolly's dead. No one knew about my trip up north other than you.'

'I don't know what you're talking about and get that bloody thing away from me.'

'You set me up.'

'No.'

'I went to Scotland to keep an eye on Connolly, see if I couldn't talk him into telling his side of the story, and the next thing I know, he's been shot and the police are all over my car, sniffing around a bloody sniper's rifle.'

'I don't know what you're talking about, Scott.'

Eight minutes past eight.

The last of Radnor Road's office staff were leaving for the day.

'What we should be asking is, why are you here now?'

'Miss White. Alperton said she's to be invited to a meeting. Okay?'

'Okay. No time like the present I suppose, let's go.'

They looked up Radnor Road. Parked outside Miss White's house was an elderly Volkswagen and from behind the Volkswagen emerged a figure.

Hunter recognised her immediately.

'Samantha. Now what the hell is she up to?'

The pretty girl Hunter had last seen pouring him a drink in her flat was walking quickly towards them. She was clearly agitated, struggling to prevent herself breaking into a run. As she reached the car Hunter threw open the passenger door, catching her and throwing her to the ground. He sprang out and grabbed her wrist with his free hand, pushing the Glock into her ribs and forcing her into the back of the Audi. Healy locked the doors.

'Hello, Samantha.'

'Scott, you shouldn't be here.'

'I wish people would stop telling me that.'

Ten minutes past eight.

'You need to go. Now.'

Michael Healy turned from the driver's seat to face her.

'Who are you? Who are you working for?'

'My name's Samantha Fairchild. I'm a student, I'm not working for anybody.'

'Bull.'

'It's the truth, look here's my student card.'

'Sam, who's Kazimir Malevich?' Hunter asked remembering one of the books he'd seen in her flat.

'I told you, I don't know. I'm just an arts' student at Middlesex Uni.'

Healy and Hunter exchanged glances.

'Who are you working for, Sam?'

'I don't know. I've never even heard of Malevich I swear. I need to get back.'

'Shoot her,' Healy snapped at Hunter.

'What?'

'Shoot her. If she won't tell you, shoot her.'

Hunter racked the Glock whilst Healy scrambled to find his mobile phone.

'Do it now, Scott.'

'But...' Hunter hesitated.

'She's an arts' student who's never heard of Kazimir Malevich, shoot her.'

'Please,' Sam was shrieking, 'they did the same to me. Put me in the flat below yours, then out every day doing a bunch of pointless exercises.'

Eleven minutes past eight.

'Someone must have been training you?' Healy barked at her. 'Just not very well.'

Hunter pushed the pistol into her stomach.

'Come on, Samantha. For Christ's sake tell him who you're working for.'

'I can't. He'll kill me.'

'He may not get the chance. Scott, shoot her now or I will,' Healy said producing his firearm.

'Bennet. Robert Bennet.'

'Fuckin' hell.' Bob Bennett, his ex-partner? Jesus, Healy thought the old bastard was dead. Well, not dead exactly, but retired, which to Healy amounted to one and the same. He'd gone to some half-arsed drinks' party to mark the occasion, shaken his hand, wished him all the best, only part of which he'd meant. Christ, he'd even bought him a bloody present.

'We shouldn't be here. It's not safe.' Sam was pleading now.

'Why do you keep saying that? What do you mean it's not safe? Samantha? What's going to happen? What were you doing by that car?'

'We watched the same house for weeks. Bit of a drive, out in the country. Nice old guy. Then Robert had me doing the drop,' she was rambling.

Healy pointed his PPK at the girl's head.

'Explain. Tell me what the hell is going on or so help me God I'll blow your pretty little head off.'

'Pull up at the target, out of the car, make like you've dropped your keys, take the box and stuff it under the driver's side wheel,' she continued as if no longer hearing Michael Healy.

'Wait!' Hunter shouted, 'let me out of the car!'

'What?'

'Let me out of the car, now!'

Healy waved the gun at the girl. 'Don't get any funny ideas, missy. You stay put. Scott, what the hell do you think you're doing?'

'What's the time?'

'Eight twelve.'

'Sam, have you ever been to this address before?'

'Never.'

'Ever heard of it until the text this morning?'

'No.'

'There's a bomb under that car. It's set to go off in less than thirty seconds, and the only way she and Bennet could possibly have known where and when to place it would be from the information *we've* been gathering. Where does that information go, Michael?'

Healy shook his head.

'Who does it go to Healy? There's a lot more at stake than I think you realise.'

'There always is,' he said. 'I pass everything up to a man called Harper.'

'Let me out of the car now. Warn my father and call an ambulance!'

The locks clicked up and Hunter sprinted towards 28 Radnor Road, shouting at bemused passers-by to take cover as he went.

The explosion lifted the tiny Volkswagen off its wheels and tore through the front of the house showering the pavement with glass. The windows of surrounding buildings were sucked from their frames by the blast wave. And then a quite sudden and equally shocking stillness. The most unnatural stillness, before a choir of car and burglar alarms and the screams of terrified local residents rend the air.

***

A clean white noise tore through Hunter's head. He ran his hands slowly over his extremities, making sure he was still in one piece. A thick coating of dust and rubble covered his face. He daren't open his eyes until he'd brushed away as much as he was able. And then there was the deafening ringing in his ears. He was about to try and get to his feet when he felt hands over his face, brushing away at the dust. Soft, feminine hands.

Hunter opened his eyes.

'Samantha!'

Her lips were moving noiselessly. He shouted her name again. Now she was gesturing frantically at him. It took a moment.

Was he alright? She was waving her fingers in his face.

'There was a bomb,' he shouted back.

I know, she nodded. And then he was remembering and with the remembering his hearing began to return too. He tried to grab her leather jacket but his body wouldn't let him and she stepped easily out of his grasp

'You! You did this!' Hunter screamed at her.

'Come on, Scott, we did this. You provided the intel, I just showed up with the box that went bang. How many fingers?' she continued waving her hand in front of his face, 'Oh who cares, you're fine.'

He lunged for her again, still on unsteady legs.

'It's the job, Scott,' Samantha was shouting, grinning from ear to ear and giddy with the excitement. 'Don't tell me you didn't get a hell of a kick out of that?'

Hunter had been brought up never to strike a lady, but he was considering making an exception for Samantha.

'That was great! What a noise. And you,' she laughed, 'you were like, running into the middle of it all, like some bloody lunatic, and then, blam!' She shot her hands up to where the ceiling ought to have been and mimed the devastation at their feet.

'Where's Michael?'

'Your friend with the short temper and the winning smile? He got a phone call just as things were getting explosive round here,' she said with a smirk, 'and set off like a bat out of hell.'

'What about White?'

'Who?'

'The woman you tried to blow up. Where is she?' Hunter was shouting against the lasting deafness left by the explosion.

'Hear that siren?'

'What?'

'The *siren*. That's her leaving in an ambulance. She was thrown clear of the house by the blast.'

'How was she?'

'Impossible to say.'

They walked away from the front of the house as masonry continued to fall. 'You're a piece of work Samantha.'

'Listen, they did to me what they did to you. I think you can call me Sam now, don't you?'

'The quiet little village?'

'Yeah, with the nice old guy?'

'Is it called Sarratt?'

'Yeah, Sarratt. How could you know that?'

'Just a hunch. What were you doing there?'

'I told you. Watching the old boy. Can't imagine why though. Seemed to spend most his time in the garden.'

'And?'

'And what?'

'Once you'd finished observing, then what?'

'I don't know.'

Hunter grabbed her roughly by her biker's jacket.

'Then what, Samantha?'

'I don't know, honestly, now get off me.' Hunter loosened his grip. 'Maybe he was going to get one of those boxes under his car,' she grinned, 'but we should probably tame the next one down a touch. Jesus, that nearly destroyed the whole street.'

Hunter's phone beeped as a text message came through and he turned and began to walk away.

'I'll be seeing you then, Scott Hunter,' she called after him.

'I sincerely hope not.'

'Hey, come on now!' she was protesting.

Hunter turned on her.

'The nice old guy you seem to like so much and were thinking about blowing up.'

'Yeah, what about him?'

'That's my dad, Sam.'

'Oh.'

'Not cool, Sam. Really not cool.'

'Okay, I get it.'

Hunter turned and walked away.

'But we're good right?' she shouted after him. 'I mean, you know, I didn't blow your old man up, did I? Scott? Scott!'

Hunter raised a hand but kept walking. 'Bye, Samantha.'

'You're not still pissed off about the other night,' she shouted after him. 'Don't take it so personally, it was just training!'

'For what?' Hunter shouted back, never slowing his pace.

'Oh, come on!'

***

Events were now moving with an unbridled swiftness, a swiftness David Hunter was recalling with all the pleasure of recaptured youth. Following his conversation with Ewen Connolly, David was more certain than ever that his life was now in danger. Then he'd received an anonymous phone call which had only confirmed his suspicions. He drew the sitting room curtains and looked past his beloved Volvo and into the lane. Any doubts he'd had that the car parked menacingly on the track beyond contained a spook sent to keep an eye on him, or worse, long gone. It was difficult for David to be absolutely certain, but today the man in the driver's seat appeared to be alone, which would make his task a little simpler, although he still had to presume the driver was armed.

David made a quick and rather awkward telephone call to Jerry the neighbour to whom he rarely spoke. In all the years of living next to the man, this was one of their longest conversation. Then he went to the small wooden shed at the end of his garden.

The next time he looked out and past his Volvo he was pleased to see the situation had changed dramatically. Sat atop Nixon, a 16-hand heavyweight cob, his neighbour was remonstrating noisily with the man in the car. David eased open his front door, slipped past the Volvo and was quickly and quietly at the rear of the black Audi.

'I couldn't give two fucks about your rights. This is a bridle path and you are blocking it. If you don't move your car, I shall have no alternative but to call the police.'

David listened with amusement to the heated exchange as he eased the three-pronged cultivator fork under the Audi's rear wheel. A quick push down on its ash handle and two of its three prongs sank satisfyingly into the tyre. David twisted the fork out and went to work on the other one. Then he sat and waited for his neighbour to finish his routine.

'I tell you what, why don't you just bugger off back to London, you complete...'

The final words of their exchange lost as Jerry pulled on Nixon's reins and the animal under him shuddered noisily, churning up the gravel as it turned. David caught his neighbour's eye as he steered Nixon back to the paddocks, a huge grin painted across his face. Now David had to act quickly, whilst the driver's window was still down. He leapt to his feet and stepped briskly forward, pushing the muzzle of the Super-Star into the base of Bob Bennett's neck and praying the man would not call his bluff.

'Hands. Up where I can see them, please.'

Bob Bennett instinctively reached for the keys swinging temptingly in the ignition.

'I wouldn't bother,' David continued, waving the fork in his other hand. 'Now, if you wouldn't mind stepping out of the car, throwing your keys into the bushes, and walking slowly up to the house, I think we need to have a little chat, don't you?'

Bennett sighed. Why hadn't he taken it? He'd been offered a

healthy retirement package, so why hadn't he just done the sensible thing and taken it? His wife would have thanked him, and he could have been sitting in his local having a pint and watching the football.

Following a firm and frank conversation, David Hunter climbed into his car, crunched it into first gear and headed for London.

***

Michael Healy, Bennett's old partner, sat in his Audi and did his job. He waited. He was getting used to waiting outside The Traitors Gate Pub in Bermondsey. Today though, well today was quite different. In recent months, since Bennett's supposed departure, he'd grown used to taking orders from Toby Gray. But then today Healy had almost been blown up and discovered that not only had Bob Bennett not retired but that he was still extremely active. Then, quite out of the blue, he'd received a message from Bridget Crowther, his old boss's secretary, asking him to get down to Bermondsey as quickly as he could. He hadn't questioned her, well you didn't, but he was beginning to wonder what the hell was going on.

Healy was quietly pleased to be working for Sir John again. Toby Gray was fine, succinct and clear with his instructions, some might have said bordering on the perfunctory, but there was something about him which had always unsettled Healy. He was guarded, well who wasn't in their line of work? But he was duplicitous too. Ditto, he thought with a smile. Healy simply wasn't convinced that if push had come to shove and the shit had really hit the fan, Toby Gray would have been there to stand by him, pick up the pieces and do what needed to be done. He might do what was best for Tobias Gray, but for Michael Healy, he doubted it. He doubted it very much.

His thoughts wandered to Scott Hunter, he wondered how he was getting on. He'd left the girl to pull him from the rubble on Radnor Road. Scott had certainly changed a great deal since their first meeting. The trip to China had done him good, he was much more self-assured, confident and able to take the lead, all things which Healy realised he valued. All things he was looking for in a new partner. Certainly there were still some rough edges. He was impulsive, drank too much and, as his trip to China had proven beyond doubt, had a staggering disregard for authority and an inability to take orders without question. But secretly Healy wholeheartedly approved and with time and a little more of his help, he was coming round to the idea that he could work with Scott Hunter. After all, his old man had been in the service, asked to leave in disgrace after letting a traitor slip through his fingers, but in the service never-the-less. They'd been friends, this traitor and Scott's father. Never a good idea to form friendships in their line of work he reflected.

In the Audi's wing mirror he saw the first of them approach. Sandy Harper, marching purposefully. Healy had always found Harper to be ineffectual and bitchy in equal measure. Next, from the opposite direction, Tobias Gray. Today he appeared ill at ease, twitchy, not his usual calm unflappable self. Healy watched his former boss check his sports jacket, padding at his breast pocket. Perhaps he was checking for his cigarettes. But then Toby Gray didn't smoke, did he? He hadn't smoked for years, or drunk. He was pure as the driven bloody snow, wasn't he? Then, suddenly content, Gray smooths down his jacket and heaves open the swing doors to the pub.

This meet was of the big guns, Healy reflected. Perhaps he should drag Hunter along to Bermondsey, introduce him to The Traitors Gate, a piece of the service's history, and then, once all the big nobs had left, over a pint, offer him the role as his new partner? Having come to terms with his decision Healy flicked open his phone and sent Hunter a text.

The caller of the meeting was always the last to arrive. That was the way of things, always had been. Sir John Alperton filled Michael's mirrors. Healy wasn't much of a follower of fashion, he was happy with jeans, a T-shirt and his black leather jacket, but even to his untrained eye, John Alperton cut quite a dash. A beautiful Italian grey suit and waistcoat. Healy could see how his trouser moved next to his shoe. These were hand tailored trousers; not too long, catching at the shoe making the wearer appear clumsy and awkward, but not too short either, the perfect cut and length, allowing Sir John's highly polished toecaps to glisten as they cleaved the air. Healy watched him take one last drag on his cigarette then flick it to the kerb.

Sir John walked straight past him without breaking stride or giving him a second glance. So, they were all assembled he had to assume. The purpose of their meeting, well that was certainly none of Michael Healy's business. He would carry on doing what he was being paid to do and wait. And wait.

***

Sandy Harper sat alone in the basement of The Traitors Gate. He hated Bermondsey, everything about it; the people, their accent, even their overly aggressive choice in pets. He'd seen Michael Healy sitting in his car. This was to be an important meeting then. He examined the frayed sleeve of his well-worn jumper. The money had gone, all of it, along with his wife, the kids and the house. He was still wed to the bloody service though wasn't he? He'd been forced to find somewhere else to live. Moved out of the family home. She'd even got the bloody dog. He pulled distractedly at a loose strand of wool. Four chairs around the table. John Alperton had called the meeting, so who would the other two be? He felt the wool tighten and distend and so nipped it between thumb and forefinger and sulkily snapped it off. Now, where to dispose of the long burgundy strand? The door opened and Toby Gray entered.

'Sandy.'

'Tobes.'

'Any idea what we're doing here?'

'I'm as much in the dark as you I'm afraid,' Sandy's response, except that he already has the feeling Gray knows more than he's letting on.

The door again. This time, in a whirl of silk and finely woven wool John Alperton enters the room. He, or Bridget his secretary, have called this meeting. Tradition decrees that he should not be here though, not quite yet anyway. A break from their unwritten procedure, a breach of protocol. So, who *are* they missing? Sandy wonders.

'Gentlemen.'

'John.'

Alperton pauses to observe the vacant chair.

'I have a feeling Pat won't be joining us today.'

'Pat?' Sandy's enquiry is genuine.

'Hedley-King.'

'Oh really, and why is that?' Toby Gray asks, uncharacteristically quick off the mark.

'Spot of car trouble, I believe.'

'Oh, shame,' continues Gray. 'And to what do we owe this great pleasure?'

'Thought it might be interesting to have a little chat, vis-à-vis regarding Landslide.'

Gray shoots a questioning glance around the room. *Should we be talking of such things in front of Sandy Harper?*

Alperton reads his mind, 'Oh, Toby, it's alright. Sandy here is very much up to speed on Landslide, aren't you Sandy?'

Harper is racking his brains. Landslide, to everyone's relief, had long been forgotten, until recently when that Yank had turned up and there had been quite the flurry of activity. They'd met, not that long ago to discuss bringing in Ewen Connolly for a friendly little chat. They'd sent Alperton's latest find, David Hunter's boy, in what had seemed like a nice attempt at making things right and squaring a rather embarrassing circle. 'Yes, all dealt with, to the best of my knowledge,' Sandy decries, unaware of recent events.

'Not quite,' Sir John offers, flirting with them a little.

'Really, John, how so?' Gray enquires.

Alperton turns to face a bewildered Sandy Harper.

'Why was David Hunter's boy sent out to China, do you recall?'

'To track Connolly down and bring him back here,' Harper replies innocently.

'Not to kill him then?'

'No,' Harper exclaims, his bewilderment in danger of becoming flat out incomprehension.

'That was my recollection too,' Alperton continues, 'and unwittingly that was exactly what he did.'

'Oh, so Connolly's here then? I should like to have a little chat with him,' says Harper.

'As would I,' sticks in Toby Gray angrily.

Alperton smooths down his tie and is about to reach for his cigarettes.

'He *isn't* dead then?' Harper blurts out again, inadvertently putting his finger on it.

'Funny you should say that,' Alperton replies, enjoying Harper's anxiety.

Sandy Harper turns a quizzical eye on Gray, his lord and master, hoping for any light the great man may feel willing to shed on proceedings.

'But listen to me,' Sir John continues 'I'm getting ahead of myself, isn't that right, Toby?'

'If you say so, John.'

'I do say so. I'm about twenty years ahead of myself, aren't I?'

'Will someone please tell me what the hell is going on?' Harper's exclamation one of genuine confusion.

'Shall we, Toby?'

Gray is up and out of his seat and pacing near the door. 'Listen John, I don't know where the hell you think you're going with all this, but I do wish you'd get to the point.'

'Why, is there an AA meeting somewhere minus one drunk?'

Gray stops in his tracks and faces Alperton across the room. Sandy Harper looks between the two men, shocked at the supposed insubordination which he has just witnessed.

'Spit it out, John, whatever you think *it* is,' Gray says with thinly disguised ire.

Sir John flexes in his seat, carefully crosses his legs, his unblinking gaze never leaving Tobias Gray, then he folds his arms across his chest and breaths in deeply through his nose.

'You decided to send Connolly out to Istanbul in '99 as I recall?'

'That's right.'

'Knowing it would all go wrong and hoping he would take the fall I suspect, which I suppose he did in a manner of speaking, just not in the way that you would have liked.'

Gray's face hardens as he waits for Alperton to finish.

'Disappearing like that meant he was a loose cannon, likely to reappear at any moment and start shooting his mouth off as to the true identity of your super-source Landslide. So, through the years you made various unsuccessful attempts to silence him. Just jump in if I'm missing anything, Toby. You sent Pat King with him to keep an eye on things and hoping for a bit of pillow talk when she got back no doubt.'

Gray has heard enough.

'Don't be preposterous. In any case Landslide's dead. You ought to know that, we found his body.'

'No. We found *a* body. And when you say *we* I take it you mean *they*? That was a cool play Toby, I grant you. I'm guessing your friends in Moscow had a hand in it? Who was he? Some poor soul found frozen to death on a street corner, taken out to Turkey in a crate, a bullet put through his already dead head before sawing him into little pieces and dumping him in the river? Or was he diplomatic? An inconvenient guest who

Moscow were delighted to see just disappear off their radar? Either way, poor sod was certainly not our man, was he?'

'John, really this is ridiculous. I don't understand what's happened to you. Ewen Connolly and Pat King were sent to Istanbul by me to recover Landslide and bring him back here. They failed quite miserably to do so, resulting in his murder. If anyone has the right to be pissed off about Istanbul, it's me.'

'No, Toby. No, they were sent out to Istanbul like lambs to the slaughter. You sent them with one intention and one intention only; to fail and save your sorry arse. Landslide was never there, never left the motherland and quite probably never even knew about the operation.'

'Rubbish. This is all nonsense. He was there and your people failed to pick him up. *Your* people, John. Because of their ineptitude he was kidnapped, I'd imagine by the Turkish SIP and killed.'

'In which case, would you mind explaining who it was that turned up on George Wiseman's doorstep about this time last year?'

'I have absolutely no idea, and we can't ask poor old George, can we?'

'No, no that's true. The same of course goes for Ewen Connolly and Pat Hedley-King. Both dead.'

'What?' Sandy pipes up for the first time. 'I thought you said Connolly was here, and my man Healy's been keeping a close eye on King.'

'Ewen Connolly was assassinated yesterday whilst on a fishing trip in North Scotland. Pat King had a car bomb parked outside her house just this morning.'

'Well,' Gray continues, calm and reasonable to the end, 'that is all deeply troubling I grant you, but you can't possibly think I had anything to do with it.'

'No? Perhaps dear old Sandy here can shed some light on that. Sandy, what happened to the reports Healy made for you on Pat's comings and goings?'

'Typed up and filed sub rosa, just like any other report,' Sandy replies cautiously.

'Pass over anyone else's desk before disappearing up to floor four?'

'I will have seen those reports,' Gray puts in helpfully, 'as you could have too, if you'd so desired.'

Alperton nods. 'True, true. The order to kill Connolly, I'm guessing that came directly from you though?'

Gray shakes his head and listens as Sandy Harper incoherently pleads his innocence. Once Harper has stopped babbling Gray turns his attentions to Sir John. 'And you say Landslide defected?'

'That's right, Toby. Sadly for you though, you were utterly unaware of it, and with good reason. He turned up on George Wiseman's doorstep less than a year ago bearing all sorts of goodies. You see, he never died in Turkey and for one good reason, you never intended for him to die in Turkey, you never intended for him to die at all, you simply needed for him to disappear for a while whilst the situation in Moscow blew over. So, you faked his death.'

'This is preposterous.'

'You faked his death and believing his file has been closed and forgotten, left to gather dust on floor four, you press on as if nothing has ever happened. The only problem being when, about a year ago, the real Landslide, or as close as there ever was to one, decides he's had enough of his life in the east and turns up in South Ken. with a bottle of single malt, a box of the finest cigars Cuba has to offer and an overpowering need to talk. I understand, due to his new-found status in The Federal Assembly and thanks to some old acquaintances from his time in the KGB, he was able to uncover some rather unsavoury information about a favourite uncle of his who'd disappeared during the Purges. It was just enough to push the poor old bastard over the edge. That and the death of his stepdaughter of course.

'He and George spent a most enlightening weekend together putting the world to rights. It seems he was particularly eager to talk about a certain high-ranking member of our secret service who'd been such a love to him, back in the day.'

'Where is he now?'

'Oh, come come, Tobias. He's perfectly safe. Living the good life as it happens, many miles from here. Transpires in his little chat with poor old George, that he'd always fancied the Californian coast. He was so taken with the idea in fact, that he happily spent days recording his life's work for us in return for a plane ticket. One way, you understand. Once we'd finished with him he got on the first available flight to Washington where he had a rare old time, in between spilling his guts to the FBI and anyone else who would listen and being wined and dined in Georgetown by good ole Uncle Sam. As a consequence I feel it only fair to warn you that there are more than a couple of our freedom-loving cousins who are desperate to have a little word in your shell-like once we're done with you. Anyway, once he'd had his time in Washington and our American friends had picked him clean I understand he buggered off to warmer climes, sandy beaches, clam chowder, valet parking, mojitos and terrible,

terrible coffee, poor sod. Oh, and before you try and get word to your friends in Lubyanka Square, I ought to remind you, this was several months ago now and I expect he will have tired of cocktails and bikinis and moved on. And that puts us rather neatly just about here.'

'Whilst this has all been highly entertaining, John I don't see a single scrap of evidence.'

Alperton reached beneath the table and produced a thin and aging manila file. He threw it violently at the centre of the table.

'There you are. There's your proof.'

'What's this?'

'George, God bless him, was good enough to give me this before he died. It's a file on Landslide.'

Tobias Gray reached across the table and, with one outstretched digit, dragged the folder toward him.

'This is no proof,' he said inspecting its contents. 'This is an intelligence file on Aleksei Kadnikov. I thought you said it was on Landslide? Really John, and you say George gave you this?'

'That's correct.'

'But sadly for us, he's no longer around to tell us how it came to be in his possession. This could be anything, could have come from anywhere.'

'But it didn't. It came from me.'

Patricia Hedley-King stood, battered and bruised in the doorway.

'I gave the file to George,' she said advancing across the room on Gray, 'I'm surprised you don't recognise it, Toby? And shall I tell you who gave it me, you bastard?'

'That won't be necessary,' Gray replied reaching into his jacket and removing a snub-nosed Walther PPK.

13

In the past, when he and Bob Bennett had been called upon to babysit during meetings such as these, they had played a guessing game to see who would be the first to emerge. Bennett had always plumped for the most junior, and invariably had been right. Healy, having only ever been given second dibs, and enjoying winding his partner up, had made a habit of electing the least likely candidate. Neither of them however could have predicted that Toby Gray would be the first to emerge. The pub's swing doors flew open and he barrelled out, red faced and blowing hard. Not a good meeting then, Healy surmised. Hardly surprising following the earlier events of the day. There hadn't been a car bomb on the streets of London in over ten years, and never one that had targeted one of their own. Gray checked his jacket pockets again, probably making sure he had collected his mobile phone from the shoebox under the bar, and then he's looking up and scanning the street. Healy cranes his neck, wondering if he can work out what his ex-boss is looking for. And then he realises. Gray is looking for him. Spotting Healy in his

Audi Gray nods as much to himself as to Michael and bounds across the road. A moment later and he's in the passenger seat.

'Drive, Michael.'

'I think I should wait and see Sir John, that was our arrangement.'

'Drive, Michael. It's not a request, it's an order.'

Healy looks down at the ugly Walther PPK Tobias Gray is pointing at his stomach.

'I'm sorry, Michael.'

***

There was the pub Hunter's father had told him about; The Traitors Gate, its sign creaking slowly in a spring breeze. The name fitted well with the gallows' humour he'd witnessed so far. What should he do? What would his guide and mentor Michael Healy have him do, charge in there like a bull, or sit it out patiently and see what transpired? Hunter was just about to opt for the latter when something caught his attention. Opposite and along from the pub were a row of parked cars. This part of London was as hectic as any other, so a parking space, any sort of parking space, stuck out like a grinning child's lost front tooth. Healy was always nipping at him to look for the unusual, the out of the ordinary and there on the opposite side of the street, a decent distance from the pub's double front doors, sat the most wonderfully incongruous parking space Hunter had ever seen. He crossed the road, drawn as if by some invisible force to examine the spot.

Once in the void left by the departed vehicle Hunter realised he had the perfect view of the pub's entrance. If Healy had been there, this would have been just the vantage point he would have wanted Hunter to adopt. The front of the pub was framed like a painting, giving him a perfect view of the routes away in either direction. It was as Hunter looked back up the road, towards the tube station, that he saw, mingling horribly with the dust and grime of London in spring, blood.

Hunter followed the drops to a neglected semi. The front gate had been pushed open with a bloody hand, a crimson smear cruelly decorating its aging paintwork. Reluctantly he followed the carmine trail, his heart sinking with each step. The house featured a tiny entrance porch, home to moulding and abandoned telephone directories and wind-blown crisp packets and confectionery wrappers. And in this porchway, the crumpled body of his friend and mentor, Michael Healy, his head resting, quietened, on his bloodied chest, a huge red circle spreading from the centre of his crisp white shirt. Instinctively, Hunter checked his gun.

He knelt next to him, already fearing the worst and gently pushed back his head. Healy let out a low groan of pain and Hunter saw for the first time the huge crack he had taken on the side of his head. The skin was badly split and blood was stickily seeping down his cheek. As Hunter dabbed at the wound with his handkerchief, a bright little girl skipped by, briefly looked in at them, and then, seeing nothing of interest, continued on her way.

Healy mumbled something and Hunter realised he must act quickly. He found his phone and called an ambulance to the pub. It sounded as though Healy were trying to say someone's name, his wife perhaps or one of his daughters. Hunter was ashamed to admit he didn't know.

Sorry, Michael, Hunter thought, but today's Monday and so I can't concern myself with you or your family. I'm here to do a job and so I'm just going to get on with Monday, but I do promise you one thing, I will find whoever is responsible for this and I will kill them.

Healy had been sent to keep an eye on the pub and its occupants. Hunter looked down at the crumpled body lying in the porch.

As he stood to finish the job he had come to do, Hunter caught himself in the dark red panel of stained glass making up the house's front door, his features horribly bent and distorted. What had he become, he wondered. Today is today and so fuck tomorrow and fuck yesterday. Surely Michael Healy hadn't meant that. The man who lay at his feet, the family man with two small girls, who would have given anything to see another Tuesday. Anything. Surely he had not meant that?

It started to rain.

Hunter bent and gently took Michael Healy's body in his arms. He stumbled across the road to The Traitors Gate Pub whilst the rain washed away the blood.

As soon as the barman saw him struggling through the doors with Healy's body in his arms he leapt out from behind the counter. Others moved towards him too, eager to help, leaving drinks and conversations. But then, once Hunter laid down the body they, like Shoeshine Ian began to back off. He recognised Healy, had seen him standing at the bar with Tobias Gray and, before that with Sir John Alperton. The young lad who'd carried in his body could have been anyone, but as Hunter bent to try and make Healy more comfortable the barman caught a glimpse of a weapon tucked in the back of his jeans.

'You have to help me. I need to get down to the basement room.'

'What about him?'

'I've called an ambulance, it's on its way. The basement, now.'

'I don't know what you're talking about.'

Hunter opened his hands to the man. 'I haven't got a lot of time to fuck about. I know about the meeting room, I have to get down there right now.'

'Who are you?' the barman said retreating to the safety of his counter.

'Scott Hunter.'

That name, Hunter, that did ring a distant bell, but it wasn't Scott and in any case, the lad barely looked old enough to buy a round of drinks let alone know about the basement.

'I've never heard of you.'

'I know there's a meeting going on and I need to get down there immediately.'

'I don't care. I've got my instructions.'

'So have I. I need to get down to the basement right now.'

'I've been told they're not to be disturbed, by anyone.'

Hunter saw the man edging closer to the bar and he could only presume, a weapon. He had to act and he had to act swiftly. He withdrew the Glock and pointed it at the barman.

'Hands. I want to see your hands. On the bar and then don't you move.'

Obediently he turned and placed his hands flat on the counter. Hunter waved the gun at the one remaining customer and shouted at him to get out whilst keeping the Glock levelled at Shoeshine as he rounded the bar. There, on top of a box of crisps, lay a sawn-off shot gun. Hunter grabbed it, broke it and let the cartridges fall to the floor. Then he took the belt from the barman's trousers, winding it round his wrists, drawing it tight, before pulling his trousers down and around his ankles. 'I'm sorry,' Hunter said remembering how Healy had cautioned him against apologies, 'but I have to go downstairs.'

'Are you going to kill them?'

'No. I'm going downstairs, and you're going to help him,' Hunter gestured towards Michael Healy, then kicked Shoeshine Ian firmly on the backside sending him sprawling into boxes of crisps and crates of empties.

***

At the bottom of a steep flight of stairs Hunter found a tall thin steel fire door, an axe jammed under its handle. Inside, three tired and anxious faces. Two already familiar to him, one new; a slight, skittish man in a threadbare cardigan who had been pacing determinedly upon his entrance. Sat at the table a woman he knew only too well. Miss White, who had been smoking, stubbed out her cigarette and spun to face him. Her cheek was burnt and badly bruised from the explosion, a cut running across her forehead. She wore a pashmina. Healy would have liked that tiny detail, and Hunter noted, kitten heels, not stilettos. However it was the powerful looking gentleman in the £2,000 pound suit who had once offered Hunter a lift and seemed to know everything about him that was the first to speak.

'Where's Michael?' as though by Hunter's very presence, he already knew.

'Upstairs with a nasty lump on his head.'

John Alperton stopped and instead turned to address the blonde-haired man in the threadbare sweater.

'Sandy, you know him better than most. Where would he go?'

'First guess, 15c.'

Hunter pushed past Sir John Alperton. 'You must be Harper?'

'What is it to you?' Sandy said barely acknowledging him.

'You sent Samantha. Did you kill Ewen Connolly, was that you too?'

'And I can only assume, from your behaviour at least, that you're David Hunter's boy.'

'Did you have Ewen Connolly killed?'

Hunter looked to the man who had only that morning introduced himself as his boss. John Alperton shook his head.

'It's okay, Scott. The information you and Michael collected may well have ended up in Sandy's hands, but he's a nobody, a snivelling little pissant who's only fit for the knacker's yard.'

Harper offered no stroke and so Hunter turned his back on the man.

'Just like his father,' Sandy muttered. And just like his father would have done, Scott chose to ignore him.

'We need for you to go and find Sandy's superior, Tobias Gray,' Alperton continued fumbling in his pocket before withdrawing a scrappy piece of paper and pen. Hurriedly he scribbled down an address and handed it to Hunter. 'And Scott, be careful.'

And then Miss White was by his side and pressing something into his hand.

'Here, take my car. It's a...'

'Red Astra estate, HN 54 DFW, I know.' Headley-King and Alperton turned and stared at him. 'What? Oh, I see. HN looks a bit like the Greek for Eta, 54 is the perfect round of golf and DFW is the code for Dallas Fort Worth. I like the airports, there's always an airport.'

Alperton raised an eyebrow and Hedley-King shot him a reproachful look. Sir John had surprised himself just how pleased he'd been to see the old girl still in one piece.

'We had to be sure. You do understand?' he said to her.

She did she nodded. 'It's parked back towards the main junction, and Scott,' Hedley-King continued 'thank you.'

14

Tobias Gray was tired. Initially, after Aleksei had entered his life, and given him meaning, given him power and purpose there had been exciting years. Exciting years of checking and balancing, impartiality and equilibrium, the little grey man in the bank clerk's suit who nobody saw or wanted to see. Aleksei had through their friendship and shared ideals created Toby Gray, put him on the map, on the path to greatness, where people, admittedly only a select few, but people nevertheless, knew who he was and respected him for it. Some even grew to fear him. For the first time in his life he was someone. Someone doing great things, with great intel direct from Moscow, someone who was needed, indispensable. But then the graveyards were full of indispensable people. Gray thought on that and laughed. Laughed out loud at the ridiculousness of his situation.

And then along had come Alperton. John bloody Alperton and his love affair with the Russian girl which had ruined everything, and he'd been forced to act, left with no choice. No one else put in his position would have done anything different, but the girl, she'd been his real downfall. It had never occurred to Gray that Kadnikov might have a stepdaughter, never crossed his mind that his hot asset in Moscow could be related to the girl carrying the intel and who he seemed so happy to run as an agent. But then that had always been the nature of their relationship, professional but nothing more. Dedicated to their one shared objective. The discovery that Aleksei had a stepdaughter had come as a most unpleasant shock and resulted in the need for Istanbul, which in turn had allowed the years of their achievements to be left untarnished, by Alperton or anyone else. Istanbul had thrown everyone off his scent, everyone except the Scot, Ewen Connolly. Then Connolly had fled, perhaps knowing too much, possibly suspicious he was in jeopardy from both sides. And so, following the death of Viktorija Molchalin and the fallout from Istanbul, Tobias Gray, feeling spent and powerless had really started drinking in earnest. He had filled the void left by Aleksei's priceless intel, good or bad as it may have been, and made up for the loss of face and the dent to his reputation with the one thing he'd been truly able to rely on.

Ultimately their work was nearly done. Stability of a sort, equilibrium, the status quo all existed and all thanks to Tobias Gray and Aleksei Kadnikov. In the late eighties Mikhail Gorbachev declared Glasnost and then the Berlin Wall had come down, and with it the end of the Eastern Block, and so Gray and Kadnikov's dream, born in the shadow of the Cuban missile crisis, that there should be peace and harmony throughout Europe had been realised.

Gray loosened the stopper on the bottle of Glenmorangie.

After Michael he'd needed a drink. He'd stopped the car at the first off licence he'd come to and grabbed the first bottle he could find. The whisky was made only a stone's throw from where poor old Ewen Connolly had lost his life. He had truly regretted having him killed, but anyone who could tie him to Landslide was living on borrowed time, even if Connolly had had twenty years of it out there in the Far East.

Gray lifted the bottle to his lips. He closed his eyes and slowly inhaled the clean spiced fruits, the toffee and vanilla. The sting and burn as the alcohol hits the back of his throat and nose. One day at a time, wasn't that what they were always telling him, one day at a time.

***

David Hunter hadn't been back to 15c since that day. The day when he'd been shown the door by, of all people, Sandy Harper, and his life had, he could see now, started to crumble around him. It had changed enormously over the years, the east end of London, once the preserve of wide boys and thugs in dinner jackets masquerading as nightclub owners, now home to wine bars, delicatessens and the capital's banking headquarters.

The exterior of 15c seemed much as he remembered it, but once he had been buzzed inside David realized just how much it had changed. Instead of stolen traffic cones, hazard lights and City of London signs misappropriated from the Barbican Centre up the road, a fancy new rack displaying an expensive and gleaming road bike. The stairwell, like everything else, had received a much-needed lick of paint and the old wooden banisters had been sanded and varnished. Once functional metal fire doors replaced with more welcoming wooden front doors sporting Rennie Macintosh name plates. He scaled the stairs, every now and then looking out, into the empty courtyard, at the grey flagstones and the grisly secrets they contained.

Three flights of stairs later and panting lightly with the exertion, David Hunter arrived outside 15c. At a glance he could tell he was in the wrong place, the latest in designer prams propped up like a medal of honour next to a hedgehog shaped foot scraper. He rang the doorbell anyway, listening as it chimed discreetly in the middle distance.

The woman who opened the door so suspiciously was in her thirties, well dressed and exhausted, the signs of another, younger occupant, littering the highly polished parquet flooring behind her. David recognised some of them; Lego, Matchbox cars and even a cardboard book he had once read to Scott. But there were other toys too, the likes of which he'd never seen and now could barely comprehend; a miniature drone and robots which were planes, all garishly moulded in Chinese plastic.

'Can I help you?' she asked politely but sharply from behind her security chain.

'I'm sorry to bother you,' which David genuinely was, 'but I used to live here.' Not quite true, but the other explanation was too complicated and probably broke the Official Secrets Act. 'I wonder, would it be possible to come in and have a quick nosey around, just for old time's sake?'

The woman considered this gentle man's request.

'I'm sorry, but no.'

David looked at her face. A face which, he fancied was incapable of hiding her every emotion. 'It's just me and the boy you see and it's not a good time and... well, you understand? It's been a long day. I've kind of got my hands full.'

She didn't wait for his answer or explanation, just turned and closed the door.

Perhaps he had been wrong. The new owner of 15c and her son seemed to be alone. Perhaps this wasn't where he would come. There were plenty of other places dotted about London and beyond, but David Hunter had always been of the impression that 15c was in some way special. That was all he had based his hunch on, and, as was the nature with hunches, sometimes they were just plain wrong. He began back down the stairs, looking out at the courtyard below through the huge glass panelled windows at the bottom of each landing. However much the developers had managed to alter the insides of the flats, the courtyard-cum-graveyard would have to remain untouched, both historic and sacred. And there, kneeling in the far corner, working at something, was Tobias Gray.

'Your legend, Toby?'

Gray looked up, unsurprised by the intrusion. He'd prised up a heavy flagstone and had been about to remove a plastic wrapped parcel.

'I thought someone would come, but I never expected it would be you, David.'

'When did you realise?'

'When did I realise what exactly?'

'When did you realise you'd signed Viktorija Molchalin's death warrant?'

'It was about a week before I heard from Aleksei. I knew

something must be wrong. He was always as regular as clockwork. John Alperton was still at home recovering and I hadn't spoken to Connolly. The flash came through from The British Embassy, they said all hell had broken loose. One of Russia's foremost politicians, once of the KGB, now top mover and shaker in The Assembly's lower house and all-round traitor, his stepdaughter's been found beaten to death and people were starting to point fingers. Jesus David, I didn't even know he had a stepdaughter. In any case the Russians were supposed to rough her up a bit, not kill her. You should know that much.'

'Was that when you decided to kill off Landslide?' Scott Hunter asked joining his father. 'Was that when you decided to sacrifice my father and my godfather to save your own neck?'

Gray brushed some dirt from the package he had come to retrieve. 'Alperton said he was good, your boy. Seems he may have been right. Not that it matters now, but I've always had the hugest amount of respect for your father. He has been a good friend and protector to me. Istanbul was deeply regrettable but necessary.'

'Ewen Connolly?' Scott asked.

'He should have kept his hands to himself and minded his own God damn business.'

'And Michael Healy, was he a regrettable casualty too?'

'Scott?' David looked at his son.

'I'm assuming that was you? Was he a regrettable casualty, the father of two? And for what, for his car?' Hunter reached behind him and withdrew the Glock. 'Give me one good reason. One!'

But it was David Hunter, Scott's father who positioned himself between Gray and the weapon.

'There are many good reasons, Scott, that you are not going to do this, do you understand?'

'But what about Ewen?'

'It's more complicated than that, I'm afraid.'

'Don't Dad. Don't apologise for him. What do you mean it's more complicated? You of all people should want him dead, after everything he did to you.'

David Hunter held out his hand to his son as he had done once before. 'You're going to give me the gun and then we are going to allow Tobias to leave.'

Gray had finished extracting the plastic wrapped package from beneath its tombstone. He retrieved a pocketknife from his jacket and slid it along an edge. Scott saw money in a variety of currencies, a passport, not British, and a set of keys. Happy with what he had found, Gray pushed the slab back into place, pocketed his finds, dusted down his trousers and stood to address father and son.

'David,' he nodded grimly. For a moment Scott thought he might offer his father his hand. 'You should be very proud of your boy.'

'I am.'

'Sorry things didn't work out differently.'

'Promise me one thing, Tobias,' David said amicably.

'Of course.'

'Don't come back.'

'I shan't.' He grabbed David Hunter's elbow affectionately. 'Scott, perhaps, one day, you'll understand and then perhaps you'll be able to forgive me? Goodbye.'

Hunter watched as Gray walked away, his head thrown back, his arms swinging proudly.

'There is a very brave man, Scott. Now, I don't know about you, but I could do with a drink? Come on.'

***

As they sat in David's Volvo and prepared to leave the City of London, Scott suddenly experienced a tight wave of pain from the wound to his elbow.

'Should we get you to a hospital?'

'I think I'd rather go home, Dad.'

David smiled and slipped the Volvo into gear. They drove back to Sarratt and the house full of secrets in total silence, as Scott was becoming to understand was the way of agents with one another.

'I could do with that drink now,' Scott said.

'There's something I have to take care of first. Follow me.'

David led his son into the kitchen. Strapped to a chair with heavy black gaffer tape, a resigned and exhausted Bob Bennett.

Father and son set about loosening the bindings.

'Go home,' David said. 'They'll call you a cab at the pub. You can tell John I'm sorry about, well everything really.'

Scott and his father watched as Bob Bennett wordlessly gathered himself, stretched his racked limbs and prepared to leave. As he reached the door he turned back into the kitchen, looking as though he was about to speak, but then, thinking better of it, opened the door to leave the pair and an awkward silence.

An exhausted Scott Hunter pulled up a chair at the kitchen table, propped his head in his hands and distractedly massaged his scalp.

'How did they meet,' he yawned, 'Gray and the Russian?'

'I don't know, but I can speculate. The bump, at a café, a chance encounter in a bar, the shared interest, perhaps a book or a paper, a dropped comment. That's how I'd have done it,' his father explained returning to the table.

'And why did we let him go?'

'Because it was the right thing to do, Scott.'

'I don't understand.'

'And I wouldn't expect you to, not right now. Drink?'

'Please.'

'You still on the Scotch?' David asked trying not to appear overbearing.

'I thought I might try something different. White wine?'

Scott's father found a couple of glasses and poured two healthy measures.

'Ewen would have liked this,' he said observing his son.

'He would,' Scott replied recalling Amber and his evening in The Golden Dragon. 'What do you know about Aleksei's time in the KGB?'

'Precious little really, but we do know he was in London for a few years at the end of the seventies, studying at the LSE and recruiting likeminded individuals, until George got wind of it and politely issued him his marching orders. Seems he may have overstepped the mark somewhat. George intervened, a little chat on the dos and don'ts, a spot of social etiquette handed out gratis and the suggestion that he get on the first Aeroflot back to the motherland, spend some time with his family and not show his face here again anytime soon. Reading between the lines, and Toby Gray's recruitment to one side, I get the feeling from his file that Aleksei may not have been the greatest of field agents. Certainly if George had realised his true intentions things might have played out very differently, but as it was he left London in 1979. Gray was possibly his one and only success, and I know what you're thinking, but both he and Kadnikov were men of principle striving for just one thing.'

'Let me guess, even numbers not odd?'

'What?' David asked a trifle bemused.

'Just something Michael said.'

'In the '80s and '90s Aleksei and Gray found themselves uniquely positioned to influence the shape and direction of Europe, but unlike many of the men around them, their motives were peaceable and largely altruistic. After his stint in London Kadnikov returned to Moscow and begins his slow yet inexorable rise through the ranks of the KGB. In his thirties he's already been picked as the next big thing and it should have been a golden age for him, but at about this time his first marriage hits the rocks. We lose track of him a little at the start of the '90s, around about the time the KGB underwent its own private perestroika and stopped being the KGB, but then he resurfaces again in an entirely new role at the recently formed SVR from where he's able to pass huge amounts of invaluable intel as Landslide. A short stay there as deputy director and then more plaudits and promotions until he reaches the holy of holies, The Federal Assembly. In the intervening years he remarries a Lubov Molchalin, ten years his senior and, sadly unbeknownst to us or clearly Toby Gray, Aleksei inherits a stepdaughter, Viktorija.

'Then, after the episode with John Alperton, the next time Aleksei really comes to our attention is when he shows up on George Wiseman's doorstep. It's quite possible he never even knew about Istanbul or Landslide. It seems that in an effort to cover his tracks, Toby Gray did a magnificent job convincing anyone who would listen that Viktorija's death had been the result of some ancient Russian feud. Aleksei himself believes this for many years until, thanks to some old friends in the SVR, his suspicions are roused. In all that time he never stopped looking for his stepdaughter's killers, but until a couple of years ago it never occurred to him they could be anything other than Russian. Following this fresh lead he quickly identifies two heavies. Muscle for hire. They disappear in no short order, bodies found within days of one another, but not before he extracts some vital information from them. Where had they been paid from and by whom? A little more digging and Aleksei has a name closely linked with the British Embassy back in the early '90s; one Sandy Harper. Fortunately for poor old Sandy, Aleksei knows a monkey when he sees one and decides to go after the organ grinder.'

'What about John?'

'Alperton would have been on his radar certainly, in fact I believe they actually met once, but anyone who saw him following Viktorija's murder could never have believed he had anything to do with it. Her death destroyed him for years you see. As, in fact, it did Gray, once he'd realised what he'd done. That was when the drinking really started. With hindsight, and even despite their friendship, Gray must have known Aleksei would come after him. He's probably spent the last twenty years looking over his shoulder. As it was, Aleksei was a much shrewder judge of character than we ever gave him credit for. When it came to exacting his revenge he chose to hurt Toby more deeply than any physical attack. He went after the one thing which meant more to him than anything else, his job and his reputation. Two years ago Aleksei's wife died of cancer and so, with no real need to stay he starts to put the wheels in motion. I suspect, for instance, that your friend Frank Cassatto may not have just bumped into Ewen in that bar in Hong Kong? Aleksei knew that once he'd been reunited with George Wiseman and shared his side of the story George would never let Gray go unpunished. He knew Wiseman would undermine him from the inside out and, he knew that once those wheels were turning, it would only be a matter of time before John Alperton got wind of it and exacted his own personal form of retribution. Aleksei walked away, hands relatively clean, happy to let us sort out in house and confident that, at the end of the day, the right thing would be done, which in a sense it has been. Gray circled the wagons for a while, poor old Ewen paid the price for that, but in the end justice of a sort was served.'

'But we just let him walk away and after all he'd done?'

'With Gorbachev's glasnost, the fall of the Berlin wall and subsequent breakdown of the USSR and the Eastern block, Russia ceased to be the political panacea Toby hoped it would be. I think, at about the time he stopped drinking, he probably lost faith in the whole enterprise. To him, you see, Russia had become as fetid as the West. London was brimming at the seams with Russian billionaires made rich on the decline of Gray's ideals gone bad. That must have left a particularly sour taste in his mouth, to see everything he'd thought could be a cure for the guilt of being born with a silver spoon in his mouth fall around his feet.'

'Who are you?' Scott said lifting his head to look at the man next to him.

David laughed. 'I'm your father, Scott, like it or not.'

'You know what I mean.'

'Yes, I do.'

'So, who are you then, really? How do you know all this?

Alperton called you an incredible man, and Gray said you were a friend and protector.'

David Hunter smiled as he considered his son's request. 'I'm the Lord God all Bloody Mighty, Scott' he said with a self-conscience laugh, 'that's who I am.'

'I don't understand.'

'I know, and believe me, that's no bad thing.'

'Will I ever?'

'I'm not sure.'

'I still don't see why we let him walk?'

'Because Scott, whilst he may have lost faith in the great communist machine of the USSR as it crawled towards free speech, none of us know what the hell he's been up to in the intervening years. I know Toby better than most. He may be a quiet man, he may not court the limelight or shout his opinions from the highest roof tops, but I can guarantee you this, he won't have been sat on his hands either. And the only way we have any chance of finding out what he's been up to, is to let him go and hope he doesn't notice if we tag along.'

Scott considered long and hard before he asked his final question for he already suspected he knew what his father's answer would be.

'The orders to the Russians, the men who killed the girl, where did they originate from?'

'London.'

'Who in London, if it wasn't Sandy Harper or Tobias Gray, who gave the order?'

'I did, Scott. The order came from me,' David said twisting the wineglass in his fingers. After a lifetime of guilt and hesitation, David Hunter had surprised himself with quite how easily he'd shared that little secret. 'Now, how did it go?' he mumbled, 'I heard him say it so many times... I take this glass into my hand...'

'No Dad.' Scott looked into his father's tired, watering eyes and offered up a different toast. 'Absent friends,' he said quietly. And in that cursory moment of calm resignation and acquiescence, he finally let her go.

Scott Hunter's in a race to find the truth.

The Scott Hunter Spy Series Book 3

With wealthy Russian mobsters threatening to overrun London, Hunter's investigations force him to consider the very people he's working for and a murder The Service appears all too eager to cover up.

"Another cracking read ... Get it and clear your diary. Brilliant!"
☆☆☆☆☆

Praise for Birth of a Spy

A modern take on the classic spy novel.

☆☆☆☆☆

Absolutely fantastic read... a plot and sub-plots that will keep the reader page-turning until the very end

☆☆☆☆☆

The world created by the story became more deliciously dark with each chapter

☆☆☆☆☆

As good, if not better, as any John le Carré story.

☆☆☆☆☆

If you like a thriller packed with drama and shady characters this is the book for you!

☆☆☆☆☆

Read the series from its beginning.

The Scott Hunter Spy Series Book 1

Out of work Cambridge graduate Scott Hunter breaks Second World War Enigma codes. His girlfriend is desperate for him to find a job and settle down, so when a fresh code lands unexpectedly on Scott's doorstep, he promises it will be his last, little realising that revealing the dark secrets it has protected for over fifty years will shatter their lives forever.

About the Author

Success as a writer of short stories led to the creation of the Scott Hunter Spy Series where the globe-trotting Swindells cleverly combines factual knowledge with fiction and a main character thrown unwillingly into the strange, murky world of Britain's Secret Service.

Buoyed up by critical acclaim for Birth of a Spy, Absent Friends and A Crown of Thorns, quickly followed, continuing Scott Hunter's burgeoning career as an agent in The Service.

A fifth-generation classical musician, Swindells studied at The Royal Academy of Music. Following a successful free-lance career in London he is currently Principal Bass Clarinet with the Royal Scottish National Orchestra.

In 2022 he established Ex Libris Digital Press, a company aimed at aiding self-publishing authors format their paperbacks and ebooks prior to publication.

He lives with his wife, two sons and a couple of demanding black and white cats in a small village outside Stirling.